**Praise for the Star Risk, Ltd., Novels**

"The genius of the Star Risk, Ltd., series is that it is unrepentant action and fun. . . . *The Scoundrel Worlds* makes for great vacation reading." —SF Site

"Bunch's pacing is superior, his characterization is better than that of most others who produce similar books, and hardware as well as characters display some nice authorial touches. . . . Well up to Bunch's standards for intelligent action SF." —*Booklist*

### And for the Last Legion Series

"Lovers of military science fiction could hardly find better fare." —Painted Rock Reviews

"The books of Chris Bunch . . . are well-written books with complex plots, intrigue, and great descriptive narratives of battle and combat. *The Last Legion* is no exception. . . . Fans of Bunch's previous books will not be dissatisfied." —SF Site (featured review)

"A powerful piece of military science fiction that includes a well-crafted universe that seems starkly real. . . . Bunch's military tone and sense of atmosphere will delight fans of military SF."

—*Affaire de Co*

"Good, fun n

ities to Davic

**Praise for the Other Novels of Chris Bunch**

"Bunch knows how to mold heroes, how to keep the pace fast, and how to create exciting scenes of battlefield mayhem and convincing webs of political intrigue."

—*Publishers Weekly*

"Remarkable."

—*New York Times* bestselling author
Michael A. Stackpole

"Glorious swashbuckling . . . absolutely riveting."

—*Locus*

"An excellent fantasy adventure."     —*Chronicle*

"A fantasy sex-and-violence fest, courtesy of Bunch's sure grasp of military history."     —*Kirkus Reviews*

"Fast-paced action and aerial battles as well as a smattering of romance and intrigue. Fans of military fantasy . . . should enjoy this fantasy adventure."

—*Library Journal*

"Bunch's military background stands him in good stead as he concocts strategy and depicts battle in the air and on the ground. A good bet for military SF and fantasy fans."     —*Booklist*

Chris Bunch's

# THE GANGSTER CONSPIRACY

••••••••••••••••••••••••

A Star Risk, Ltd., Novel by
## Steve Perry and Dal Perry

A ROC BOOK

ROC
Published by New American Library, a division of
Penguin Group (USA) Inc., 375 Hudson Street,
New York, New York 10014, USA
Penguin Group (Canada), 90 Eglinton Avenue East, Suite 700, Toronto,
Ontario M4P 2Y3, Canada (a division of Pearson Penguin Canada Inc.)
Penguin Books Ltd., 80 Strand, London WC2R 0RL, England
Penguin Ireland, 25 St. Stephen's Green, Dublin 2,
Ireland (a division of Penguin Books Ltd.)
Penguin Group (Australia), 250 Camberwell Road, Camberwell, Victoria 3124,
Australia (a division of Pearson Australia Group Pty. Ltd.)
Penguin Books India Pvt. Ltd., 11 Community Centre, Panchsheel Park,
New Delhi - 110 017, India
Penguin Group (NZ), 67 Apollo Drive, Rosedale, North Shore 0745,
Auckland, New Zealand (a division of Pearson New Zealand Ltd.)
Penguin Books (South Africa) (Pty.) Ltd., 24 Sturdee Avenue,
Rosebank, Johannesburg 2196, South Africa

Penguin Books Ltd., Registered Offices:
80 Strand, London WC2R 0RL, England

First published by Roc, an imprint of New American Library,
a division of Penguin Group (USA) Inc.

First Printing, July 2007
10  9  8  7  6  5  4  3  2  1

PUBLISHER'S NOTE
This is a work of fiction. Names, characters, places, and incidents either are
the product of the author's imagination or are used fictitiously, and any resemblance to actual persons, living or dead, business establishments, events, or
locales is entirely coincidental.
    The publisher does not have any control over and does not assume any
responsibility for author or third-party Web sites or their content.

This book is for Karen
—CB

And for Dianne
—SP

And for Pop, for being there when I needed him—
and for my boys, for needing me to be there
—DP

# ACKNOWLEDGMENTS

Our thanks this time to Liz Scheier, Jean Naggar, Jennifer Weltz, and Shawna McCarthy, for help aiding and abetting.

And Chris, wherever you are, we miss you, buddy.

Gangster: 1) A member of a gang of violent criminals. See also mobster, thug, brigand, bushwhacker.

# ONE

If you had to go broke, there were worse places to do it than the new Star Risk Ltd. offices. The team ought to know, since they had *been* to many such places. . . .

Their conference room was a perfect example: genuine Naugahyde pleather-covered tuck-and-roll seats filled with biosensitive memory gel set under full-spectrum lamps, adjustable to the solar radiation of a being's choice. A huge inlaid wood table held the latest issues of *Modern Mercenary* and leather-bound volumes of the current *Jane's Spaceships of the Galaxy*. The fact that the hardware catalog was no longer routinely published in hard copy made it all the more extravagant.

Plush, hand-knotted carpets representing years of work by a family of the multiarmed aliens of Ferris V waited to soothe the feet of potential customers. Of which, lately, there had been exactly none.

"Just one score," said Chas Goodnight. "One little job, and we'll be set for months. Bills paid, tanks topped up, happy as clams—whatever they are, and however happy they can be."

Goodnight was tall and handsome. He had been, among other things, a successful jewel thief before being rescued from a death-row cell by Star Risk. His criminal success had been due in part to having been an Alliance covert ops specialist, a variety known as a "bester"; he had been surgically modified to be able to see in the dark, listen into radio frequencies, and operate at triple the speeds and reaction times of Olympic athletes—for about fifteen minutes, after which the battery at the base of his spine ran out. At which point he was pretty much worthless until it was recharged.

His amorality was almost as much an asset to Star Risk as his physical abilities. Or at least it usually was. Sometimes they just shook their heads at what he thought. Or did.

"My boy, a job will come along. They always do, eventually."

The speaker, Friedrich von Baldur, was a dapper man with gray hair who looked like someone's kindly uncle. Von Baldur's appearance was deceptive: In addition to being adept in a handful of martial arts, he was an accomplished con artist who had skillfully embezzled his way out of the Alliance military one step ahead of a court-martial. He was a pretty good card-sharp, and not unacquainted with other forms of gambling. As the founder of Star Risk, he had more than a little say about the company's direction, despite the fact that they were all equal partners. In theory.

The current conversation had been going on in various forms for the several months since peace had broken out in their little quadrant of the galaxy. With no large conflicts nearby, being mercenaries just wasn't paying.

In addition, during their recent clash with archrival Cerberus Systems, their former forty-second-floor offices had been crushed and then blown to pieces, necessitating a move. Whether potential customers were leery about coming to see them, fearing another such event, or just couldn't find them, the result was the same.

So Goodnight, in the same way that a surgeon sees most problems as steaks, had suggested augmenting their limited funds with some burglary.

"I believe the excitement of being 'on the lam,' as it is known in some of your epic poems, could be quite stimulating," Amanandrala Grokkonomonslf—generally known as Grok—said.

The nearly two-meter-tall alien was also nearly two meters wide, most of it claw, fang, and muscle, covered with silky fur that seemed to never need care. Grok's race was known as great philosophers, thinking deep thoughts—and then acting on them with a ferocity to match. A good combination in a lot of cases, not always so good in a merc.

"To see the lights strobing as the fuzz close in—what thoughts it might promote!"

"Well, yeah—one being the realization that you're going to prison," said Goodnight. "When the lights start flashing, it's game over. What is a 'fuzz,' anyway?"

"It is a reference I scanned from an ancient law enforcement manual," said Grok. "It apparently referred to the hirsute nature of prominent law enforcement officers."

"Well, hairy or not, I'm with Freddie," said Jasmine King, their research specialist. Jasmine had the blond hair, as well as the body, of a male fantasy—an appearance which made her seem ill-qualified for the job. Said perfection had caused her no little grief; her former employer, Cerberus, had accused her of being an android, and therefore property that did not need a paycheck. She'd been pissed off enough to quit, and go to work for Star Risk. But she was more intellectually fit and physically adept than she was beautiful, something that still boggled all their minds. Still, it didn't hurt that she was easy on the eyes, Goodnight felt. A side benefit.

"Principles aside, pulling a job here would be stupid—you don't crap in your own backyard. And the cost of getting us all offworld would eat up one of the two months' expenses we have left. How smart would that be?" Jasmine asked.

The conference room went silent for a moment as they regarded her comment.

"Well, hell's bells. Smart or not, I'm getting bored enough to try it," said M'chel Riss.

Riss, a tall blonde with emerald green eyes, also looked like she could be a runway model, but was in fact formerly a major in the Alliance Marine Corps. She'd left when her commanding officer insisted that her next assignment should be in his bedroom. A decision he regretted pretty fast.

"Exactly!" said Goodnight. "Why be bored *and* broke?"

He started to say something else, when they suddenly heard a loud *brrrriing!*

"What is that strange noise?" asked Grok.

"Got me," Goodnight said. "I never heard it before."

Even the ultraefficient Jasmine looked stumped for

a moment—until she and Freddie looked at each other and simultaneously said, "The front door!"

Grok, moving surprisingly fast for a being of his size, reached across the table and tapped a button on a control panel.

Immediately, a high-resolution image of a somewhat elderly man standing at their front door appeared. Given their location, this might not be unexpected—there were a lot of old people about—but this one didn't look as if he had gotten lost, Goodnight thought.

The man was dressed in a uniform of sorts, black with a white collar. It looked vaguely familiar.

The man pressed the button one more time, filling the room with the noise yet again.

The five of them were almost too stunned to move. A customer?

The man looked at the locked door, shook his head, and turned to go.

Goodnight reached a hand toward his chin to trigger bester mode, but Riss had already made it to the front door, which she opened.

"Good afternoon!" she said. "Welcome to Star Risk, Limited."

She didn't sound out of breath or anything.

The man looked at her and smiled.

"Well, it is a minor miracle, then. I had about given up hope when I saw your old offices. The rubble, I mean."

Riss forced a smile and ushered the man down the stairs to their greeting room.

"We decided to look for something more, um, down-to-earth," she said.

In the case of their new office, they'd taken the sentiment literally. One of the curses of being a developer on a holiday world was finding new land. Too much vertical growth spoiled the view, so a few years back an entrepreneurial sort had done the opposite—and gone down.

Developers, in cahoots with local lawmakers, had tugged at the tapestry of law and created a loophole that allowed them to sell both above- and below-the-ground rights on a single section of land.

Star Risk's new building was underneath a retirement village that commanded an astonishing view of the western sea. Unfortunately for the developers, they'd neglected to realize how unpopular having no windows would be.

So the building had been perfect—cheap, bunkerlike walls, and buried under another target. And if baddies did decide to attack, von Baldur had noted that the collateral damage would be minimal—at least in terms of years of life lost. A lot of the old people up there were teetering on the abyss anyhow.

Riss thought that sounded a tad insensitive, but it *was* true.

The man walked slowly down the stairs with the shuffle of a low-gravity dweller, placing each foot carefully.

When they reached the meeting room, Riss noticed it had been tidied in a hurry.

Von Baldur sat at the conference room table staring at a blueprint on the monitor. Jasmine leaned over and handed him some papers. Goodnight and Grok were nowhere to be seen. It looked almost as if they had things to do.

"Freddie, this is—um . . ." Riss turned to the man. "Mr., ah . . . ?"

"*Reverend.* Reverend Josiah Williams."

"Well, Reverend Williams, this is Friedrich von Baldur, our founder, and Jasmine King, our research specialist. Our other two members, Chas Goodnight and Grok are—"

"A preacher?" Goodnight's voice came from the doorway. He stood next to Grok—or rather in front of him, since the alien's bulk would have filled the doorway and then some.

"I like to think of myself as more of a helper," said Josiah. "Helping each man do his best to do good to each other."

There was an uncomfortable silence.

Riss picked the conversation back up before it died completely.

"Ah, yeah, so how can Star Risk help you? Not being in that line of work, and all. Have a seat, Reverend."

The man did, and she sat across from him.

"I come from a system called Artegal. A rather corrupt place."

The members of Star Risk seemed to let out a silent sigh. Corruption. Comfortable territory at last.

If the reverend noticed, he gave no sign.

"Some of my flock—a good many—work for the loaders' union on Artegal's four key space stations. They wish to be allowed to live better lives.

"So they have decided to strike, and freeze the ports. They feel that this will air their grievances in a peaceful, yet meaningful, way."

Williams spoke in a resonant tone, his words almost

musical in their cadence. All that practice to the congregation, Riss supposed.

"Yet within their organization there are men, evil men, those who are afraid of making a change, who wish to stop such growth. These are powerful folk, and they are willing to do anything to keep their pockets lined and the status quo as it is."

Riss nodded and smiled to keep him talking.

"These people have been working to break the strike, to steal our ability to choose our own destiny." He paused for what was surely dramatic effect. "We must stop them."

Riss heard Goodnight mutter something under his breath.

Von Baldur spoke. "Indeed, Reverend, I agree this is terrible. Not everyone shares your morality, however."

Out of the corner of her eye, Riss saw Goodnight open his mouth, no doubt to say, "Like me," but she glared at him. He stayed quiet. Not a good idea to alienate the customer.

"However," continued the Star Risk founder, "it is a hard universe, and sometimes truly difficult to know when to take action."

The reverend smiled. "Indeed Mr. von Baldur, indeed. The Lord works with what He has, however, and my beliefs are nothing if not pragmatic. I wasn't always a preacher," he added, sliding his sleeve up to reveal an Alliance Marine tattoo.

They were still absorbing that when Williams reached into his pocket and pulled out a piece of paper, which he carefully set on the conference room table.

It was a check. A real, paper check—you didn't see a lot of those bank drafts these days. It had a lot of zeros in it—one, two, five, *six* . . .

A million credits!

All of them stared.

"I understand that money won't make you agree with my beliefs, but I'm hoping it will hire me some serious support for them."

"Supporting beliefs is our specialty, Reverend. Consider us hired," von Baldur said.

# TWO

"For once," began von Baldur, "it's going to be simple—"

And then a bomb went off. A really *loud* bomb.

The skylight imploded and, in the sudden absence of sound that came from auditory overload, pieces of safetyplas cascaded down in silence—the nanorounded spheres and oblongs resembling large droplets of water.

But by then the team was already in motion.

Riss waved at Grok, von Baldur, and Jasmine and circled her hand over her head. She pointed at Goodnight and then the front door.

Goodnight triggered himself into bester and blurred for the door, drawing his sidearm. Grok, Riss, von Baldur, and Jasmine hopped up on the table as Jasmine touched a control. The table started to rise—

Grok pulled a panel off the table and removed a terribly large hand weapon. Riss had already pulled her blaster, as had von Baldur, and Jasmine tapped more controls on the table.

Within seconds the conference room table had served

its secondary purpose, and they were at the top of the skylight. Grok leaped off first, followed by Riss, while Jasmine worked the console on the table to check the sensors they'd carefully hidden around the rest home.

Goodnight shot up the stairs, the walls seeming to blur as he moved. The top of the stairwell, where the entrance had been, was missing. The entrance, which turned nearly ninety degrees once you were past the first doorway, had passed the blast through—it had shot through the door and then past the wall, carrying debris and carving holes through every wall facing the sea. He could see blue sky at the end of the newly made tunnel.

Goodnight flew through the opening, his senses vibrant. His hearing was still not up to par, but he could see. His LOSIR signature scan lit, looking for targets.

Bullets filled the air through which he'd just passed. Had he been moving at a normal pace, he would have been toast. He ran toward the source of the shots. His advanced neural computer had already calculated where the shooter was, and the best cover was just ahead.

More small missiles zipped at him, missing by a hair. A centimeter was as good as a parsec—

He reached the cover, but didn't stop. He jinked, first to the left, then dived and shoulder-rolled to the right. It was a good thing—the shooter had corrected much faster than should have been possible. Which meant that he—or they—was either physically augmented or running on some chemical accelerant.

*Well, that puts a different light on things.*

When he came up from his roll he snapped off five or six shots at the third floor across the street, where the attacker's fire came from, and then dived again.

Actinic light strobed behind him, and the vehicle he'd just moved out from behind blew up as a CP beam destroyed its batteries.

*Crap, another one!*

One behind, one in front, a classic cross fire. *Move!*

He sprinted toward the entrance of the building that held the first shooter.

As the ringing in her ears subsided, Jasmine could hear von Baldur speak.

"—ing idiots set a shaped charge on our front door. Fortunately they were too stupid to realize our place is almost straight down."

Jasmine's hearing improved yet more—now she could hear screams.

"Oh, dear—looks like they got some of the old folks," von Baldur said.

Jasmine kept checking the readouts. While it was probable that the charge at the front door had been intended to kill them, it was certainly possible that there were other plans in play.

She would certainly have a backup plan in case the bomb didn't work.

Ah, there it was. A fishing vessel—at least that was what its ID tag said.

Which wouldn't normally raise any eyebrows, except that there were no edible fish in large numbers on this particular stretch of coast, and this was a big boat. The local resorts had built up a highly colorful selection of underwater fish for tourists to look at, and didn't want the more ugly and edible bottom-feeders nearby. Not the least reason being that the bottom-feeders on Trimalchio IV had a tendency to eat tourist-sized prey.

Jasmine had seen something about it late one night on one of the local entertainment networks. Always nice to make use of random information.

She toggled the coast-side sensors to zoom in on the craft. Sure enough, once you were past the electronic ID, it didn't look like any fishing boat she'd ever seen—not many fish she'd heard of required what were obviously disguised missile turrets to catch.

One of which turrets seemed to be pointed right at them . . .

Riss and Grok rushed toward the front of the building. The grim specter of death had come a bit sooner than expected for some of the inhabitants of the retirement home. There was an old geezer who'd apparently been coming back from the gym—in pretty good shape, too, thought the ex-marine, except for, well, missing his head.

*Who says exercise isn't bad for you?*

The unlucky fitness buff had taken another one with him—a woman lay nearby clutching her chest. Nothing like a headless corpse to spawn a heart attack.

Grok and Riss moved in short jaunts, each covering the other, until they'd reached the front of the building. They were just in time to see the white flash of a particle-beam weapon.

*That came from* our *side of the street—*

Riss glanced at Grok, who nodded, and led them toward the stairwell. They rushed up the stairs, two and three at a time, and onto the second floor. She tried to focus on what was in this corner of the building. The coast side had the dining area and lounge, and the land side had—

The library.

And here it was, an inviting, plant-lined entrance.

Their attackers were following good doctrine—Riss almost missed the trip laser for the antipersonnel device they'd set in the entrance. But as her drill instructor had said, " 'Almost' is as bad as 'nearly'—except when the target is *you*."

Rather than take the time to deactivate the device, she picked up two cushions from a chair near the entrance and tossed one inside.

*Spatspatspatspatspat!*

Hundreds of flechettes shot across the doorway, burying themselves in the wall opposite. The cushion, now shredded like breakfast cereal, didn't slow them down.

*Nice. Haven't seen one of those lately.*

She chucked the other pillow and the same thing happened.

*Crap! How many more of those were there?*

They weren't going that way.

She pointed at the wall a dozen or so feet away from the entrance and Grok growled his agreement, the sound like a heavy lifter taking off.

The alien made an adjustment on his weapon and fired it. The result was a sudden door-sized opening in the wall, and a cloud of smoke to cover their entrance.

Riss and Grok dived though.

Goodnight managed to reach the door of the building where the first shooter was located, but the beam-weapon team was right on him, firing as fast as their capacitors could recharge. Which was impressively fast.

To make matters worse, the entrance was sealed. Apparently the owners of the building had overbuilt—his blaster didn't even scratch the thick plas of the front door.

Not that he could take much time to look, since the beam weapon was due to fire at any moment. His internal clock had patterned it to 1.1 seconds between shots, which made it a crew-served tripod mount of some kind. It was time to take cover.

Which gave him an idea.

He stood still until he heard the pulse of the sonic targeting unit touch him, gave it a microsecond longer, and dived to the right.

The beam strobed and the thick plas of the doorway melted behind him.

"Thanks, guys!" he yelled.

He leaped over the melted plas and rushed for the stairwell.

*Chas has entered the building.*

In the library, Riss and Grok moved cautiously. The decor was classic Imperial, with rows of actual bookcases, large maps, and thickly padded chairs.

However, the tripod-mounted beam weapon facing what was left of the window was probably not a feature the interior designer had intended. Three men stood around the mount. One, wearing what looked like a silver hat, was hunched over the weapon, aiming it. One of the others was checking readouts on a fat power supply, and the third—the third had already reacted and was firing at them.

Riss dropped to the floor and fired twice, two smoking holes appearing in the man's chest.

One shot from Grok's weapon took out the other two.

They stood and moved toward what had been the beam weapon, watching carefully for other attackers, but it looked like they were done.

Goodnight found the sniper team's position without much trouble. It was on the third floor of the building, facing what had been the entrance of Star Risk's headquarters.

Had he entered the third floor from the stairwell the trouble would have been worse, but he'd taken the less expected route, going up to the fourth floor and then climbing down on the landward side of the structure.

He needed to be careful—it would be nice to collect a prisoner so that they could find out who these yabbos were.

The building had been built in pre-Colonial style, one feature of which was windows that could be opened. Using a thin stiletto, he slipped the catch and moved inside.

Outside of the office the room was mostly open, which let him see the two members of the sniper team. One was guarding the stairwell entrance, weapon ready to fire. The other stood at his back, scanning the room.

*Oops.*

—*Brackabrackabrackabracka*—

Bullets stitched the wall behind where Goodnight had been.

*These guys are pissing me off.*

The former Alliance commando jumped up and fired twice, both head shots.

*Well, crap. So much for prisoners.*

Jasmine's passive sensor array read prelaunch signatures on the missiles.

"Is that what I think it is?" Freddie asked.

"Not for long."

Her fingers moved over the controls quickly, activating several devices that had been placed on the roof of the retirement village. The placement had ostensibly been for astronomical research, and generated income for the building, which the building's manager was only too happy to accept. Don't ask, don't tell.

The manager probably wouldn't have been nearly as excited to see the short, barrel-shaped telescope suddenly open both ends to reveal deadly, stubby-looking rockets.

"I think they're waiting for a signal of some kind," said Jasmine. She nodded at the boat.

"A fail-safe," von Baldur said, nodding to himself. "Sad to see how little other people trust their employees," he continued.

There was an abrupt spike on Jasmine's console.

"Looks like they just got the signal," she said.

"Well, I guess we'd better do something about it. We don't need any more civilian casualties."

"Done."

Six stubby missiles flew from the rooftop, far more gracefully than their shapes would have suggested. The dual-stage engines were the best money could buy, and just about the fastest. Jasmine's monitor screen went white, returning to color seconds later to show debris where the ship had been.

"You were saying it was going to be simple?" Jasmine said.

"My dear, simple doesn't necessarily mean it won't have *some* difficulties," said von Baldur. "And we are getting paid."

She nodded. Better than being shot at for free.

# THREE

It was a happier organization that reconvened in the Star Risk, Ltd., HQ conference room some hours later. Much of the debris had been cleaned up, and a new skylight was in the process of being grown. The authorities—such as they were—had come and gone, pissed off, but aware that what had happened here was not Star Risk's fault. Sort of. By the time it was all sorted out, that's what they'd find.

With any luck.

"Now where was I?" von Baldur said. "Oh, yes—this time it should be simple."

As before, it was just the five of them. The reverend had already shipped out to Artegal, after some small encouragement from von Baldur, explaining how they should travel separately if they were going to keep the baddies from finding out about their plans.

Although it seemed *some* of the baddies might already know, given the attack on their new HQ.

"However, while it should be simple, that's not to say there won't be a *few* difficulties, as we've seen. Jasmine?"

Jasmine, looking like she'd stepped out of the pages of a glossy men's magazine instead of a battle in which she had just blown a large boat to small bits, tapped a few controls on the edge of the table. A schematic of the Artegal System appeared in the air over the table. The five main planets were highlighted in the diagram and grew larger as she circled them with a pointer.

"Here we have the Artegal System—Una, with it's capital city of Sarcid, then Zweiten, Terzo, Vierde, and Abesse, the farthest planet out.

"The four space stations the reverend's loaders work are here, here, here, and *here*," she said, waving the pointer in the air.

Four stations shimmered into existence.

"The big one here is called Deep Space One, and serves to catch the majority of the spacer-only traffic in the system. The gravity wells of the planets are too high for really big freighters."

She indicated the two smallest stations.

"These don't look so big, but they each serve as the key import and export points for their respective plants. Somehow—neither Freddie nor I are sure how—the locals managed to build beanstalks without using substandard materials or allowing the rampant corruption to otherwise halt their construction."

Beanstalks were orbital elevators—giant towers that literally pulled cargo up from the surface of a planet to orbit.

"Probably somebody realized how much more money they could steal when they got working," Goodnight said.

"Spoken like a true thief," said Riss.

"It takes one to know one."

Jasmine glared at them. "If I may continue?"

Goodnight and Riss looked at Jasmine and shrugged.

"Each of the small stations hold about a hundred thousand souls, about a third of whom are loaders."

Riss whistled. "That means the bigger ones must be huge."

"Two hundred thousand for Deep Space One. Similar proportions of loaders on each. Likewise the other worlds."

"Great name, Deep Space One," said Goodnight. "So original."

"I'm more interested in the complications," said Riss.

Grok nodded, his huge, furry head casting shadows from the overhead lights onto the projection.

"Well," Goodnight said. "She's just given us one. There are four stations and five of us."

"Who doesn't get one?" asked Riss.

"*If* I may continue?"

Everybody shut up.

"Our expense line is what we just got from the reverend, plus our reserves. That mess with the bank has been sorted out, but we still don't have what we usually would."

"Which means we shall have to be inventive—and cheap." That from von Baldur.

"Poor Freddie," Riss said. "Always worried about the credits."

"I am sure that working in the Artegal System will afford us the chance to make up for being poor. If we are careful."

"Goodnight already pointed out the other complication," Jasmine continued. "Four stations and five of us."

She looked over at the group. "That could spread us pretty thin—*really* thin with our current budget."

"Maybe not," Goodnight said. "Give me a few seconds—"

He toggled bester, then leaned his head into his hands and shut his eyes—the latter motions so fast as to be a blur.

One of the side effects of being a bester was the ability to analyze complex situations at high speed—a bonus that the military designers hadn't counted on. Since the besters could think faster than they could move, it was even more effective than combat.

Like now.

A few seconds later he opened his eyes and tapped his chin again.

"Rather than try to hit all of the stations at once, we knock them over in sequence, and use the timing to apply heat to our strike-breaking friends."

Grok grinned, a sight to make strong men feel queasy. "Four of us against many thousands. I can hardly wait."

Jasmine tapped the table with her pointer and the stations vanished, to be replaced by four circular graphs.

"Not many thousands, Grok, sorry—just a few." She indicated the graphs.

"Oh. Too bad."

"Each of these shows the relative proportion of the reverend's people to the strikebreakers and backers. The current situation is that the people who want to go on strike have been bullied into continuing to work—via the usual tactics, threats, terror, etc. The reverend's people outnumber the strikebreakers by a large margin—and the difference is greater as we move away from the principal planet.

"All we have to do is remove the threats and those who are making them, and the majority will proceed with the strike.

"The baddies, however, according to Williams, have some serious firepower.

"Our job," she continued, "is to do all this and"— looking straight at Goodnight—"do it without destroying the station or its ability to do business."

"At least you didn't say we couldn't kill anyone," Goodnight said.

She shook her head. "M'chel did a little digging on the hired muscle."

Riss took the pointer and tapped it on the table. The four stations reappeared.

"The Artegal Shipping Consortium, ASC, the company that runs the stations, went big on this one— they hired four mercenary units, with a strength of about five hundred each. Those five hundred are the ones who are tipping the balance in favor of breaking the strike on each station. That's the bad news.

"The good news is that they gave each unit its own station."

Goodnight laughed.

"What is good about this?" asked Grok. "I do not see."

"They will be at each other's throats, trying to prove each is the best," said Riss. "It means they won't play nice together, which is a weakness."

"That we shall exploit," Jasmine said.

"Ah," said the big alien. "Yes, ego of the group mind. It is a fascinating aspect of your race."

"Yeah, well, it'll work for *us* this time," Goodnight said.

"Anyone from Cerberus?" asked Jasmine.

"No," Riss said. "And I'm glad for the change."

"Instead, we've got four fairly diverse groups—the Doom Dogs—they're from Bretton VI and most of them have some genetic mods; the Daggar Clan from Zachary IX, which specializes in unarmed combat; a group of cybernetic fanatics from Helen VI who call themselves the Machine Guns—they were the ones who hit us here; and a group from Westlake who call themselves the Professionals."

"I hate that kind of crap," Goodnight said. "Funny names."

"Not like 'Star Risk,' hey?" Riss said.

Goodnight gave her a sod-off look. "Here's a question: Why did they hit us? How did they get set up so fast?"

She shrugged. "Some ambitious soul took it upon himself to follow the reverend. He's been here a while, asking around, trying to find us. Somebody overheard him, figured it out. Doesn't matter, since none of them are still with us, and therefore won't be sharing their error with the other mercs anyway."

"Point taken," Goodnight said.

"Let's talk logistics," von Baldur said. "Since we are going to be working to destroy—ah, I mean *halt* all shipping in the system, I think we'll need another way to get in and out. Funds are tight, but I suggest we contact Redon Spada."

"Yeah," said Goodnight, "I second that. A stealth ship would be ideal."

Grok scratched under his chin with his long nails, a

sound vaguely reminiscent of a carpet being scraped by knives.

"I know where we may be able to obtain a ship," he said. "One of my colleagues was studying the war on Killian V and needed to be able to move in secret. Unfortunately, he was busy documenting a ground-level command post when the hillside in which he was hiding was destroyed. The ship automatically returned to our embassy. A friend of mine at the embassy offered to send it our way—for a price."

"How much?" asked von Baldur.

"A simple bribe," said Grok.

"Your last simple bribe cost a former client a hundred thousand credits," Jasmine said. "And this time we don't have an expense account."

"We do get expenses—if we win," said Jasmine.

"My dear, clients have a way of forgetting details like that," said von Baldur. "Which is why I prefer to work strictly on a pay-as-they-go basis. But you have to play the cards you're dealt."

Riss nodded. "That we do."

"We'll travel together—no need to hide on our own ship," she added. "Drop Freddie at Artegal, and then scoot back to Deep Space One and help get the strike started."

"Thanks to Reverend Josiah we have more on-the-round intelligence and contacts than usual," said Jasmine. "Which means we'll only be spending marginally more time than normal on background research."

Goodnight grinned. "Your devious mind is more and more attractive, Jas," he said.

"Better us than them," she said.

"So," Goodnight said, "all we have to do is stop

two thousand or so mercenaries across four space stations from putting pressure on the godly so that they can go on strike. There will be six of us. We have very little money, no major resources to speak of, almost no one who we trust, and we have to be sure we don't destroy the station. That sound about right?"

"Perfect," said Jasmine.

"Like I said before," von Baldur added. "It's going to be simple."

# FOUR

Grok routed the call to the basement of the Star Risk headquarters, the deepest room in the building. Before connecting with the embassy on Grimaldi, he toggled several switches that sent coded pulses along the signal path checking for lost or tampered-with packets of information. Nothing. Once he was sure the path was as secure as he could make it, he opened the connection.

The viewscreen showed another of Grok's race, one who might have been his twin had the alien not had a large scar on his face, and been slightly thinner.

"A meaningful day to you, Gorbochandrov Rhyannoniankan."

"And to you, Amanandrala Grokonomonslf. What a pleasant surprise."

"Indeed? Then your message to me about the impounded ship was purely a courtesy? My call is unexpected?"

Rhyannoniankan grinned, exposing a mouth full of sharp teeth. No weakness there. "Well, perhaps not entirely, my friend."

"So now we are friends, eh, Ryan?"

"As I have learned in the diplomatic trade with humans, the enemy of my enemy is sometimes my friend."

"Ahh. So who is my new enemy?"

Ryan laughed. "You are too good at this, Grok—you really are. Let me get right to the point: You need a stealthed ship, and I need someone dead. Trade?"

Grok didn't hesitate. Their budget was low; the rest of Star Risk would no doubt be pleased. Besides, he would welcome the action. Whoever it was, if it was just the one person, how difficult could it be?

"Trade."

Goodnight and Riss hung upside down like spiders from thin monofilament lines. Below them lay the warehouse where the weapons were stored.

Said warehouse was owned by a weapons dealer who went only by the name Mel—and, more importantly, who had screwed them over during the financial troubles they'd suffered from Cerberus Systems only a few months before.

The screw in question had been a few crates of Mark V blaster rifles, destined to be used by guards at a temporary headquarters. The financial problems caused by Cerberus had not, in fact, been a problem for the arms dealer—he had been paid.

But when he had heard that Star Risk was persona non grata with the local banks, via a local collection agency, he'd filed a claim against Star Risk for the cost of the weapons. Assets seized by the bank had covered the cost. No doubt Mel had been pleased—after all, he'd been paid twice for them *and* kept them.

But even though they had been unable to take action at the time, Jasmine had made a little note in her database: *Score to be settled.*

And now that they needed some specialized weapons, what better time? It was justice.

They were seeking SS weapons—otherwise know as "Station Safe," a term which indicated that the weapons could kill or maim without the risk of breaching the walls or bubbles of a space station. In practice this meant low-powered dart throwers, short-range shockers, poly-plas shooters, and even nonpowered edged weapons.

Goodnight pressed a button on his spinner, which began generating more of the thick-molecule web, and he began to descend toward the building below. Both he and Riss were wearing skinsuits, thin, intelligent-fabric garments that covered them from head to toe and would keep DNA in, mostly. Plus they looked good, if you were in shape. . . .

They were just above the skylight nearest their target area. Riss tapped Goodnight's arm and he nodded, stopping his descent. She pulled a plas-cutter from a pouch at her waist while Goodnight checked for sensors.

He shook his head. *Nothing.*

*The kind of idiot that doesn't have alarms* deserves *to get ripped off—double cross or no,* he thought.

Riss attached a small suction device to a section of the window and then fired up the cutter. The tip of the cutting arm immediately began generating intense heat, enough to melt the clear plas of the skylight.

As Riss finished circling the suction cup, Goodnight pulled. Wisps of material accompanied by the distinctly unpleasant odor of burning plas wafted upward as he removed the cutaway.

He set the panel carefully down on the roof nearby and pulled out his sensor array again.

The former Alliance special forces agent leaned forward, carefully putting the fiber-optic probe of his device into the panel. His sensor array lit up most dramatically.

"Crap!"

He leaned over toward Riss.

"Bastard has sentry guns set to roll—above the crates, and on the ground," he whispered.

*So much for being an idiot.*

Jasmine sat with Freddie in the recently repaired conference room. The huge hologram normally projected at the end of the room was now centered over their worktable. Multiple layers of data covered the display, two or three deep in some places. King and von Baldur had been at their research for several hours.

"Well, it looks like that's him, all right," Jasmine said.

The "him" in question was a holo of a dark-haired man wearing a suit that looked like it might have cost more than one of the starships operated by their regular subcontractor, Redon Spada.

"And he is . . . ?"

"Keven Makko," said King, "the power behind the power of ASC. At least as far as we know—there is almost certainly somebody holding his leash, but we don't have the particulars of that yet.

"Although ASC is officially a government entity,

ASC has, through the issuance of public bonds—and a unique rider in the fine print of the referendum which passed them—become effectively owned by Mr. Makko."

"Well, well," said von Baldur. "I do love corruption on that kind of scale. Gives me all kinds of places to play."

"He's our man, and apparently he hates to be told no—he's the one whose funds are paying for the mercenaries."

"Well done, my girl. I don't suppose you found any glaring weaknesses in his profile?"

"No—and not many enemies either. Most of them have had a tendency to vanish mysteriously, usually immediately after some public statement against him.

"I did, however, find out that public shipping is not all he owns. He has a chain of nightclubs which, in addition to regular entertainment, claim to offer the widest variety of offworld smoking pleasures available on the planet. Apparently Mr. Makko enjoys a good cigar."

"Ah," said Freddie, "very interesting."

Grok lay in the sand on the private island that belonged to his target. Ryan had explained that the man he wanted killed was a rich industrialist—one who had supported several antialien factions in the last election.

Grok had stopped him at that point. "I care not why you want him killed," he'd said. "Just tell me who and where."

Ryan had laughed. "I could use more of your thinking in politics, Grok."

So now he was on the island, having swum the last

kilometer without the aid of mechanical devices that could be detected by the perimeter security.

The magnitude of sensors surrounding the island had made the big alien grin. All he'd been able to get past them was a plastic sensor array and a large ceramic knife. It pleased him to be getting back to the basics.

Of course, for Grok, the basics also included useful fangs, claws, and a musculature that exceeded human strength by close to seven times. He'd considered leaving the ceramic knife to be more sporting.

He glanced at the sensor array. At least four separate colors were blinking on the device, indicating multiple sensor networks.

Well, if the target was going to play with technology, so could he.

The big alien checked the readout again and moved forward through the trees.

Goodnight considered the sentry guns. Officially frowned upon by most Alliance worlds, they had radically fast step-flex motors that moved at speeds far beyond what human flesh and blood could hope to achieve. Electric current moving through conductive nanotubes made the gun emplacement *flex* rather than spin, helping achieve the guns' amazing speed, directed by near-AI vector targeting systems. The gun was housed in a strong composite armor that could take enormous abuse before being damaged. His bester sergeant, a grizzled old bull named Thorp, had effectively illustrated what a sentry gun could do during training: He'd taken a handful of clay targets and thrown them in the air in front of one of the guns. All the recruits had been told to go bester so they'd see what happened. Thorp had thrown maybe seven or eight of the clays in a wide fan in front of the machine. None of them had hit the ground. Goodnight could still remember the smell of the clay dust that had drifted back over the recruits, and could remember seeing the clays vaporizing in a sequence almost too fast to follow, even in bester.

One of the stupider recruits had had to ask of course. "So, Sarge, what do we do if we run into one of these?"

The answer had been succinct. "You die. Best to avoid running into one."

And here were not just one, but two, with overlapping fields of fire. Attempt to get one of the guns and the other would get you.

There had to be a way. No way Goodnight was going to let Mel get the better of them.

He fed the fiber-optic strand back down into the warehouse and panned it around. The picture on his handheld mapped itself to a floor plan of the warehouse.

As he'd thought—no way to get right over the guns, but he could get closer to them.

Hmmm . . .

Jasmine tapped the SEND icon hanging over the conference room table and a thousand credits moved from a shell account owned by Star Risk to Heiner and Associates, an information broker on Mission that regularly accessed and backed up offworld databases. At least that was one way to look at it—the other was that they broke in and stole data from a myriad of systems and sold it to the highest bidder.

In this case the data concerned shipping manifests for the last six months of goods into the Artegal system. A large chunk of data, to be sure, which was why Jasmine was going to cook it down before passing it on.

She pulled the data off Mission and routed it through several other systems, logging in remotely at each location to confuse anyone who might want to trace the transaction. With the distances involved she wasn't truly real time on the other worlds, but the tachyon grid lag for Trimalchio IV wasn't too bad. She'd been on some worlds where actions executed took up to an hour.

A green light flashed on her left workspace, a layer or so back. The top layer went translucent until she pulled the data to the surface and acknowledged receipt.

*There.*

The records would show average volume on each station, typical trade good patterns, and lag times from station to planet. She and Freddie had taken the research a step further, however, and had tracked where a good deal of the cargo that arrived had been stored and, more importantly, how much was there *now*.

The research specialist tapped the SAVE icon in the air over the table, and the conference room computer began burning five identical copies of everything: ASC, Makko, contacts Josiah had given her whom she'd vetted, shipping records for the last six months, and manifests she'd hacked for the upcoming two months.

She waved her hand and executed an action that broke the new records down into cargo categories, sorting the data to previously identified key markers. There.

Forewarned was forearmed, after all.

Grok slid over the windowsill on the second floor of the huge mansion and grinned into the darkness. He'd made it to the house. Ah, what fun!

Not a huge challenge, however. Slipping past the sensor nets had been so easy that he'd almost not needed the personal detector unit.

The only remotely tricky part had been passing over a series of electric eye beams at the large fence surrounding the property. Just beyond them was a large field of pressure sensors.

To be sure, there were probably no humans who could have leaped as far over the sensors as had Grok—even after using a huge tree limb as a springboard.

However, it was sloppy security to design only for your race, as his target would soon find out.

Still, perhaps he could make things more challenging—take the target out and move all the way off the island before anyone knew. Or better yet, take him along. Wouldn't that make for a mystery?

He checked his detector before moving forward in the room.

*Hmm. Most interesting.*

There was a hidden room just to the left. Heavily alarmed, as well. Grok moved forward and used a simple shut-off function of the device to defeat the alarm. There was a click as the lock released and the door swung open on silent hinges.

The big alien stepped inside and closed the door. There were no windows in the room, so he turned on the lights.

*Well, well . . . look at this . . .*

It was a trophy room—but instead of the usual predators and herbivores, it was filled with the stuffed and preserved remains of aliens.

*Sentient* aliens . . .

There was one of the Lichens of Regula V; a skeleton of what could only be a Flier from Santiago, and over there—

The big alien slid forward, eyes narrowing, a deep rumbling growl starting in his chest.

It was the body of one of *Grok's* people. Frozen forever in an attack position. Oh, this was *vile*!

His detector pinged. Someone was coming.

Goodnight and Riss moved to try out his idea.

If it didn't work, they'd have to get out fast—if they were still alive.

They'd moved much closer to one of the sentry guns—the one that was closest to the roof. Goodnight had selected a skylight that was just about dead even between the two guns.

Riss cut out another panel, and he pulled it up. Then he attached two dabs of anchor putty to the panel and linked it to M'chel's and his spinners.

As near as he could tell, he'd need to drop it just *there*.

He touched his chin and went bester, and then dangled the thin plastic edge-on between the two guns.

The plas had no metallic content and was nearly

invisible to normal eyes. On edge, as he had it, it was unlikely to set off ultrasonics, either.

However, when he turned it *so*—

Both sentry guns suddenly noticed the large panel that had appeared between them and was moving.

Goodnight kept the movement quick, swinging the panel to and fro, keeping the swing on a line between the two guns. Now—were they paired or independent?

Both guns fired at the panel.

Not paired. Good.

Once it disintegrated—almost immediately—the bullets were shooting through the space where the panel had been.

And toward each other.

The appearance of mutually hostile targets and the impacts of the bullets triggered each gun into self-defense mode. Both kept firing.

And, as he had hoped, destroyed each other.

He turned toward Riss and indicated the skylight with a flourish.

"I do believe Mel's is open for business."


The lights came on in the trophy room, and two men entered. One spoke, indicating a huge, elongated skeleton.

"Now this one I took on the estate here. Brought him back and chased him down. Of course, he'd been drugged, and the venom sacs removed."

The second man chuckled. "Must have wished he'd never entered human space."

"Yeah. I couldn't understand it, of course, but he could have been crying for his mother."

"Wow, that one looks fierce."

Both men looked at Grok, who stood stock-still, just in front of the dead and stuffed member of his people.

"Uh-huh—one of the toughest alien bastards I ever took. Nearly got me."

The man pulled the collar of his shirt down, revealing several parallel scars.

"Of course, man *is* the greatest hunter of all—just ask them." He indicated the rest of the room.

His friend moved forward, a little drunk, walking carefully.

"Wow, Bobby, I guess you really like taking chances—don't see any other duplicate species here."

Bobby, the target, frowned. *"Duplicates? Where?"*

Grok roared.

The look on his target's face was worth more than the ship he was going to be paid with.

They screamed—but the screams were cut short.

Before he left, he repositioned the trophy of his fellow being in a more appropriate fashion.

As the big alien left the building, he wondered what the forensics people would make of it—two dead men clawed to death by a stuffed trophy.

He grinned and, had anyone seen it, there would have been no doubt in their minds which race had the greatest hunters of all.

# FIVE

"Our ship has, as you say, 'come in,'" said Grok. Sunlight from the overhead skylight dappled the alien's fine fur as he entered the conference room.

Freddie and Jasmine were sitting at the table going over cargo manifests while M'chel and Chas played with the SS weapons. Goodnight had taken a thin tube and was holding it to his mouth. There was a "phhhft" sound and a dart appeared on a target across the room.

Grok grinned.

"Which port?" asked Jasmine, "Did you go local, or tuck it out of region?"

Grok's grin seemed to get wider, a sight that would have terrified many who did not know him, and worried some of those who did.

"It is local. Very local."

M'chel looked over, not missing the emphasis.

"How local?"

"Oh, just outside."

That got their attention.

Everyone got up and headed outside, much to the big alien's obvious satisfaction.

He followed, and came out behind the group.

Goodnight was looking around at hummingbird speed, his head darting back and forth, and von Baldur held a finger on his lips, bemused.

Between the entrance to their underground headquarters and the building across the street that had been part of their recent run-in with Artegal's hired guns was a wide street. To the left of the old folks' home was a small grassy area dotted with benches for picnicking and enjoying the view. To the right was another building—an emergency clinic for urgent care that von Baldur called doc-in-a-box. The building was set back from the street and had a small garden.

In accordance with Trimalchio IV urban development rules, the insurance building across the street also had open areas nearby: a small grove of tropical trees surrounded by sand on one side, and a sport court on the other side. There was no ship to be seen.

Goodnight seemed to blur slower, and then said, "You're conning us, Grok. Nothing is that stealthed. There's no impressions on the sand, a game in progress on the court, no couples smashed to a pulp under the picnic tables, and cars moving back and forth on the street. Oh—and none of the flowers are smashed."

Riss nodded. "I think he's got it covered, eh, Grok?"

Freddie grinned. "I'll take that bet if you want, M'chel."

Jasmine frowned. "I don't see how you could win," she said.

Grok laughed, a deep rumbling in his chest.

"Look at the players," he said, indicating the sport court.

Their heads swiveled as one, and they watched the two teams going at it, each bouncing a ball as they ran toward the goal at the other end of the court.

It was Jasmine who spotted the pattern.

"They're staying away from the left side of the court," she said.

"What the hell?" That from Goodnight.

"Maybe from hell," said von Baldur. "Certainly not Alliance."

Grok nodded.

It was true that, of all the forces in the civilized galaxy, the Alliance tended to have the best equipment. The many member races of the group all shared their technologies, which gave Alliance engineers the cream of the galactic crop to put in their ships. At least, that's what the PR spinners promulgated.

But like martial arts masters, most races held something back—an ace in the hole, something that only they had.

So it was with stealth technology.

"This ship was a gift from the Pr'ar," said Grok. "One of my people had dealings with them, and earned the right for a favor.

"How much do you know about Alliance stealth?" he continued.

"Well," said Goodnight, rolling his eyes, "although I was never officially on board any stealthed ships, which of course don't exist anyway, my understanding is that various frequencies of light—visible and invisible—are diverted around a ship with a cloak, which effectively renders it invisible. Of course, the problem is that you don't want to divert all of them—otherwise you can't see out."

Grok nodded.

"Yes," he said. "So it is with this ship. However, the Pr'ar are also telepathic—and have devised technology to compliment that. Their cloaking devices include a 'look away, stay away,' compulsion which functions within several hundred meters of their ships, even when visible."

"Fantastic," von Baldur said.

"We could just sell the ship and retire forever," said Goodnight.

Grok laughed. "Ah, sadly no. The ship is only on loan until our current needs are met. Besides, their devices use part of a Pr'ar brain and are impossible to replicate. At least so far as I have been told."

"Who'd you have to kill to get this?" asked Goodnight.

"Someone who deserved it," Grok said. He didn't smile.

The others all turned to look at him. He shrugged. "You asked."

After dark, they started loading the ship, which gave them their first look inside. However, looks weren't what they noticed first.

The ship—not to put too fine a point on it—stank.

"What *is* that dreadful smell?" Freddie asked.

"The Pr'ar have a home world which smells much the same," said Grok, "and feel it is a racial necessity to have it wherever they go."

"Whew!" Goodnight said. "Now I'm sure I've never met one of them—I'd remember that stench."

"They are somewhat low profile," Grok admitted. "Not real members of the Alliance at all."

"If there were any doubt about how good their cloaking technology is, the fact that we didn't *smell* the ship should count for something," said Goodnight.

"Great," Riss said. "Any other surprises?"

"Well, actually," Grok said, "there is the matter of *plumbing*. The Pr'ar are a very efficient race and seldom—meaning in terms of months—need to void waste."

Freddie shook his head, getting it. "No toilets?"

Grok nodded. "Just so."

"Ah. Well, it looks like we'll be needing to add a few more items to our travel supplies. I really, really miss our old battleship."

With chem toilets aboard, along with a whole lot of whirring deodorizer units, they left at midnight.

Their first stop was an out-of-the-way space station in the Denebian system, where they picked up Redon Spada. Spada wrinkled his nose when he got on board. "Gah! Usually it's just a figure of speech when I say my stinking clients, they aren't paying me enough," he said. "Not this time. Can't you use a deodorizer?"

"We have *several* working round the clock. You should have smelled it *before*. Don't worry," said Goodnight. "You hardly notice it at all unless you need to breathe."

Jasmine had contacted Spada several days before, and he had arranged to get the detailed orbital charts for the Artegal System.

When he saw the alien controls he grinned. "On the other hand, where else can I be paid to play with toys like this?"

Once they were away from the station and the cloak

had been engaged, Spada spent several hours practicing with the controls and nav systems.

After several amusing incidents, including one near miss of a large asteroid, he announced he was ready to get started.

"Next stop, Artegal System."

# SIX

The Star Risk crew took the normal precautions when arriving at a place where they would be working. The ship was logged into the port under one of the myriad covers they had established. In this case, they were ostensibly a group of well-off amateur ornithologists come to view and catalog the species that the planet Una had to offer, and as long as they were here, they were going to do a little business and thus be able to write off the trip. At the moment, they could leave the ship visible. Soon enough, the cloak would come out and they'd disappear.

They had the requisite starlight scopes, binocular-cams, and guides, along with recordings of the local tweeters, though they wouldn't be doing a lot of that activity.

Grok, who might be the last person anybody would look at and think "bird-watcher," had listened to the recordings and demonstrated a gift for mimicry by replicating the sounds.

It was passing odd to hear a creature who looked like a nightmare cheep like a songbird.

"That was the orange-tufted boobmouse," Grok said. "And here is the blue-necked nutcrusher." Whereupon he commenced an eerily accurate match to the recording of that feathery creature.

"Tell you what," Goodnight said. "You call 'em, I'll cook 'em. Probably all taste just like chicken."

Grok just shook his head. "Sometimes you seem to have no appreciation for beauty whatsoever, Chas."

"Sometimes?" Riss said.

"Oh, I appreciate beauty. A nice emerald-cut blue-white diamond, fifteen carats or so? Beautiful. Especially when it arrives in my pocket at a five-finger discount. And there have been a few women I've known I'd qualify as beautiful—those wearing big blue-white diamonds even more so. But birds are just rats with wings, far as I am concerned. Ever stand near a statue in a park? Bad idea. Exterminate 'em all; wouldn't bother me any."

"Probably best if you don't strike up a conversation with the local birder society, then," Grok said. His voice was very dry.

"Not a problem," von Baldur put in, "since I'll be on the planet while you toodle off to the stations. Not a lot of bird-watchers there, I suspect."

"Now that I think of it," Goodnight said, "why *aren't* there rat-watching groups? Might as well be—lotta different kinds of those, aren't there? Brown ones, gray ones, white ones . . ."

Riss just shook her head.

"Well, von Baldur can talk to the bird huggers while we give the nice security teams at Deep Space One something to worry about," Goodnight said. "What was our cover there going to be again?"

Jasmine made a rude noise. "Don't you ever bother to listen at the briefings?"

"I hear the important stuff. How much will I make? Who do I get to shoot? Who is paying for dinner? Like that."

He was pulling her leg, she knew, but sometimes he kept such a straight face that it was hard to tell. Plus, he *was* sociopathic to a certain degree . . .

"We work for a shipping company looking for cheaper routes to move our cargo," Riss said. "I'm the head of the team, you are the labor guy, Grok represents our client, and Jasmine is the accountant. I have appointments with low-level functionaries set up. We'll go to meetings and grumble about the high cost of reaction mass and cargo containers.

"Oh, yeah. I remember."

"Try not to shoot anybody before we get out of the beanstalk."

"Me? Whatever do you mean, M'chel? I wasn't the one who fried a guy once because he insulted my intelligence." He looked pointedly at her.

She flushed. He was never going to let her forget that. "No, because it would be almost impossible to insult *your* intelligence."

That was lame, and everybody knew it, but it was the comeback she had. Goodnight grinned at her, and made a point-for-me sign in the air with his forefinger.

She also made a sign at him, but using a different finger.

"Okay, let's mount up," von Baldur said. "Keep me posted on the secure channel."

"Yeah, let's go places and hurt people," Goodnight said.

He wasn't joking.

The space station was large as such things went, probably fifty kilometers around and shaped something like a squashed orb. It was standard construction, basically a small city in a Lagrange area where the forces of gravity from the planet balanced and made it easier to keep in position. The beanstalk shaft carried most of the cargo to and from the planet, along with passengers in pressurized and heated elevator cars. Really large items could either be broken down and shipped in pieces, or trucked up via ship.

Given that they weren't overly large cargo, they booked a lift on a passenger elevator. This was more like a bus or a shuttlecraft in design. They went business class, which jammed them in fairly tight, the seats not being particularly roomy for such a short trip.

Grok, even with two seats booked, lifted the separating arms and spilled over into a third and a fourth chair, and nobody begrudged him the space—at least they didn't do so out loud. As always, he got a lot of curious looks. He had gotten used to that. The idea of him sneaking around unnoticed in public was fairly silly; then again, when Grok was around, nobody paid much attention to the rest of them, so that sword cut both ways.

Goodnight was reminded of an effective and cheap disguise when robbing a place: Put a big bandage on your face, and that's what people remembered when the law came by later to ask.

*What did the robber look like, sir?*
*Um, he had a big bandage on his face.*
*How tall was he?*
*The bandage was flesh-colored . . .*
Which disguise also came off two steps out the door . . .

Goodnight took his seat and promptly fell asleep, an old military habit. He'd known guys in the service who could nod off standing up and eating a bowl of hot soup, and they'd never spill a drop even though they were deep in dreamland.

Riss, meanwhile, considered their plan for the four-teenth time. Freddie was right; this ought to be simple, at least in theory. "Simple" and "easy" weren't even close cousins a lot of the time, but this was right; out of the most basic texts on guerrilla warfare, tried-and-true tactics that anybody could use with only a little bit of skill and luck. They had plenty of skill, so all they needed was luck, and as everybody knew, chance favored the prepared mind. The Six-P Principle: Proper planning prevents piss-poor performance. . . .

Jasmine would have no trouble being the bean counter, she could do that with no effort. Her real job would be a bit more involved, but it was more up her alley. Anytime there were a bunch of people in a small space, information was easier to suss out, and that's where she would be—finding out the who, where, what, when, why, and how of all the things they needed to know.

This job was practically in the bag—it ought to be like a paint-by-numbers kit.

Of course, she'd thought that a few times before and had it not turn out quite that way, so she wasn't going to buy into Freddie's offhand nonchalance completely. The job was never over until it was over . . .

# SEVEN

For a man who owned a chain of nightclubs, there was one item that was an absolute necessity: liquor. And Keven Makko, being such a man, knew this fact well. He always had two backup suppliers on standby. If his primary delivery service had problems—a hovertruck blew a lifter or there was a wildcat strike by the damned drivers or loaders—he could make a call and have a standing order on the way in minutes. He had a pretty good supply of drinking stock in each club, enough so that he could squeak by for a few days even without new cases arriving to replenish stock, but past a certain point, things would become dire.

People didn't go to nightclubs to drink *water*.

Makko looked up at Neves from behind his hand-carved molowood desk, the dark and swirly wood still aromatic after ten years. His desk smelled like the finest smokeweed, pungent and earthy, and had cost a year's salary for an average worker. "Say it again. I'm not sure I heard you properly."

His assistant, Neves, who was two meters tall and built like a brick—you could bounce credit coins off him he was so tight—said, "None of the delivery vans are running today from any of our suppliers."

"How is that possible?"

"I dunno, Patron. Something to do with the routing dispatch computer systems. Some kinda virus got into 'em and bollixed the delivery addresses."

"Don't these people have backup systems?"

Neves shrugged. "Some kinda problem getting 'em online. So the supply hovercraft are all grounded while they try to fix it."

"This won't do. We need to shift some of our stock around. Call the clubs, find out what they have and don't have, and get some vehicles in the air moving it."

"Already done that, Patron. Biggie's has the most extra—it's been slow there this week—so a van is loading that and taking it to the Starshine and Bright Moon, which are almost dry. Everybody is okay until tomorrow."

Makko nodded. He couldn't control everything, which was too bad, but crap happened and you had to deal with it. At least it wouldn't make any difference to the paying customers.


Von Baldur, decked out in his bird-watching gear, stood on the edge of a city green space next to a busy avenue. He wore a little bit of a disguise that he would maintain for the rest of this part of the caper: a fake mustache and different hair color, a little bioflesh to change the shape of his ears and nose and brows, lifts in his shoes—simple stuff. FaceTrace software behind public spycams had a handful of measurements it used, and with just a little work you could rascal the matching criteria. The bird-watcher might look enough like Freddie von Baldur so a keen human eye could detect it, but the software would stick to measurements, and enough of those would be wrong so it wouldn't match two side-by-side holographs.

Traffic blew past, the hover fans and repellers kicking up what dust there was, sending a lube-scented breeze in his direction.

Fortunately, the pocket park behind him actually did have a few birds of assorted varieties living in it. He had aimed his binocular-cam at several of these and captured numerous holographic images, duly stored in the binocam's large memory. A blue bird, one that was brown and yellow, and another one that was black as mortal sin. He had run a comparison of the images with the interactive guide hooked to his belt, identified the avians, and knew enough about them to respond knowledgeably if questioned.

*Why, yes, I did get a snap of the Okonono Fiscus— you don't usually see the males so bright this early in the season, eh?*

If he could fool a real bird-watcher—and he was sure he could do that much regarding the birds in the park—then any passing law enforcement officers who bothered to query would be no problem.

And he had reason to believe that, very shortly, the area would be replete with LEOs.

A hovervan heavy with cargo and only a few centimeters above the roadway labored into view on the street, the fans working hard to maintain that little height. Traffic was light and the van was moving slowly but steadily, a big load weighing it down.

"Ah, there we are. Mr. Makko's liquor van, on its way to deliver its precious cargo of happy juices."

Von Baldur looked at his wrist chrono, ostensibly

to check the time, but what he was watching was an LED proximity flash. As the van drew nearer, the blinking diode pulsed quicker and began to shade into the cooler end of the spectrum. Red to orange to yellow to green . . .

When the blinking green light stopped flashing to hold steady, von Baldur pushed the reset button on his chronograph in a quick pattern—twice, pause, then twice more.

The back of the hovervan exploded into a shower of castplast, glass, and a spray of assorted varieties of potable alcoholic beverages. The fans failed, and the van dropped like a brick and skidded on the road, then slewed to port as it screeched to a smoking halt in the middle of the avenue.

A truck, two passenger vehicles, and a monocyclist behind the downed van all plowed into it or each other; von Baldur saw protective airbags and hardfoams erupt inside the vehicles, and even the cycle rider's helmet ballooned into an impact-resistant hardfoam halo that protected his head as he left the seat of his wheel. Nobody would be seriously hurt, he was sure. He hoped they all had insurance to cover the vehicle repairs.

A hoverbus coming the other way managed a neatly done drift-turn wide enough to miss the crashed van, but had to leave the tarmac and move over the slidewalk to do so, and, as a result, took down a light stanchion and smashed flat a public fresher before fanning to a stop, still airborne. Fortunately, the fresher was empty. That would have been most surprising, von Baldur thought, to look up from one's private business to see a bus coming at you sideways . . .

There was no fire, which was good, given that the high-proof liquid that drenched everything would burn with colorful flames did it ignite. The aroma was quickly potent, even a hundred meters away. Several hundred thousand credits worth of distilled liquors being blown apart by a shaped charge disguised as a pothole patch would do that. Von Baldur smiled as he inhaled the heady fragrance. The odor was like a moonshine mash barrel on a hot day, but it smelled a lot better than that ship they'd brought for this caper. Terrible waste, though. All that booze.

Police sirens began their mournful wails, joined by the slightly different tones of fire engines and ambulances.

Time to go back to bird-watching, von Baldur thought. He smiled. Mr. Keven Makko was probably not so stupid that he wouldn't quickly figure out he had been marked and attacked, but that didn't matter.

Knowing that one was a target was not nearly as important as knowing who was doing the shooting.

Some clumsy fool bumped into Goodnight as they were leaving the beanstalk elevator, and were it not for Riss's hand snaking out to grab his arm, Goodnight probably would have broken the stumblebum's neck. That would have been quicker than pulling his hidden blaster and incinerating the idiot, but he was mindful that he had made a point of not being quick to stomp somebody for minor reasons, so he relaxed and just glared at the guy, who had no idea how lucky he was.

Jasmine looked at her handheld flatscreen and began her disguised search for information even as they waited for their baggage to be unloaded. Already the history of the station was being downloaded into a file, and a passing tidbit caught her attention.

"Hmm," she said.

"What calls forth such a terse remark?" Grok asked.

"During the station's construction, there was a major accident in one of the corridor's downlevels. A seal either malfunctioned or was damaged and there was a blowout. Fifty-seven workers were killed."

"Yeah, too bad," Goodnight said. "So?"

"Well, there is a portion of the populace that believes the corridor where the accident took place is haunted by the spirits of the dead."

Goodnight snorted. "Yeah. Right."

"Is such a thing possible?" Grok asked.

"Probably not," Riss said. "But I see where Jasmine is going with it. It doesn't matter if it really is haunted, only that people *believe* that it is."

"Ah," Grok said. "I see."

"Well, I don't," Goodnight put in. "I repeat, so what?"

"Well, imagine if a bunch of strikebreakers decide that going down that corridor isn't something they want to do. If they demand an escort of security guys."

"Ah," Goodnight said.

"In bester, with a little costuming, you'll make a pretty convincing ghost," Riss said.

"I can't wait."

"Meanwhile," Jasmine said, "I will get the specs for the security team's offices and living quarters, and we'll see what's what there. I expect they haven't gotten much resistance and aren't expecting much from a bunch of cargo haulers. Maybe they've gotten a bit lax."

"One can hope," Riss said.

"Doesn't matter," Goodnight said. "Sharp or dull, they all fall when Chas enters the hall."

Riss and Jasmine looked at each other and shook their heads.

"Full of himself, isn't he?" Jasmine said.

"Full of something," Riss said. "Chas will do what he does and the rest of us have our own chores to accomplish, don't we?"

Grok and Jasmine nodded. This would involve some travel, Jasmine one way, Grok and Riss another, and once they had all set their initial plans in motion, they'd gather together again with Freddie to move to the next step.

So far it had been a breeze, and the next part should be easy enough.

"Blew up? My van full of liquor just *blew up*?!"

Neves said, "Well, it didn't just blow up, Patron. It had help. LEOs have it pegged to a shaped charge somebody put in the road. Dunno if it was aimed at that particular van, or just a coincidence. Some kind of terrorist thing, maybe."

"Not bloody likely it was a coincidence!" Makko said. "Our delivery supplier's vans are all grounded— three different companies—by a computer snafu, and then my van gets blasted? That's too much of a reach. Somebody is out to damage me. Question is, who?"

Neves shook his head. "Shouldn't be anybody left. We've taken out all the competition in the biz."

Makko ran his hand through his hair and rubbed the back of his suddenly stiff neck. "Something to do with the strikers. Some malcontent got hold of a bomb."

"Maybe." His assistant shrugged.

"What?"

"Gotta be a malcontent with some skill, Patron. Managed to get the delivery vans stopped, figured out we were shifting stock, set the bomb up on the right route and blew it? Doesn't sound like your basic cargo loader's kinda smarts."

"No, it doesn't. But it's somebody. Go nose around and find out who."

"Yes, Patron."

After Neves was gone, Makko considered the implications of the attack. He had enemies, though as Neves had said, the ones he knew about who were any kind of real threat had been eliminated. But there were always new ones showing up. Life was unfair that way. He was just trying to make a living, and yeah, every now and then he had to step on somebody's toes to do that. Or squash them like bugs and wipe out everything they had. Maybe if they could see the big picture like he did, they wouldn't be so upset.

What was more important here was—What was Susa going to say? Makko knew he had better have things fixed by then, because even though he was on another world, Susa would already know—he had eyes everywhere.

He sighed. Whatever he had to do to keep body and soul together, that was just how it had to be. If somebody blocked his path, he would take them out, end of story. . . .

# EIGHT

Barry Jarvis scooted his dual-drive container lifter down the darkened row of huge shipping containers, looking for E13–11. Although all of the containers in this sector were destined for outsystem, some were destined more quickly than others, a fact he had always ascribed to someone somewhere having to pay a little more.

*Not that we see a damn extra demi-cred,* he groused to himself. And with those goons ASC had hired, it was unlikely he ever would. Hard to tell your shift leader you were going on strike when a guy with an automatic dart thrower and a big knife was standing right behind him. First to speak would be the first to get darted, and who wanted to be him? And the law was in somebody's pocket, so that would be that.

Damn, where *was* that container? Most of the Es were in this row, so he should have seen it by now, despite the poor lighting. One more thing to thank ASC for, cheap bastards. They'd issued extra headlamps rather than paying to light up the entire warehouse.

Jarvis stopped the double-D and tapped the locator on the dash, looking around before he punched the button. Everyone was supposed to use the damn things, but the loaders took it as a source of pride to avoid them as much as possible. No one in sight. Good.

The little device pinged and he hurried to turn the volume down. A tiny representation of the warehouse appeared on the screen, with his loader plotted on the map as a tiny pink triangle.

*Aha!*

He'd gone right past it.

The loader started to turn his vehicle around to head toward one of the rows back just about thirty meters. Suddenly his rig died. All the electric lights—dim as they were—went out, and for a moment everything went black. But only for a moment.

Then Jarvis saw him. A bluish-white glowing figure in a coverall, carrying a huge spanner in one hand. The figure seemed to blur as he moved toward Jarvis.

*Holy crap!*

Every station he'd worked had its share of bullshit stories, urban legends that ran the gamut from alien eggs to angry computers. On Deep Space One, it was the ghosts.

Years before, during construction, there had been a blowout and a lot of guys had died. Supposedly, some of the ghosts had hung around. Whenever things went south, people had a way of ascribing the cause to the ghosts. Jarvis had never believed in that crap himself, but—

The loader felt a cold chill in the air as the figure drew closer, and he could feel the hairs going up on the back of his neck, goose bumps popping into place all over his body. The apparition raised his wrench, then let out a shriek that made Jarvis's bowels go liquid.

The figure gestured again, and a cargo container—weighing at least six tons—rolled off of the fourth row up, falling within ten or fifteen feet of the double-D.

Jarvis yanked at the controls frantically. Nothing—

Bag this!

Somehow he found himself on foot, running as fast as he could away from the apparition. He might kill himself by running into something in the dark and, somehow, he had enough presence of mind to switch on his helmet light, but he didn't slow down to do it.

He didn't stop running until he was back at the main hangar.

A couple of loaders looked up at him. One of the guards saw him.

Dart thrower or not, there was no effing way he was going to be going back into that bay by himself. No way.

Goodnight smiled from behind the containers where he had hollowed out a nice resting place. The loader had been too easy. "Booga-booga," and he took off, moving at almost bester speed. He figured they'd send a goon, maybe two, to check out the man's story, and the deal was that he was supposed to take 'em out but not kill them.

He hadn't understood the why of that, and Riss had acted like she was explaining it to a child: "If they are dead, they can't go back and pump up the story. What we are after is making it so nobody will go into the warehouse bay."

"They will just send more goons in," Goodnight had said.

"Yes. And when they send in a squad or a whole platoon and you have to take them out, then fine, do it however you want, but you have to keep it quiet and you also have to clean up afterward. Ghosts don't use blasters and, to keep it mysterious, they have to vanish completely."

"How do I take out a whole platoon without making any noise? Where do I put them?"

"That's your problem. Nerve gas, poisoned darts, I don't care. As to where you put them? Somewhere they won't be found, at least not for a few weeks. Once they come up with enough guns so you can't get them all, you move to another bay and start over. Pretty soon, nobody will go anywhere away from the main without demanding a huge security team, and they don't have enough bodies to cover the whole station."

"Nobody will believe a ghost is doing it."

"Oh, yeah, some will. A platoon of armed guards goes into a loading dock and doesn't come back? Nobody can find them? That will spook a lot of folks—at least enough for our purposes."

Yeah, well, that did make a certain kind of sense, Goodnight figured—

He heard voices. Oops. Company.

He shifted back into bester, popped his head up and back down so fast nobody would likely notice even if they'd been looking in his direction, and smiled. Two of them. Noooo problem.

He touched the remote cutout switch and the lights went out.

The two goons said the expected "What the hell?" and "Hey!" and Goodnight tapped himself back into bester. He took a deep breath and gave out his best imitation of a demented spirit condemned to walk the halls of the station forever.

Then he moved . . .

Nude dancers swayed and gyrated in pools of light, each one further defined by the smoke in the air. All manner of smoke could be found—old-style pipes, cigars, cigarettes, and hookahs, as well as more modern air injectors, burn-shoots, and particle hazers. A complex system of intake and outtake vents kept the disparate flavors mostly separate, generating very little overlap.

And there was still enough booze to keep the customers lubed, at least for now.

The place was crowded.

Two obvious bodyguards followed Makko everywhere, stationing themselves no less than a meter from him, and no farther than two. There were other bodyguards of course, undercover, dressed or not dressed. Some of the unclad waitresses were experts in martial arts and could break a neck without raising a sweat. Never think it to look at them, but that was the point, wasn't it?

Makko had long ago gotten used to naked flesh—if he wanted it, it would be available when and where he wished—and he paid the gyrating bodies scant attention as he headed for his office. Halfway there, he saw Neves angling across the floor. He nodded at his assistant.

With the guards outside the door, the two men were alone.

"News?"

"The police don't have any suspects, Patron. I have a copy of all the interviews they did with witnesses and passersby at the site of the explosion. Nobody leaped out as the bomber."

"This helps us how?"

"I did a cross-check on the witnesses and other interviewees. Most of them are locals, in-city or at least onplanet residences. All of them had good reasons for being where they were."

"And . . . ?"

"I came across one who was a little hinky."

"Neves, I know you are not stupid and I pay you well for what you do, so you don't need to impress me with your sleuthing abilities. Drop the other boot."

Neves grinned. "There was an offworlder in the park, a bird-watcher. He seemed to check out—came with a group of guys doing some shipping biz. Had their own ship. But when I tried to backtrack it, I hit a wall. Shell corporation owns the ship, and that corporation is owned by a shell corporation, and that one, which is as far as I could get."

"Ah. Suspicious on the face of it. Could be a tax dodge, but maybe we should have a little talk with this bird-watcher."

"Already in the works, Patron. A couple of the boys have gone to pick him up."

"They are taking him to the Quiet Room?"

"Yes."

"Good. Go and find out if he knows a pinfeather from a pineapple. . . ."

# NINE

Goodnight knew he was good at what he did. Not just because of the military enhancements that gave him superior physical speed and quicker thought processes, but because he had natural strategic and tactical abilities. And, while taking on a couple of normal goons was easier than falling off a two-legged chair, a squad was a little tougher.

There were a dozen hired guns in the squad that came after he had taken out the two. He'd started with a nice lay-down of emetic gas. When they were all puking their guts out—which took all of ten seconds—he went into bester and capped them. It was hard to return fire when you were heaving up everything you had eaten since you were nine all over your boots. . . .

The bodies he had stuffed into a durasteel refrigerated cargo container and resealed, so that nobody could tell it had been opened. Probably somebody would have gotten around to checking eventually, but that was not going to happen because pretty soon that crate wasn't going to be here. . . .

Cleaning up afterward was the hardest part. A dozen guys tossing their cookies creates quite a reeking mess. If he had thought about that before, he would have just used nerve gas.

What came next was a platoon.

Taking out a platoon of nervous, edgy, shoot-first-and-don't-ask-questions guys, even a short one of only three squads, was, even given his abilities, not gonna happen in a stand-up fight.

And worse, the platoon came in geared for war—they wore good armor, and had full filters and their own air supply, so puke gas or nerve agents weren't gonna get 'em. Even a recom-DNA nanotech scrambler would be hard-pressed to drop 'em all, and it wasn't likely that he could lay his hands on such a nasty bit of work in any event. Possession of such outside top secret military environs was worth brainburn pretty much everywhere, and that might as well be the death penalty since it accomplished the same thing. Nobody home, your body kept on ice and sawed up for spare parts as needed . . .

No, taking out a platoon all by himself without making a mess?

Not in the cards. Unless he came up with a clever—no, call it brilliant—plan, which, of course, he had. . . .

Technically, it didn't quite satisfy Riss's requirements for mystery, but it was close enough.

So here they were. Thirty-six suited wazoos armed to the teeth, heavy shoulder weapons ready to cook anything that moved. Jumping out and going booga-booga? That would get you turned into fried fool, no matter how fast you were. Some of them had to be able to shoot straight, and it only took one.

The trick was to get them bunched up where he wanted them, and really, that had been fairly easy. He had spent a few hours using a forklift to move cargo crates around. Most of the storage room looked the same, big corridors through stacks of cargo containers stacked three or four deep, so that they formed walls thirty or forty meters high. Once you were in the maze, you couldn't see much. A smart commander would split his troops into teams and spread out, and apparently the guy in charge of this platoon wasn't completely stupid, because that's what he did. No way one guy could take them all out.

Half an hour of slow searching, even with a couple of guys up on top, and they wouldn't find anything, because there wasn't anything to find. They'd be radioing back to let the higher-ups know, and Goodnight wouldn't mess with that tactical channel—not yet.

Goodnight hurried ahead of the approaching sweep toward his hidey-hole, which was just inside the sunward pressure door at the hull. It would take them a while to get there, it being the farthest away from where they'd started.

He had built a channel of containers leading directly to the door. Nothing so obvious as a funnel, just a nice, container-length-wide corridor seventy-five meters long; nothing there to make a platoon leader nervous, and nowhere for an ambusher to hide.

On the top of one of the containers lining the corridor, he had mounted a holographic projector. A tiny little thing, run on batteries, good for an hour.

Everything else was in place, and all he had to do was wait. . . .

*       *       *

The expected knock came at his hotel room's door. Von Baldur, still in his bird-watcher's facial disguise, opened it, smiling. "Yes?"

The two muscle-bound dweebs didn't even bother to pull weapons. He could have beaten them to the draw and cooked them both, no problem, but that wasn't in the plan.

"Bird-watcher?" one of them said.

"Yes?"

"Come with us."

"Why?"

"Because we say so and if you give us a hard time we'll break something. An arm, like that."

"Oh, dear. I simply can't abide *violence.*"

The two men smirked at each other. He could almost read their thoughts— Got us a little sissy here . . .

They didn't even bother to search him.

Von Baldur wanted to shake his head at such stupidity, but he kept his face blank.

The ride, in a sleek and expensive hovercar that probably was worth more than these two made together in a year, took fifteen minutes. They didn't bother to opaque the windows or blindfold him, so von Baldur figured that meant this was a one-way ride.

That confirmed his suspicions, and made his course of action morally supportable. Goodnight might not need that, but, now and again, knowing the opposition would just as soon shoot you as look at you helped von Baldur sleep better. The Golden Rule had a slight variation in his book: Do unto others as they would do unto you, only do it first. . . .

When they got to their destination, a squat, squarish, windowless block of a gray everplast building in a warehouse district, the dweebs accompanied him to the entrance, one on each side.

The door was thick and heavy. Soundproof, von Baldur reckoned. He expected you could make a lot of noise and nobody outside would hear you. Or, probably, care if they did.

Inside in the entrance atrium, a taller and wolfish-looking man waited.

"Did you search him?" the man asked.

The two dweebs looked at each other. "Um . . ." one began.

"Aw, damn, Mulun! What do we *pay* you for?"

The one called Mulun had the grace to look embarrassed. He turned to von Baldur and patted him down. Found the little pocket blaster and held it up.

The tall man sighed. "Creesto on a cross-shaped crutch!"

"Sorry, Neves," Mulun said.

"Oh, you are that." Neves looked at von Baldur. "I apologize for Mulun and Nonutti. If you had killed them both, you'd have done us a favor."

That drew a smile from von Baldur. Neves wasn't stupid, and he was addressing von Baldur as a fellow professional, based, of course, on having the hidden blaster. A bird-watcher wouldn't need one of those, would he?

Neves would therefore be more careful than his two henchmen.

"Would you step into my, uh, office, Mr., ah . . . ?"

"Von Baldur. Friedrich von Baldur."

"Not the name on your hotel registration."

"Nor the one I was born with, but it serves."

Neves gave him a tight smile. "A relief to be dealing with a pro." He glared at Mulun and Nonutti. "I am Aldo Neves."

Von Baldur nodded. "As you say, Mr. Neves."

"You two wait out here. I believe Mr. von Baldur and I can conduct our business without your help."

Inside the office—and that's what it looked like—Neves gestured at the couch as he moved to sit behind a nicely carved desk of some golden wood. "Sit, and let's discuss events of violence."

Von Baldur sat on the couch and crossed his legs. Cloned leather, and quite comfortable, the couch was. "Such as liquor vans exploding on the public avenues?" he said.

Neves smiled. "I really do appreciate dealing with a man who takes the easy path."

"Saves having to start with torture?"

Neves nodded. "Exactly."

"Which comes later," von Baldur said.

"Truly a pleasure, Mr. von Baldur. You are caught, collected, and we don't need to pretend. If you are forthcoming with all that we need to know, we can do this quickly and relatively painlessly."

"I suppose I should be grateful for that. Will your employer, Keven Makko, be joining us for this discussion?"

"Alas, no. The Patron leaves such matters to me."

"Too bad."

Neves shrugged. "Shall we get down to basics? Who sent you, and why?"

"Well, we could, but maybe you should ask another question first."

"Which would be . . . ?"

"Knowing you planned to torture and kill me, why *didn't* I shoot Lump and Lumpier out there?"

Neves considered it for a couple of heartbeats, and he was both sharp and quick—he jerked open the drawer of the desk—

But with his legs crossed, the toe of von Baldur's right shoe pointed directly at Neves's chest, and the tap-tap of a finger on the shoe's heel triggered the one-shot blaster in the sole and put a quiet bolt through the man's heart. His eyes went wide in shock as von Baldur stood and moved to the desk to remove the more conventional blaster for which the dying man had been reaching.

He examined the weapon, made sure the charge indicator showed green and the safety was off, and then, in a passable imitation of Neves's voice, said, "Mulun, Nonutti, would you step in here for a moment, please?"

As the door opened, he raised the blaster.

The platoon finished its sweep through the main cargo area, and, there being nothing to find, found nothing. The squads met at the corridor Goodnight had built and, when they did, Goodnight touched a control on his remote and lit the holoproj.

The image of Goodnight glowed into being, a wrench in one hand, and a small, hidden speaker uttered a ghostly moan.

Somebody was quick on the trigger, and a blaster bolt zipped through the ghostly image and splashed against the durasteel hatch. The image was, of course, unaffected.

A barrage of blaster bolts followed, with as little

effect, but Goodnight thumbed the projector control and the "ghost" vanished.

The thud of approaching boots down the corridor was loud in the hidey-hole.

Goodnight smiled. He looked at the tiny monitor on his remote, and the spycam on the ceiling showed that most of the platoon had entered the corridor and were double-timing toward the hatch, leaving only a couple of men at the entrance.

"Showtime, folks!" Goodnight said.

He hit three buttons on the remote, one-two-three, in quick succession.

Several things happened.

The lights went out.

The hatch opened—and the sensors showing the hatch's functions at Central went down. Air in the hold whooshed out into the hard vacuum, making quite a breeze, little wisps of it freezing as it met the cold of space, turning into little faceted jewels . . .

A radio jammer blared and shut down all tactical opchans in the hold—nobody was calling for help or even talking to one another.

A series of shaped charges attached to the back of the durasteel container at the end of the corridor went off and, assisted by four directional rockets also set there, effectively turned the container into a huge piston that shot down the corridor toward the now-open hatch, fast and gathering speed—

Like a plunger, the container shoved the men in front of it toward the hatch. The vacating air pressure alone was enough to move them, but the impact of several tons of steel box, made heavier by the bodies of the squad Goodnight had stuffed into it, slamming into them? That was, under the circumstances, irresistible.

The men splayed across the face of the container as it shot into vacuum and directly toward the sun at a speed well past that needed to escape the station's puny gravity. By the time somebody realized what had happened and sent a ship to check it out, the hapless platoon and the container would be a hundred klicks away.

So maybe it wasn't a total mystery like Riss had wanted, but how a ghost blew a whole platoon of armed men out of the station? That would be food for thought, hey?

Goodnight smiled. He loved to pull off tricks like this.

# TEN

While Madam Refinger's little boy Mital was more comfortable running a complex con, or playing a game of cards with his own rigged deck, he knew how to make things go *boom!* when necessary. Since he had given up his former identity and become a new man, sometimes it had become necessary. Such as now.

Von Baldur hummed softly to himself as he worked, a classical piece by Paul Lennon—or was it John McCartney? he never could remember which one was which—something about a blind bird with a broken wing calling in the night or some such. He was uncomfortable in the camosuit. It was heavy and better suited for a cold climate, and he was hot and sweaty, but he was certainly a lot harder for somebody who saw in the visible spectrum to notice. The camosuit was essentially a series of tiny vid screens, each the size of a man's thumbnail, carefully set into a flexible mesh coverall, including a hood. An array of small cams sensed the nearest object—a tree, a wall, a vehicle, whatever—then took that image and projected it onto the screens, computer-augmenting it a bit, so that the suit essentially matched whatever it was in front of. It wasn't perfect, and it didn't do much for one's heat sig or fool a decent motion sensor, but at any kind of distance, especially in low light, the chameleonlike effect was very good at fooling an organic eye. Not as good as their ship, but it was useful.

Fifty meters away, a pair of armed guards stood smoking chemstiks and bitching about having to be out here, and von Baldur, crouched down next to the back of the nightclub, was effectively invisible, even though he was right out in the open.

Wonderful thing, technology.

Of course, if it started to rain, he'd get a bit smeary-looking. The cams worked best against a static background; there was a lag of a few milliseconds between the pickup and projections, but at night, holding still against a dull background such as a permaplast wall painted a flat green? Invisible.

He finished making the connection to the final shaped charge, a newton-bleak explosive that, somehow, channeled most of its force into more or less a flat plane. It was the last of a dozen such charges that ringed the nightclub.

The place was busy, and were he to stand back and trigger the explosives now, a couple of hundred people would die. While killing people was sometimes necessary in their occupation, unlike Goodnight, von Baldur avoided such things when possible. Especially civilians, which was bad for public relations, and thus for business.

He edged his way slowly along the wall until he was near the parking ground, then stood and boldly walked to a van he had rented. He climbed in, worked his way out of the uncomfortable suit, and picked up a one-time throwaway communicator. He thumbed the unit to life.

"Nighthawk Club," came a recorded voice. "We are located near the intersection of Hopper and Americana—" Von Baldur hit the three-digit override code. A human voice said, "Manager's office."

"Let me speak to the manager, please."

"Regarding . . . ?"

"The bomb planted in your club, set to go off in three minutes."

"What?!"

"Oh, sorry, two minutes, fifty-eight seconds. Fifty-seven. Fifty-six—"

Which was as far as von Baldur got before the voice started yelling for somebody named "Robby," loudly and repeatedly.

Von Baldur broke the connection and smiled. He removed a remote from his little carry pack and touched a control. The remote powered up and a green diode lit above a small, circular stud. The bombs weren't on a timer. He would detonate them manually, but if the people inside the club thought they had less than three minutes to—ah, here they came now . . .

The exits burst open and people fled the building, moving at speed, streaming from the place as if, well, as if they had just heard there was a bomb inside about to go off . . .

Von Baldur waited thirty seconds after he saw the last person bail into the night from the nearest exit, and then he pressed the firing stud.

The resulting blasts, coming as one and more or less

erasing a three-meter band of the supporting walls, were most satisfying. The top of the club, fairly intact, dropped suddenly, and while there were sections of the roof that collapsed, and the odd bits of exterior walls that gaped, what the place looked like was now a very squat building a meter or so high. A place now more suitable for extremely short people or, perhaps, mice . . .

Very satisfying, indeed.

# ELEVEN

Keven Makko was not, under the best of circumstances, a particularly patient man. When he found the bodies of his two strongarm boys and Neves in the safe house, and while he was still cursing like a ship full of sailors, he dispatched a full squad of his hired goons to find the killer. He knew who had done it, or at least part of it, and the squad triple-timed it to the hotel where the guy had been staying. He didn't have a lot of hope that they would catch the guy there, and in that he was right.

Then he started putting touches on people he owned, rented, or who owed him favors. He got the local police looking, had security working the beanstalk, and spaceship ports watching, and basically put as tight a lid on the planet as was possible, at least regarding this so-called bird-watcher.

He didn't say anything to Susa who, fortunately, was on another planet doing business and not looking over his shoulder, though Susa certainly already knew about it from his spies.

The next evening, when the first of his clubs had

blown up, his rage was hot and instant, and he thought it couldn't get much worse.

When the third club had been blasted, he thought he was going to have a conniption.

Somebody was messing with the wrong guy! When he caught up with them, they were gonna be sorry they had ever been born!

But he had two problems: First, other than the old guy Neves had collected, who was he looking for? Who was behind it?

And second, with an army of people combing the planet and the station up the stalk, where the seven hells *was* the bird-watcher? His people should have collected him by now! Every gutter rat and cutpurse scum, every street cop, the port authorities, all of them were looking for the guy.

Where could he possibly be?

As he sat fuming in his mansion, he knew he had to calm down. That was the only way he was going to get the answers he needed. Sooner or later, Susa would query him. It would be subtle, but the iron fist was always under the velvet glove, and when that question came, Makko needed solid answers. If he could wrap this up before the raised eyebrow in his direction, he was platinum. If not, he'd have to vamp and spin the story hard to keep himself out of deep crap . . .

With a major effort of pure will, Makko relaxed his breathing, slowed his heart, and put the anger into a box down a dark corridor of his mind. Later; he'd get back to that later.

Somewhat calmer, he considered the matter as dispassionately as he could. And with that, he remembered one of the earliest lessons his father had taught him. Poppy had been a crooked police detective and a rotten bastard, who'd steal the implants out of a dead man's corpse, but there were a couple of good lessons he'd imparted along the way. One of them was the simplest of questions the LEOs asked themselves when they were looking for somebody who had committed a crime: *Who makes out on the deal?*

Quickly he ran through his list. There were only a handful of competitors in his biz. The dangerous ones, he had eliminated. He had spies watching, and there weren't any newbies out there who had the balls or the brains to get away with stuff like this. It didn't make any sense . . .

Wait. Hold on a second . . .

There was that guy, the religious guy who had gotten all pissy over the labor biz, that Susa put him onto. Josiah. Josiah Williams. He wouldn't make any money out of this, but he and his people would benefit if they could strike and demand better pay and benefits.

Son of a bitch! The preacher, he had to be behind it!

"Yeah, well, we will just *see* about that!" Makko said to the empty room. "We will just freakin' see!"

Some days, no matter how sharp you thought you were, something happened to show you that you weren't.

How Riss's personal sensor had missed the detection-scan was a question, but obviously it had missed it, otherwise these guys wouldn't be here—she didn't think any of them could find their butts with both hands, and she hadn't made any noise or walked in front of any security-cams, she was sure.

Whatever. The thing was, they *were* here, and that was a problem.

People often underestimated M'chel Riss because of her appearance. On the one hand, she hated it that men were that stupid; on the other hand, it worked to her advantage more often than not. If they offer, might as well use it . . .

The three men facing her in the warehouse now weren't even a little bit worried. They had put away their blasters once they saw she was apparently unarmed, and in the jet-black skintight and midcalf orthoflex boots she wore, where could she hide a weapon? They were bigger than she was, stronger, armed, and there were three of them. Maybe they'd feel the same way if she were a man, but somehow she doubted it. They hadn't bothered to search her yet, though one of them obviously couldn't wait to slide his hands over her. He was practically drooling.

She had a short knife in the left boot and a tiny, snub-nosed, five-shot flatpak blaster tucked into the right, but it would be an iffy move to get her weapons out before these three could pull their own.

Back when Cerberus Systems had decided to stomp Star Risk into the ground, Riss had been studying an ancient Terran martial art called salat. Somehow, Cerberus had put pressure on her instructor and she had been kicked out of the class. She hadn't realized why at the time, since her teacher was notorious for booting students for no apparent reason. But in that art, she had learned some interesting things. Salat was designed to allow a small person to overcome larger, stronger opponents. Lots of them. And salat taught that deception and guile were useful things in a fight. She was no expert, but she had a few moves.

Plus plenty of built-in deception and guile . . .

"Okay, lady, now you're gonna tell us about the people you work for, right? Who sent you here, and why?"

This was from the tallest of the trio, a large and heavy fellow who was apparently the leader.

"Yeah," one of the others said. He was shorter, had thick, curly hair, and a nasty leer. "Otherwise, we might have to do some things you won't like. Or maybe you will like it, who knows?" He cupped his crotch meaningfully.

"I don't think it will come to that," the third man said. "I believe the little lady here wants to be cooperative." He was a cherubic-faced man who was obviously playing the role of the sweet cop in this scenario, the carrot, not the stick guy.

*Little lady?* She wanted to spit.

Immediately, Riss thought of them as Heavy, Curly, and Sweetie. And if they were wont to underestimate her abilities, then she would go with that. In a quavery voice, Riss said, "Oh, yes, I'll tell you whatever you want, just don't hurt me, please."

If they were relaxed before, this meek-little-girl act made them even more so. Riss lowered her head and allowed her shoulders to slump, looking as fearful and defeated as she could.

The three men edged closer. "What do you want to know?" she asked, allowing herself to shiver slightly.

Curly was the closest, just itching to touch her anywhere; she could feel his lust like a warmth on her skin. But Heavy was almost there, and Sweetie, to her left, was also nearly in range. Probably as good as it was going to get.

She took a deep breath, relaxed as much as she could given the circumstances, and pointed behind Heavy. "What about your friend there?" she asked.

Savvy guards would have ignored that, but, of course, these three all turned to look, just as she had figured.

"Who are you—?" Curly began.

That was as much as he got out before she kicked him square in the crotch, hard enough to feel the rubbery orbs mash almost flat under her boot instep.

The next sound he made was a cross between a swallowed scream and an inhaled squeal, but she ignored that and jumped at Heavy, clearing his startled block with her left hand and jabbing her stiffened fingers into his throat. As he started choking, she stepped to the side, blocked the slow punch Sweetie launched on the inside with her left forearm, and threw the marble-elbow into the man's temple.

It made a most satisfying *thunk!* as it connected.

The name marble-elbow came from how it was taught. "Imagine," her teacher had said, "that you have a marble in the crook of your bent elbow. Now do the strike so that you don't drop it." The technique was necessarily a short-range one because of that, but delivered properly, it was quite effective.

Sweetie went down like a laser-cut tree and Riss dropped with him, jammed a hand into his pocket, and came out with a small dart gun. Could be knockout or poisoned needles—that didn't much matter to her—

whatever they had been willing to give her, she'd give them. She shot Sweetie, spun, and put one into the gagging Heavy, who went boneless and fell. Then she took a couple of steps to stand in front of a very pale Curly, on his knees and making whimpering noises. He looked up at her through wide eyes.

She pointed the darter at him. "Hey, Curly, maybe you'll like this, who knows?" Then she shot him. Right between the eyes.

She wiped the needler clean and tossed it onto the floor. None of the three seemed to be breathing, so the darts were apparently poisoned. Too bad for them.

She was pleased with her performance. Three hits, three seconds, three down.

"Not bad for a simpering little *girl*, eh, boys?" she said.

Them being dead, nobody responded.

Time to leave. Pitiful as they were, these guys had probably called somebody to report the break-in, and she didn't want to be here if anybody with more than half a brain showed up. Maybe a woman guard who wouldn't be so impressed by the body under the skintight. She knew what she'd come to find out; no point in taking any more chances for little gain.

Back at the transport vehicle, a large, recently swiped hovervan big enough to hold all of them—even Grok—in relative comfort, Riss blinked her flashlight in the UV spectrum in the agreed-upon signal. Grok could see it, but humans couldn't, and anybody who approached the truck in the night without offering the correct signal would regret it in a hurry.

Riss opened the door and slid into the driver's seat.

"All went well?" Grok asked.

"Yep. Had to take out a few guards, but other than that, no problems," she said. "Got the information we came for."

Even in the dark van, Grok's teeth were visible in his sudden fierce smile. "You have all the fun," he said. "Next time, I get to go."

"We'll see," she said. She started the van, the muffled fans Dopplered up, and they slid away on a cushion of night air.

# TWELVE

*This might be a problem,* Grok thought as he watched the giant robot roll through the alley. *Where did they get this thing?*

The bot swiveled on its tanklike treads, the upper part, including the sensor array in the head, facing the Dumpster behind which Grok and his obviously ineffective blaster crouched. He knew the blaster was ineffective because he had shot the robot a bunch of times to no good end. This was bad . . .

The bot let go with a chaingun in a fully automatic hail of caseless 50mm rounds. Fortunately, the thick durasteel container, full of scrap aluminum, was able to absorb those, even though a couple of them dented the metal on Grok's side.

Well. This was *very* bad. Now what?

"Now what?" turned out to be a direct assault. The bot, which was three meters tall and almost that wide, rolled forward on clanking treads and extended one of its heavy grappling arms.

You didn't need to be an engineer to figure out what that meant. In a few seconds, the bot was going to move the Dumpster. Grok had no doubt that it could, heavy as the thing was, and he would be sans cover against an armor-plated monster that shrugged off his blaster bolts like they were throw pillows. Even the sensor array was protected by a series of baffles, blast deflectors, and laser reflectors. He'd have to have pinpoint accuracy beyond what he could expect from his handgun to get through those unless it was right in front of him, and even then he'd only get one shot.

The only good thing about all this was that the thing didn't have any rocket launchers or industrial-strength blasters of its own mounted, and if it had been Grok's toy, it surely would have. Maybe the thing had never run into a problem it couldn't handle with the chain-gun and its own strength. Grok could see that was a distinct possibility . . .

Yes, yes, that was all fine and good, but enough thinking; it was time to *do* something!

Question was, *what*?

He needed a distraction.

Grok moved to the end of the Dumpster and risked a quick up and down. Another spew of jacketed 50mm chewed smoking craters in the brick wall behind him, and the ricochets spattered all over him, the hot metal adding a burning-hair stink to the already fragrant bouquet of the alleyway. Fortunately, the bot's reaction time wasn't as quick as he was, so he was back behind cover before the bullets got there. For the moment.

Nothing in the alley except him, the bot, and Dumpsters. No distractions there.

He definitely had a problem.

*Hurry, Grok—!*

There was enough metal scrap in the Dumpster to weigh down a platoon of bodies tossed into deep water—sheet, shavings, rod, bar—but if he tried to grab a heavy chunk, the guns would get him, fast as he was. The only way he was going to do that would involved split-second timing and a great deal of personal risk.

Grok sighed. No choice.

He waited.

The bot arrived, extended its right grappling arm, grabbed one of the Dumpster's truck-pivot handles, and lifted.

Grok hoped he was right about the mechanics of the bot. He had guessed that it would raise and move the load toward its center of mass. Since it was the right arm reaching out, that would mean it would upend the Dumpster toward its left, Grok's right . . .

It did as Grok expected. The thing was strong, but it wasn't so strong that it could just snatch the heavy Dumpster from the ground and hurl it aside; the container came up, but relatively slowly, and the contents began to spill. Grok heard the strain of bio-gears and cables in the bot's arm as the aluminum scrap began to pour out onto the plastcrete with loud *clangs* and *grinches* as it fell—

*Now!*

Grok grabbed the back of the Dumpster with his left hand, reached into the cascade of metal with the other, and came up with a heavy rod almost a meter long and as big around as his wrist. He clambered up the back of the Dumpster as the bot lifted it so that it stood on its end. The top of the container at vertical was now taller than the bot's head. Grok leaped up on the end, lifted the heavy bar over his head with both hands, and waited.

A quarter second later, the bot looked up.

Like a human splitting a log with an ax, Grok swung the aluminum rod down, using all of his not-inconsiderable strength.

The bot's sensor array was protected from blaster bolts and even bullets by the complex system of baffles and reflectors, but it had not been designed to withstand being bashed by a creature of Grok's power with a ten-kilogram chunk of solid metal.

The makeshift bat dug a channel through the protective armor and stopped when it connected with the main bulk of the durasteel dome of the head.

No real damage done, nor had Grok expected any.

The bot couldn't get enough angle on the chest guns to hit Grok, and it swung its free grappling arm over to whack him.

Grok released the heavy bar, snaked his hand down to his blaster, did a quick draw that would have made a cowboy gunslinger proud, and fired his sidearm's beam into the channel he had just made.

Easy shot at this range, with the baffles out of the way.

The head-mounted sensor array blew out in an eruption of sparks and smoke.

"Urk!" the bot's vocalizers said.

*Eat* that, *metal-boy!*

Grok leaped, landed on the small mountain of aluminum slag, took two quick steps, and then changed direction, looping around behind the bot.

It couldn't see or hear him: Its cams, radar, and Doppler were gone. But its guns still worked, and it opened up, swiveling three-sixty and laying down a circle of jacketed-steel hail that drew dust and sparks from whatever the rounds hit.

But Grok was behind the thing's torso, moving with it.

It seemed to take a long time, but eventually the bot's ammo ran out. When the guns clicked dry, Grok relaxed a bit. He ambled back to the scrap bin's dumped load, found a couple of more sections of heavy rod, and jammed them into the bot's treads. When the bot reached down to grapple the rod sections loose, Grok waited until the arms were extended, then leaned over and stuck his blaster's muzzle under the armor overlap covering the elbow—there had to be a gap there or the thing couldn't bend its arms— and, at contact range, had no trouble making the shot. First the right, then the left.

The bot was now blind, deaf, armless, and out of ammo.

Grok holstered his weapon, backed up out of flailing range, and said, "I'll just leave you here with your brother, the scrap pile," he said. "Because *that's* what you get when you mess with Amanandrala Grokkono-monslf, metal-boy."

He grinned.

# THIRTEEN

Jasmine was unhappy with herself. She had practically tripped over the guard before she saw him—the building was supposed to be empty, and he wasn't listed on the work roster!—and at that point, he had seen her. She'd thought about running, but decided that a blaster bolt in the back wasn't on her preferred menu, so she stood there. "You got me," she'd said. "I surrender."

At the moment, he'd had a grip on her left wrist, and his free hand was pulling back to slap her silly. They obviously hadn't hired the fellow for his sensitivity and appreciation of art and flower-arranging abilities. He was a thug, looked it, and appeared as if he was going to really enjoy pounding her, to judge from his wicked grin.

Time stalled, and it seemed as if the thug were moving in extreme slow motion, like a vid of a bullet piercing an apple, sooo slooowww . . .

She had all the time in the universe.

Consider, say, weapons . . .

Everybody had favorites. Riss had a boot snubbie

she usually carried when working; Goodnight liked the military-issue stuff because that's what he had been trained with; von Baldur favored an antique piezo-capacitor bolt-thrower that looked like it belonged in a Space Ranger vid and took forever to recharge. Grok had to have a large-framed blaster because his hands were so big. And those were just the shooters. For very close work, or when silence was necessary, there were other tools.

Jasmine favored the little knife the old Sufi, Mushtaq Ali al Ansari, had made for her, the Tiger's Claw.

The tiger was a smallish thing, blade under nine centimeters long, with a fat, rounded handle about the same length, making the sheathed knife easy to hide on a belt under a jacket, or even a loose blouse. Mushtaq made his knives using the lowest of low-tech methods in a traditional manner, hammering and forging the high-carbon tool steel by hand, using gas-fed, firebrick ovens and open fires and anvils and suchlike that would have been at home back in the dawn of space flight, or even before. He was more than passing adept as a knife fighter himself, so he knew how to build a knife that would hold up and do the job.

The tiger was slightly concave on the edge side, with a Turk's knot guard at the base of the blade and a handle made of exotic wood—walnut in the case of Jasmine's knife—permanently bonded to the full tang. The knife was curved from tip to butt, so that the point and end of the handle could be joined by a straight line, almost like a bowstring.

The blade had been clay-tempered so that the edge was hard and could be made very sharp, while the main part of the blade was springier and not at all brittle. The edge had a visible temper line, where the clay left off, called a *hamon*. There were styles of ancient swords wherein these *hamon* lines had become quite complex, and whole texts had been devoted to the study of the patterns, which were often given fanciful names, like "clover-tree flower mushroom-shape," or "Chrysanthemum and River."

Not being stainless steel, the tiger's blade had to be kept protected from rust. Some people favored light oils for this, ranging from standard machine lubes to exotics, like fragrant—and very expensive—sandalwood oil. Jasmine's preference for protecting the blade was for fine antique furniture wax, applied in a liquid form, allowed to dry, and then gently polished to a protective sheen. Since she handled the knife frequently, this kept her hands from getting oily and kept the steel pristine.

It also made the blade easier to clean after she used it.

Jasmine wore the tiger in a cloned-leather sheath that carried the knife point down and edge forward. She had learned to draw the knife quickly from this style of carry, holding it in what knife fighters called the ice-pick grip, point down, edge forward . . .

All of this passed through Jasmine's thoughts in a couple of heartbeats, driven by the fight-or-flight-syndrome effect called tachypsychia—the sense of crystal-sharp vision and hearing, and the subjective distortion of time so that her thoughts sped past while the man next to her moved so slowly.

The thug who had her wrist gripped tightly in his left hand as he drew his right hand back, preparing to slap her, didn't know any of this. His intent was to beat her senseless, and since he was a quarter meter taller and probably fifty kilos heavier, and built like a high-gee weightlifter, likely didn't anticipate that such a beating would be any problem.

Time shifted back to normal, and Jasmine said, "Your sister is a parakeet, isn't she?"

The thug blinked. She could almost hear the gears grinding in his head. *Say what? My sister . . . ?*

It was a nonsense phrase designed to make a listener pause for a second as he considered it. All she needed was half that.

Jasmine snaked her right hand under her blouse, found the rounded handle of her knife, and drew it, a move she had practiced a thousand times. The blade slid from the sheath smoothly, coming up in front of her just as the thug realized he might need to worry.

He changed the intended slap into a more efficient punch, making a fist and driving it at Jasmine's face—

She raised the knife to block and angled it to the side slightly. The reverse-*tanto* clip-point lined up with the inside of the thug's right wrist. Jasmine leaned her head slightly to her left, using the man's grip on her to leverage herself a bit, but kept the knife angled, just so—

The thug's arm hit the point of the knife and, because the limb grew bigger around all the way to his elbow, the force of his punch drove the razor-sharp tip deeper as the arm came in. By the time his now-open hand reached the spot where Jasmine's head had just been, his arm was flayed from the wrist to the antecubital fossa, the inside of the elbow where the biceps tendon, the brachial artery, and the median nerve all resided. A bad place to be cut.

If he didn't bleed out, it would take an ER medic quite a while to glue or staple that wound shut, but nobody was going to bother because Jasmine stepped in, reversed the motion of her arm so that her palm faced up, and gave the stunned thug a gaping new mouth, right across his throat.

Nobody was going to be stitching *that* up in time to do him any good.

She stepped back. The thug, pale and going white, fell to his knees, then collapsed, facedown.

*What a great knife Mushtaq made,* she thought as she bent to wipe the blood from the steel onto the dead man's shirt.

# FOURTEEN

In their still-smelly, stealthed ship, safely hidden in orbit, Star Risk's crew sat down for a meeting.

"All right, let's review, shall we?" von Baldur said.

They had abandoned their fake identities when they left the station, and glad von Baldur was to be out of that makeup, with his hair back to its proper color.

Makko's people were combing the place and the planet downlevels like a monkey searching for fleas on its brother's back, and no matter what new identities Star Risk might have come up with, it was too risky to hang around. They did have security cameras, and who knew but that their images might be available to Makko?

Goodnight said, "Well, nobody in my space station is going to go off and *pee* by himself these days—at least, not in a cargo area. That cargo container and the goon platoon were a thousand klicks into deep vac before the rescue ship caught up with 'em. They had protective suits and air, but they weren't rigged to take a flight in the cold. Most of 'em were frozen pretty solid. One survivor, and he got a good look at the 'ghost.' It was, if I must say so myself, inspired."

Riss said, "Grok and I managed to get the information we needed to disable the drive controls for our station. It'll take them days, if not weeks, to repair things there."

"I had an interesting encounter with a guard robot," Grok said. "Replacing that will cost a fair number of credits."

"Makko's stocks and bonds and bank accounts are about to turn to liquid nitrogen," Jasmine said. "Eventually, the local authorities will get it sorted out, but until they do, he will be limited to what cash he has or can borrow. At least a week, maybe longer before they can find the freezer worm and get things thawed."

"Any problems?"

Jasmine gave him a thin smile. "None to speak of."

Von Baldur nodded. "Excellent. I was able to remove Makko's chief lieutenant and to, ah, *renovate* three of his largest nightclubs. I expect he will be feeling the pinch all over his body by now. So far, everything is going as we expected, no major problems, by the numbers. Time for the next phase, I should think."

"We really haven't discussed that, Freddie," Jasmine said. "What *is* the next phase?"

Von Baldur smiled. "Well, we'll be spreading pestilence, and we will be going to the dogs . . ."

# FIFTEEN

Jasmine King tapped the controls that would bring the cargo freighter she was piloting into the station orbiting Zweiten—which someone had named, simply, "Z-1." Apparently there were a multitude of such wonderfully creative names in this system. She checked her hair in a mirror she'd brought up to the pilot's station and took a deep breath. Time to play.

"Z-1 Station, this is the freighter *Lucky One,* coming in. Do you have my transponder?"

"Roger that, *Lucky One.* We read you with 'C' containers. Will route you to our large-stack bay. Sorry, there's a bit of a wait for that." The voice didn't sound sorry.

Good—the voice was a man's. Not that she'd expected differently—she'd hacked the station's schedule long before getting here. But it was still nice to have something work out like it should.

Jasmine toggled her pickup on and frowned at the camera. "Come on, Z-1, I've been out for too long, the climate control is out, and I really, really want to *feel* the cool atmosphere of a great *big* station again."

With anyone else the innuendo with her emphasis on "feel" and "big" would probably not have worked so well. But the slob on duty at the receiving station was a hetero single and subscribed to a shipnet service called "hotblondes," another tidy research tidbit King had gathered long before arriving.

The fact that she was wearing the thinnest ship coverall she could find, complete with a deep V cut in the front, and that she actually *was* sweating—the toughest part of the caper so far—could only set the hook deeper.

Her viewscreen lit up, and the subject of her research became visible. His eyes appeared to be bugging out.

Still, he had to say no.

"Sorry *Lucky One,* but class 'C' is bay two only."

"Oh, come on"—Jasmine looked down toward the viewscreen and made as if she were reading it—"Chris, is it? It's hot in here. Couldn't you please, please find a way to get me off this ship? It's so *hot.* I mean, look at me!"

And she leaned forward, showing the camera beads of sweat on the portion of her chest revealed by the V-necked cut.

There was a long pause.

"Ah, let me check on something a second, *Lucky One.*"

She hoped this gambit would work. If it didn't, there was a backup plan, but it wouldn't have as much effect.

"You say your climate control systems are failing?" asked Chris.

"Yes," she said, making the word more a moan than a simple reply.

"Well, that sounds pretty serious to me. I mean, I may have to come check on that myself," he said.

"So why don't we set your ship down in bay three—we'll slide it down to the maintenance dry dock and see what we can do. Then we can slide it right to bay two for unloading."

Excellent. He'd figured it out—with no hints even.

"Oh, Chris, that'd be so great!" Star Risk's research specialist beamed at the monitor.

"Initating station takeover," he said, tapping a switch and trying to look heroic.

Jasmine toggled a release, turning the automatic piloting over to the station.

"I'm just going to try and clean up a bit," she said.

"Okay!" said Chris, trying not to sound disappointed.

She switched off the pickup and sat back to wait for phase two.

Z-1 Station followed all of the ISC protocols for ship decontamination and quarantine. Cargo not destined to stay at the station never left its container, and ships were decontaminated on arrival. Standard protocol prevented any ship from moving from one bay to another until it had been cleared. However, there were chinks in this procedural armor.

Since Z-1 was a small station with only one dry dock, elevators had been installed at all three of the main unloading bays so that ships could be moved to the maintenance area in sublevels. The system was also used for cargo transfer—shipping containers were often sent through the tunnels to be reloaded in another bay. In effect, this meant that a ship or its cargo could come in through any bay and leave through any other, if it were transferred through the internal elevator system.

The *Lucky One*'s manifest had it carrying a fairly large ship container, which meant that either the ship or the containers would have to be unloaded in docking bay number two, even though the ship could be landed in either one or three.

Ship controls eased the *Lucky One* onto the station's maglev system, and after a few minutes she bypassed inspection as her ship was towed toward the maintenance dry dock.

*Oops. You are being bad boys.*

Not checking the cargo? Not inspecting the ship? Tsk, tsk. Well, that was what happened when you thought with your little head. She smiled. She'd have been cursing them if they'd been vigilant, too.

A timer alarm sounded and she shut it off. She was approaching the junction between the maintenance tunnels—the place where all three bays connected and routed to the maintenance level. A level deep within the esophagus of the tunnel system. The passage around her was sealed end to end to keep all traffic inside; no one was going to sneak into the station by hiding here—there was no other way out.

Which was exactly what she had in mind.

Jasmine slipped into a space suit and headed toward the air lock. A few seconds later she was outside her ship, moving carefully to its topside. She had to feel her way, and counted her steps, trying not to think about what she was doing.

*There.*

She felt the doorway and triggered it.

The passageway was sealed between the entrance of the bay she'd come in and the maintenance tunnel junction, and if you were on foot trying to sneak in or out you were out of luck—unless you had a stealth ship handy.

She stepped into the Pr'ar air lock and cycled through.

"Welcome aboard Spada Airways," said the pilot as she stepped on board. "Please fasten your seat belts as soon as you can."

And then Redon Spada was all business, hands jumping over the controls of the stealth ship like a master musician playing his instrument. Even a near-magical cloaking device wouldn't save them if he rammed them into the walls.

Jasmine sat at the communications console and beamed several signals to the *Lucky One*. Then she released several packages as Spada moved them back along the tunnel toward bay three. The timing would have to be just right—the lock between the triple junction and the lock to the bay outside were only open for a few seconds at the same time.

Back on the *Lucky One* a prerecorded message was about to play.

It showed Jasmine running toward the camera in the pilot's chair, wearing only a towel.

"Chris! You've got to get me out of here! One of the containers from Sufayed Seven ruptured—there's something on me, I—"

The station controller would at this point see a spike in the internal sensors on the ship, showing a massive pressure change. But his focus would be on Jasmine opening her towel.

To scream . . .

"Aaaaah—!"

And instead of seeing what he'd hoped, the controller would see a carefully crafted simulation of her body beginning to melt, flesh pouring off her bones, which would immediately begin to melt as well.

At that point several more things would happen— the ship's seals would rupture, and a dark green paint that Star Risk had set up within several of the containers would shoot out, giving visual evidence of a ship being eaten from within by the deadly Dzzor virus, one of the modern bogeymen of space-faring civilizations everywhere.

Encountered only a few times within recent memory, the Dzzor virus was a unique, self-perpetuating and ultimately self-destructive pathogen that ate flesh of multiple DNA varieties as well as a wide variety of nonorganic materials—metals, a wide variety of plas polymers. No one really knew much about the virus, and it wasn't known how it moved through the galaxy. But one of the last times it had shown up was on a system nearby, Sufayed One—six planets away.

It was so deadly that scientists couldn't even study it—for long.

Acid bombs strategically placed within the *Lucky One* would destroy areas within sight of multiple camera pickups on the ship. And the finishing touch was the packages she was dropping off along the passageway. The fast-acting acids would dig a little into the metal of the walls and stain them green—the telltale color of Dzzor—and then would evaporate.

The real key to the plan was having the video hit just as the junction between all three bay tunnels opened. With ship seals bursting, all of the tunnels and the adjacent passageways, which in this case included the docking bays at the opposite end of each tunnel—would be included as part of the standard quarantine procedure for dealing with Dzzor. Or rather, part of the never-used emergency plan.

But for now they had to get out. Because once lockdown went into effect, nothing was getting off the station; not even a stealth ship could go through a closed door.

Spada accelerated the alien ship, nearly taking out the communications pickup on top of another freighter as they zoomed toward the docking bay and escape.

Back on the *Lucky One,* Jasmine's computer-generated double screamed and began to melt.

Z-1 didn't know it yet, but its cargo shipping days were over—at least until an Alliance team of decontamination specialists could arrive and certify the station safe.

Freddie was right. It *was* by the numbers.

Score another one for the good guys. . . .

Everyone but von Baldur sat in the stinky stealth ship, heading for the last station. They had played it pretty low-key so far—booby traps, bombs, urban legends, and the threat of plague, but by now the competition knew something was up, so more direct action was needed.

Which wasn't to say that they had to just walk right up and knock on the heavily guarded fortress's door. After all, what else were stealth ships for? But the plan, once inside, was to be simple and direct—take out as many of the baddies as possible, no subterfuge necessary.

Grok was ecstatic—at last, here were some long odds! While not as high as thousands to one, at least a hundred plus to one made things exciting.

Redon Spada leaned low over the controls, checking readouts as they approached the station. This one, orbiting Vierde, was being guarded by a group called the Doom Dogs. According to what Jasmine had been able to get from the merc organization's database, many of the group, who predictably referred to themselves as the "pack," had an affinity for canine species and performed genetic mods accordingly.

The precise range of mods was hard to pin down—that data had actually been stored in a more secure manner—but from other reports, it ranged from simple cosmetics all the way to enhanced senses and diamond-metal claws and teeth.

As they neared the station, Spada began looking for a place to set down. Unlike the earlier stations, this one was alerted that it might be under attack, so they had to tread carefully.

"Ahhh, yes, I think I've got just what we need," he said.

As their ship touched down, Spada tapped controls, and suddenly the walls around them seemed to vanish.

"One of the neat features of this baby," he said, grinning, "is that trick of making the ship disappear to everyone *inside* it as well. Too cool."

There was a thump as Goodnight stood up. He ran his hand over his head, wincing.

"Thanks Spada. Next time tell me when you're going to hide the low bulkhead, hey?"

Large-diameter ports flanked either side of the ship. As they watched, one opened and a large packet of *something* came floating out. It looked like a poly-plas bag, but whatever was inside was clearly brown, or yellow, depending on which end you looked at.

"What is that crap?" Goodnight said.

Spada laughed. "You called it," he said.

"You're kidding," said Riss.

"Eeeewww," said Jasmine.

"Do not the stations recycle all such matter?" asked Grok.

"Well, most of it," said Spada, "but a full-spectrum recycler costs more, and with the beanstalk so close, they didn't spend the money. What we're seeing is after all the water has been pulled out, and maybe one or two chem reclamations for the algae beds."

"You mean it's the crap of the crap?" asked Goodnight.

"At least we'll be in space suits," said Riss.

It didn't take long for things to head south.

The first thing they noticed was how quiet the station was. Coming aboard in the waste plant meant they weren't likely to be running into dozens of people. But so far there was no one. Everything was quiet.

Too quiet.

Goodnight was on point as they worked their way to a central maintenance cubby that they were going to use as a base of operations. The cubby had access to many maintenance tunnels, which was ideal for their purposes. From there they would identify their targets and attack when their numbers and the element of surprise would give them the victory. The former Alliance commando was followed closely by Riss, then Jasmine and Grok. With his hearing turned up high, he probably heard the noise first. He stopped and tilted his head, listening.

Then they all heard it.

"Aoorrooooooh!" A bone-chilling cry split the silence.

"Uh-oh," Riss said.

"Second that," Goodnight added.

There was no way anyone had seen them approach. The infil had been perfect.

The howls were a long ways off—maybe it was just some unloved creature on this shithole sublevel?

But no. The noise started getting louder. Whatever it was, it was coming for them.

Riss's com vibrated and she tapped the actuator.

"What did you guys do in there?" It was Spada.

"Why do you ask?"

"There are about ten people outside where I dropped you off, looking all over the area. Hard to say, but it looks like these could be some of those 'Doom Dogs' you were talking about. Haven't seen many space suits equipped with wagging tails lately. Something made them check out this entrance, which means you're blown. Do you want to exfil?"

Riss swore. How had they been made?

"You good?" she asked.

"Yeah, I was already up in the air. No problem for me."

"Okay. We'll, ah, see what develops. Stand by in case we need to leave in a hurry."

If things got hot, their directive to protect the station could hang—Riss would have Spada rip a hole wherever they happened to be.

The howling was louder.

"Perhaps we should move toward our objective?" said Grok.

"Yeah, and a bit faster," added Jasmine.

Goodnight had already disappeared around the corner.


The tunnel junction ahead was a hexagonal hub with all six sides open. Goodnight indicated the second opening on the left.

"That way," he said.

Riss stopped him.

"Grok, can you do a quick scan?" Their pursuers seemed to be making excellent progress tracking them, and that just wasn't right. Could someone have picked up a bug?

The huge alien nodded and pulled a full-spectrum receiver from his pocket. He waved the device quickly over the rest of the team.

"Nothing," he said.

"Crap!" Riss swore. "This is starting to tick me off."

Grok pulled a small spheroid from his kit and tapped a stud on the side. The sphere opened and he stuck it high up on the wall. Within seconds it seemed to disappear.

"Perhaps this will tell us what we want to know,"

he said. And they all started through the door Good-night had indicated.

They were two-thirds of the way there and Riss was cursing Spada for putting them so far away from the maintenance cubby, when Grok pulled the receiver for the bug he'd planted at the intersection.

"Aha," he said, showing it to the rest.

Two large humanoids with great, dog-shaped heads leaned over on the floor of the junction they'd passed through. They had huge noses and very long, floppy ears.

"I bet those ears are useless in combat," said Riss, shaking her head.

"Maybe," replied Goodnight, "but right now their noses are pretty useful."

"Crap, crap, *crap*!" muttered Riss.

"Or something that smells like it," said Goodnight.

"The ship!" said Jasmine. "It's that stinking ship! They've got our scent!"

As one, the three of them turned and glared at Grok.

Who was busy staring at the readout.

"There are only ten or fifteen," said the big alien, looking up. He saw their expressions and did his best impression of chagrin—a facial expression that looked like he was choking. The electronics expert reached into his kit and pulled out a small spray canister. He sprayed the air around them.

"The spray contains nanites designed to scrub scent molecules. It will take effect in five to ten minutes. However, at our pursuers' current rate, we do not have that long. Since the ship, and thus our scents, was my contribution, I am honor bound to correct this."

Riss narrowed her eyes. Did Grok sound just a little bit happy?

Never mind.

"Fine," she said. "You take care of it. We'll see you at the rendezvous point."

Grok hung on the ceiling of another six-way hub near a large ventilation duct. In addition to his side-arm he was carrying two huge knives. More than enough for these genetically modified humans.

The dog-men came into view. The two leading the rest stopped in the middle of the room and then sniffed toward each of the doorways.

"Come on, Tod," said another of the modified humans, this one with a black-and-white cosmetic mod that made his head look like a true dog. "Let's get it done."

"Sorry, Laddy," said the sniffer, "but it smells like they went to each of these doors."

"Where is the scent strongest?"

A puzzled expression came over the hound's face. He began sniffing the air, tilting his head left and right.

"It's . . . hmm . . . ?" He looked up.

"Here," said Grok, dropping on them.

The first five went quickly on his knives, but by then he'd gotten a taste for the action and had moved to his own claws, ripping and tearing and shredding mods. There would be no more tracking today.

Several of their pursuers tried to flee, and Grok had time to wonder how long genetic mods had been available to humanity. A phrase about defeating enemies had come to mind—something about the vanquished running away with their tails between their legs. Until now, Grok had always though it was a figure of speech.

He shot those who made it out of his immediate range, and within minutes all was quiet. Now he could rejoin the rest of the team.

The big alien grinned as he left the blood-spattered hub.

# SIXTEEN

Makko watched as the preacher closed the front doors of the warehouse "church" and then turned toward his cube, just a few blocks away. It was summer on this part of Una, and a warm breeze blew, making the treetops whisper in the night wind. Late enough so the streets weren't too busy. That was good.

*I hope you enjoy your walk, Preacher,* thought Makko, watching from behind some trees. *Because it's probably going to be your last.*

He was angry. Thermonuclear flash-fire hot. People had been screwing with his business, breaking the number-one rule:

*You don't ever screw with my business.*

And he was pretty sure the preacher here had something to do with it—with everything that had happened to his clubs, his men, and potentially his position in the organization. And that just wasn't going to be allowed to pass.

His boss, Susa, liked to call their business evolutionary. The first time Makko had heard it, he'd been a little puzzled.

The senior of Una's two boss of bosses had grinned. "I call it 'evolutionary' for a simple reason, Mak—survival of the fittest. The weak get eaten."

Susa would let you run whatever side ventures you wanted—even if they competed with his own. But what you figured out pretty quickly was that you couldn't compete with the boss. He'd match whatever tactics you used—and then some. Ambitious lieutenants who tried to off Susa got offed themselves. It was, after all, how Makko had gotten to where he was as well, filling a vacancy that had suddenly opened up.

The flip side of the process was that any signs of weakness could draw an attack. If some of the other district bosses decided Makko couldn't handle his business, they'd close in, and if Makko couldn't hold them off, Susa wouldn't say a word.

So he had to do something fast—send the message up, down, and sideways that anyone who messed with him paid the price. Period.

He nodded at Enin and Nett, Neves's two replacements. The boys didn't have the same smarts as his former assistant, but they were shoe-leather tough. Enin had spent five years playing gravity ball before an unfortunate incident involving insider betting and nonapproved neural accelerants, and had reflexes like a souped-up Mangess snake. Makko had seen him win a bar bet once by catching three thrown shot glasses—all from different angles, by different men.

Nett wasn't as fast with his hands, but made up for it with a ruthless, calculated cunning that proved the phrase about men, not weapons, being deadly. He'd spent some time as a bouncer at one of the clubs and had dusted a squad of drunken, off-duty commandos using nothing more than an ashtray and a broken hookah. Two of the customers never got up again, and no one had gotten out of line there since.

So, former Alliance Marine or no, the preacher wasn't walking past them, no way.

Speaking of which . . .

Williams walked slowly through the empty lot, and Makko tossed a plastic bottle cap past him.

When the preacher turned at the sound, Makko, Nett, and Enin stepped out from behind a large bin-bin tree.

Nothing wrong with enjoying the dramatic, hey?

Give him credit, his microexpression of surprise didn't stop the preacher from going for a weapon. Enin seemed to move slowly, but his hands were a blur as he knocked it hard from the preacher's hands and slapped him across the face.

*Clackmack!*—the sounds were almost one.

Nett wasn't slow either—he'd moved forward and grabbed Williams in an armlock before he had a chance to react.

*Excellent!*

If he'd wanted just to kill him, it would already be over. But Makko wanted to hurt him, so it was good they'd managed to disarm the man without knocking him out.

The crime boss stepped forward and dangled a handgrip with four glowing LEDs on it.

"I thought you people didn't hold with violence," Makko said.

"It is justified to use it against evil," Williams said.

"Yeah, well, that'd be me. You know what this is?" he asked.

Williams nodded. Stood to reason, being Alliance ex-military, that he'd recognize a remote detonator.

"A few of my clubs were knocked down recently, and I've been waiting to return the favor."

Makko nodded at Enin, who turned the preacher toward the church. Once he was sure the man could see, he triggered the grip.

The explosions were very satisfying—a loud *crump!* that split the night, moving the treetops much more than a nighttime breeze.

After the demolition charges had knocked the walls inward, a series of incendiaries went off, lighting up the darkness.

When Nett turned the preacher around again, the old man's face had gone white with shock.

Makko smiled. Even if he was wrong, that look alone made him feel better. What was it that did that? Catharsis? He'd seen it on some late-night edcom vid he'd accidentally flipped to. Something about other people's pain making you feel better about your own. Oh, yes.

But he wasn't wrong. He was almost certain that the preacher had something to do with what had happened.

What the hell? The preacher was smiling.

Makko frowned. "What's so funny, Preacher?"

"The house of God cannot be torn down with explosions, sonny. It isn't the building; it's the spirit. God will even forgive you, if you repent. The insurance company might not, though . . ."

Well, crap. Who'd have thought he'd go all philosophical? To hell with it.

The crime boss made a motion with his hand and Enin slapped the preacher with a sleepcap, the thin nipple between his fingers delivering enough to keep the man out for an hour or two; plenty of time to get to the Quiet Room.

If he was going to kill somebody, he owed it to himself to be more than *almost* certain, after all.

At the Quiet Room they didn't wake the old man up right away. Instead, Makko dosed him with a highly effective truth drug, only then administering the antidote to the cap—and none too gently either.

When they started questioning him, they hit a wall.

At some point in the past the man had been given a neural cutout. They were expensive—usually only used by governments or big corporations. No telling where his had come from, or why he had it.

Neural cutouts weren't complicated—it just took a lot of time and energy to get one set up. Nanoengineered neurons were tapped into the limbic system and trained over the course of a few months to read stress levels associated with particular brain activity. Anyone using the cutout who got stressed—or who tried to speak while under duress or certain chemical compounds—would simply go to sleep, negating the ability of any questioners to get useful information. Ask about the time of day, or what kind of tea he liked, no problem.

Do it while under certain kinds of stress—and zzzz . . .

Crappola! Makko was tempted to beat the man's

head in *without* confirmation, he was so teed off. But no.

"Boss, just the fact that he's got some wiring like this means he knows something—means he's guilty," Enin said.

Makko shook his head. "That doesn't follow. He could have had it done when he was in the military. Maybe he was behind enemy lines, like that."

Nett said, "I could try something, boss."

Makko stared at Williams lying on the floor. He had to know.

"Go for it.

It turned out that Neves might have a good replacement in Nett. The man used a clever tactic.

He woke Williams up and started asking very specific questions. Did the preacher have a local congregation? Were they happy? Did he hire a mercenary group to help put pressure on Makko?

The innocent questions established a baseline, and when he was asked something that was supposed to be secret, he would fall asleep.

After a few minutes of putting to sleep and waking up the preacher they had discovered nothing about anything—but they had found out several important facts.

They let the preacher wake up completely, this time.

Makko grinned down at Williams.

"I think we've found out what we need to know," he said, "but I want to hear it from you. Did you hire the bird-watcher?"

The crime boss held up a picture they'd taken of the man who had killed Neves.

Williams laughed. "Bird-watcher?" he said. "Why would I need a bird-watcher?"

Makko allowed himself a smile. "Game over, Reverend. Get ready to meet your god."

"Okay, you win. Yes, I hired him." His voice rasped, suddenly sounding as old as he looked.

Makko grinned. *Good-bye preacher. You're done now. So satisfying—even when unsurprising—to be right.* "Where is he? And any others he's working with?"

But then the preacher did surprise him.

Williams came to his feet and lunged at Makko. He was fast, too, damn—

Nett was faster. He stepped forward and shot an elbow strike at the preacher, following it up with another. The strikes were full, my-boss-is-under-attack hits—and they were hard.

Too hard.

Williams fell forward, his neck canted at an unnatural angle. He seemed to be saying something. The crime boss leaned closer.

"The Lord will forgive you," whispered the preacher, "and so do I."

And then he died.

Well, *crap!* This wasn't how it was supposed to go!

The caper, Riss figured, was pretty much about to be over. The shipping stations were in—well, not to put too fine a point on it—chaos. The guy who had hired the goons was having trouble accessing his money to pay them, which meant they were not going to stick around; the stations were filled with strikebreakers who were not going to do squat without armed guards, or even with them; and from here on, all they needed to do was sit back and let inertia do its work. The preacher would pass the word along to his people that all the shenanigans would stop once they got back on the job—no ghosts or plagues or assassins stalking the corridors. A final run at Makko to give him a few other things about which to worry, and it was a done deal.

Freddie had been right. Simple, for once, in and out, and wasn't it nice to have that for a change?

She was even getting used to the smell on the ship. If you thought about the odor as being like, say, musk, mixed with a little bit of masculine sweat, it wasn't so bad . . .

The intercom chirped and Spada's amplified voice said, "Folks, I have our friend von Baldur on the secure opchan, and he has some news you might want to hear."

Riss looked around at the others. "Go ahead," she said.

Over the scrambled opchan Freddie's voice sounded as if he were in a barrel. "Colleagues, it seems we have a slight problem."

Riss muttered. "I *knew* it was too good to be true."

Von Baldur continued. "Our client, the Reverend Josiah Williams, is, alas, no longer among the living."

There was a pause. Goodnight said, "Why is *that* a problem? The job is, for all practical purposes, done; we cashed the check and it's in the bank. Job wrapped, we got paid—it's not our worry."

He had a point, Riss thought. She saw Grok and Jasmine both nod in agreement. Feces flowers, and as long as it didn't happen to *you*, it wasn't your worry, right? They weren't in the vengeance business—not unless somebody wanted to pick up the tab.

Still, she was a little curious. "What happened to him?"

"Difficult to tell—all that was left of him had to be identified by DNA—somebody ran him through an industrial shredder. The biggest piece they found was about the size of your little finger."

"Unfortunate for him," Grok allowed. "But as Chas said, why does this concern us?"

"Well, as it happens, the late Josiah Williams had a son, Josiah, Junior. Something of a, well, black sheep. A gambler, smuggler, businessman, what have you, who was estranged from his father."

"And . . . ?" Goodnight prompted.

"Even though he was not close to his father of late, Junior is very unhappy that his father was murdered."

"And . . . ?" This from Jasmine.

"He would like the killer found and punished."

"What, are we the honkin' police now?" Goodnight said.

"Junior owns a chain of gambling casinos, among other profitable ventures. He is very wealthy. Money is apparently not a problem for him."

"Ah," Riss said. "Interesting. How did he find you?"

"His father apparently left some kind of note to the effect that if he suddenly turned up dead, his family should contact me."

"Ah."

"Whatever it costs to find and deal with the killer and his organization, Junior is willing to provide. Within reason."

"What, uh, ballpark are we talking about here?" Riss said.

"Low-seven-figure minimum," von Baldur said. "Plus expenses." He might have been talking about the weather, he was so calm, but he had to be excited over that amount.

"Holy crap!" Goodnight said. He paused a beat. "And why is this a problem? Let's jump on this boat right now!"

"The Artegal System is, as you recall, somewhat morally conflicted. The problem might reach planetary proportions. It will have to be approached with some . . . delicacy, else we could choke on it."

" 'Delicacy' is my middle name," Goodnight said.

Even Grok snorted at that one.

Goodnight was undeterred. "We're talking a million credits or more *plus* expenses? Hell, I'll change my first and last names to whatever Junior wants and dance in a tutu."

"I should like to see that, friend Chas," Grok said.

"Cost you a million, too."

"I'll meet you at the rendesvouz point," von Baldur said. "And I'll bring our potential client with me, if that is agreeable."

Riss said, "I'm with Chas on this one. Bring him; see what he has to say."

The others all nodded. They had done okay on this job for the dead man, but this sounded like a real bonanza—expenses paid?

# SEVENTEEN

"Must take after his mother," Riss whispered to Jasmine as Freddie came in with their potential new client.

"Junior" was tall, dark, well built, and, by Jasmine's lights, definitely handsome. His suit was custom-made dark green silk and fitted him perfectly, and had probably set him back six or eight thousand credits, easy. "Mother must have been drop-dead gorgeous," Jasmine whispered back. "Yum, yum!"

"Don't let the little man in the boat do your thinking, girl," Riss said, but she smiled when she said it. She also thought he looked pretty hot, Jasmine knew.

"Folks, this is Joe Williams, whose father was our employer."

Introductions were made, and when Joe reached out to take her hand, Jasmine noticed that his grip was firm, warm, and, well, lasted a little longer than was usual. He smiled. Nice teeth.

She smiled back. Yum. Definitely.

Von Baldur said, "I'll let Joe make his pitch, which is . . . a bit unorthodox. Go ahead."

Williams smiled, flashing those perfect teeth again.

"My father and I weren't close," he began. "He disapproved of my, um, lifestyle, and I wasn't too fond of his, either. We saw each other now and then, forced ourselves to smile, and managed to keep things civil, out of respect for my mother's memory. Mostly."

He had a nice voice, Jasmine decided. Deep, masculine, almost melodic. What, she wondered, did he look like with the suit off?

"Um. Anyhow, we agreed to disagree about things and stayed out of each other's way. I don't use the family name in public, so as not to have anybody wonder about the connection. Nobody knows we are—were—related.

"My mother has been dead for ten years, and she made us promise to take care of each other. I funneled some of my money into my father's church—without him knowing, of course—and checked up on him from time to time. Last few months, I got busy on some new business ventures and kind of lost track of him. And while I wasn't paying attention, he got himself killed." He paused, looking around to catch their gazes one by one. "Whatever our differences, he was my father, and whoever killed him, whoever caused it, whoever had a hand in it? I want them. Preferably dead, but knowing why before they go."

Jasmine held onto her sigh. Revenge. Well, they did a fair amount of that, but she was, for some reason, a little disappointed . . .

"Plus," Williams continued, "it is possible that his death might be due to something I did. I have a lot of enemies, and if one of them killed my father, it would be bad for business to let it get by."

Ah. More pragmatic than just plain, old vengeance, then. It made him seem a little sharper.

Williams looked at Freddie. "Anything else?"

"You might want to speak of the terms of the arrangement," von Baldur said. He smiled.

Williams nodded. "Oh, yeah. If my father was knocked off by some nut job all by himself for some loony tunes reason, then that shouldn't take you long to find and collect him. A million credits, plus expenses. If it turns out that he was killed by some criminal organization and if you have to take them all down, then three million creds.

"If it was some government operation gone wrong, or even intended, then I want you to destabilize the son of a bitch enough so it falls or loses the next election big-time. That might take a little more, so call it five million credits, and whatever expenses you need to get it done."

"What if the expenses are more than the fee?" Goodnight asked. He had his arms crossed and his skeptical look in place. "You can afford that?"

"If I started a bonfire in front of my mansion and kept it burning twenty-four hours a day, every day, using nothing but credit notes to feed it, I could have two guys shoveling it in for the next fifty years without making a big dent in my personal fortune."

"Must be nice," Grok observed.

"It is. But there are things money can't buy."

Goodnight smirked. "Really?"

"Can't buy my father's life back," Williams said.

"Point taken," Goodnight admitted.

"Might not even be able to buy justice—the Artegal

System is as twisted as a warehouse full of corkscrews—but I'll settle for punishment. Crime gets a piece of almost everything in the system, as I'm sure my father probably told you. I don't think you can fix all that, nor do I want you to. Just those responsible for my father's untimely exit from life."

"Sounds like our kind of deal," Goodnight said, uncrossing his arms.

"There is one stipulation," Williams said.

Jasmine felt the tension, which had slackened a bit when Williams started throwing out the big numbers, tighten again.

"Which is . . . ?" she asked.

"I want to go along. I want to be part of your operation. I want to be in on the chase and the capture and the execution."

M'chel beat the rest of them to it, but she spoke for them all when she said, "No effin' way!"

"Why not?" Williams asked. "I'm not exactly an amateur when it comes to, uh, clandestine activities involving a bit of violence. I didn't start out rich. I had to work my way up from the streets. I have knocked a few heads together."

Riss had the ball, and the others looked at her to see if she wanted to carry it. She did.

"First, what we do is specialized. We all have areas of expertise, plus we are all generalists. Grok there can knock down your average wall without working up a sweat, but he is also a communications and electronics expert."

"Plus I do bird calls," Grok said.

"Jasmine can rascal any computer built, but she can

also cut your throat and make you lick the blood off the knife before you die."

Williams looked at Jasmine. She gave him her very best innocent look.

"Goodnight is faster than a photon and as deadly as a carrier full of puff adders, and he is not hobbled by moral qualms.

"Freddie can blow up a building or cheat you at cards, and you can't see what he is doing if he *tells* you how he's doing it.

"And I have my own talents. So whatever you bring to the table, we've already got it covered.

"More important than that, you are the client. If you step in front of a blaster bolt or stumble through a laser mine-trigger and get yourself killed, we are out a big investment of time and money. Sitting around waiting for your will to be sorted out by what you have described as about as crooked a system as there is, to pay us for something that is, at best, quasi-legal, isn't real appealing."

Williams let that lie for a few seconds. Then: "That's it?"

Riss blinked at him. "That's enough."

He smiled. "Okay. I'll grant that you five are faster, tougher, better trained, and maybe even smarter than I am. But I do know the system here, and you don't. Getting up to speed is going to take you a while, but I know which wheels to grease, where not to stick your noses, and I have a shitload of local clout, all of which will be very useful."

Jasmine found herself nodding. He had a point. A big-time local operator on their side would be a help.

"Second, if you are worried I might get knocked off, I can set up a special bank account, give you the access code, and put enough money in it to cover your expenses and pay a reasonable—pardon the pun—kill fee.

"I won't get in your way; I'll stay in the background and follow orders. It's a no-lose situation for you, way I see it."

He leaned back against the wall and looked at each of them in turn.

Jasmine had to smile. He was good-looking and had brains. That had always been a lethal combination in her book.

The Star Risk pentette shot each other quick glances.

M'chel said, "Freddie?"

Von Baldur shrugged. "It makes a certain amount of operational sense. We've hired local guides before."

"Chas?"

"As long as he doesn't get in my way, I'm good."

"Grok?"

"A man who seeks his sire's killer should be allowed liberties in his quest. I would allow it."

"Jasmine?"

"He would be a big asset, from an information standpoint."

Riss nodded. "I agree. If you will play by our rules and do as you are told, you can come along. Jasmine will draw up a contract, and—"

Williams reached into his jacket pocket and removed a square flashmem card about the size of a demi-cred coin. He held the chip and offered it to Riss. "I've, uh, taken the liberty of having a contract done, along with the establishment of a special bank account with a starting deposit of five million credits, for expenses. The access code is in it, encrypted, and the password is 'Star Risk, Ltd.' "

Jasmine grinned. She saw Grok, Freddie, and Goodnight do the same.

M'chel said, "You are awfully damned sure of yourself, aren't you?"

He gave her a slight bow. "Yes, ma'am, I am. Like your business, hesitation in mine can cause big problems. If it comes to the choice, I'd rather jump off a building than get pushed—at least I control that much. I'd prefer not to have to make that choice."

Riss gave him a grudging smile. "All right, Mr. Williams, welcome aboard."

"Call me 'Joe,' " he said.

Jasmine sure did enjoy watching him smile . . .

# EIGHTEEN

Grok considered himself a pragmatist, able to shift his attitude to deal with whatever the galaxy might throw at him, but even he was frowning by the time their new client, Joe, had laid out the way things ran in the Artegal System. Yes, to be sure, they had done some basic research on the various planets, but only to the depth necessary to accomplish their particular mission.

The depths of corruption, if what the client said was correct, went all the way to bedrock in all five planets of the system.

Basically, the whole system was run by six humans, who called themselves the Board. Two of them shared power to run the primary world; the rest each ran one of the other planets. There were elected governments that did the day-to-day things—making sure the trash got picked up, building roads—but the power behind everything was the Board.

If Josiah Williams was killed by any organization of any size, then it would ultimately answer to one of the Board's members. Certainly that had to be ruled out.

As the Star Risk team took all this in, Grok could

almost hear von Baldur's mind whirring. They were technically all equal partners, but Freddie's grasp of things political was usually better than anybody else's, and they tended to defer to him on such matters. Most of the time.

When Joe ran down, Riss looked at von Baldur. "What do you think?"

Von Baldur rubbed at his forehead. "Well. Kicking in doors and asking hard questions might be a bit premature at this stage. It would seem that we need to infiltrate and get our bearings. Better that the powers that be here see us as one of them rather than as outsiders poking around where we ought not to be sticking our noses. We need to be, at the very least, surreptitious."

They all nodded at that.

"We need a disguise that allows us to move in circles of power, and being mercenaries isn't that. We need a base that will engender a certain amount of respect and freedom of movement."

Joe said, "Well. There is an old casino I've been looking at. It's on Una, in Sarcid, the capital. Rundown, needs work, suffering under bad management, but in a good location. What if you were, say, a group of pirates or smugglers looking for a place to park your money and make it legitimate? You could buy the casino, dump a bunch of credits into fixing it up, get it running, and fit right in. Money laundering is a time-honored concept here."

"Speaking from personal experience?" Goodnight said.

"Yep."

Von Baldur nodded. "That could work. Jasmine

could build us a nice background—once the locals see that we are less-than-sterling characters who aren't going to rock the boat, that would put us in a position to gather information. A crook looking to stay out of the Alliance's sights would want to know everything about anything that might put them at risk. We let it be known we are covering our asses by buying useful information to this end, and people will approach *us* rather than us having to go out snooping."

The others nodded, Grok included. Not his preferred method—he'd rather kick in doors and ask hard questions until somebody gave up what they wanted to know, but he could see the merits of the plan.

Joe said, "The casino has fallen on difficult times. We could get it for a couple million."

"Not 'we,'" Freddie said. "You don't have anything to do with it—M'chel and I will negotiate the deal. You have to say out of sight on this. We don't want any possible connection between you and us on this to become known. Once we get set up, we can bump into you as we might any other local."

Joe nodded. "Yeah, I can see the wisdom of that."

Grok looked at Jasmine, whose brow was furrowed in thought.

Von Baldur caught his look, and his gaze shifted. "Jasmine? Something?"

"I'm suddenly remembering a bit of business from when I was with Cerberus. They had a contract—a big one—to find something that might be in the Artegal System. I didn't have the particulars—who the client was, or what they were looking for. It was very hush-hush, but I recall it had something to do with some largish theft . . ." She shook her head.

Goodnight said, "Hey, now that you mention it, I remember something about that. Scut I heard was, somebody knocked over an Alliance transport. Ship was carrying plates for Alliance credits—computer chips for the currency printers at the MidGalactic Mint."

"Counterfeiting?" Joe said.

"Naw," Goodnight said. "These weren't fakes, they were the real thing. All you'd need to make money would be the right rag paper and a good printer. Couldn't tell the difference because it would be exactly the same. Nice."

"What makes anybody think the missing chips would be in this system?" Joe asked.

Goodnight said, "Story was, during the attack, one of the raiding ships got blown up. A couple of the bodies got recovered and they were Abesserites."

Grok said, "Abesse is not unknown in pirate circles. More than a few raiders have come from there. And that *is* the fifth planet in this system."

"Kind of a long shot," Riss said. "Just because a couple of bodies were from Abesse doesn't mean that the whole crew was from there, or even this system."

Goodnight shrugged. "Being able to make real money in an amount you want is a big honkin' prize. You want to find it, you gotta start looking somewhere. Any lead is better than none."

They nodded at that.

"Fascinating," von Baldur said, "but I don't see that it concerns us, unless it means we might run afoul of our old nemesis, Cerberus Systems."

Jasmine said, "That was my concern, but unless they are running in deep cover, I can't find any sign of them working in any large number in the system. And it has been a while since the theft."

"Well, then, no problem. Let us move along," Freddie said.

In the end, they decided to go with Joe's idea and von Baldur's strategy: Freddie and Riss would be the buyers—they'd approach the owners of the casino and make an offer.

Jasmine, with Joe's help, would build a fake background tailored to fool the locals—Joe would know which parts to tweak to make the Star Risk crew most appealing and least likely to get raised eyebrows. Grok and Goodnight would hit the local pubs and begin dropping hints about who they were and why they were here. They would be sufficiently badass to impress other ne'er-do-wells, but not so much so as to garner too much attention.

Star Risk was, once again, on the case . . .

# NINETEEN

Jasmine said, "I'll be going into *betydelse* space for a while."

"Okay if I watch?" Joe said.

She shrugged. "If you want. Not much to see. Not very interesting."

"I won't get bored," he said. "I can't remember the last time I was bored."

"Suit yourself."

The space she'd rented was a standard-sized office cube, three meters square; plenty of room. It was secure to commercial levels, and as soon as she lit it up, Jasmine could instill her own security protocols, which were considerably more stringent. Once that was done, nobody short of a top-grade Alliance codebreaker would be able to peep her, and he would have to be having a good day to pull it off before she got finished and shut down.

Inside the cube, which had a desk and chairs she wouldn't be using, Jasmine triggered the computer's ID cam. She stood in a white circle on the floor with her hands down by her sides while the computer's scanner painted her with anatomical plane-lasers, the bright green strobing against her closed eyelids. Once the scan was done, the computer's cam would lock on her. "You know how this works?" she asked.

"I've seen my accountant do it," he said.

"Then you know you can sit or stand or move around—the readers are locked on as of . . . now."

A soft chime sounded once, and a flashing red diode on the desktop turned to a steady green glow, showing that the space was active. Additionally, a vox-gen said, in quiet, accentless, feminine bizspeak, "Welcome to Intergalactic Business Systems. The computer is on-line. You may begin when ready."

"Trimodal," she said. "Vox, subvoke; program math, right; language left—use Galactic Trade Standard, prime, and AJ patois, secondary. Give me a holoproj read of return information."

The air above the desk shimmered and bloomed into a standard holoprojection screen, a soft blue background.

The soft chime came again. "Parameters initiated. Continue when ready."

The matching words appeared over the desk, floating in the air, black against the blue background.

Joe said, "AJ patois?"

"Asteroid Jockey," she said. "Got some nice shortcuts in it for vector stuff, and some good programming modalities."

He nodded.

Jasmine took a deep breath. The *betydelse* system was, in this mode, fairly complex. She would be offering three different inputs, one with her subvocalized voice, and one from each hand. Every finger motion had a meaning, and combinations from both hands at once could be quite complicated. To dance the dance properly, it was necessary to shift into a state of total concentration. This was usually done by autohypnotic triggers. It wasn't necessary to speak the words aloud; all Jasmine had to do was visualize them. She did so.

The *betydelse* trance claimed her.

She waggled the first and second fingers of her right hand, the pinky of her left, and, under her breath, spoke the coded name of her security program.

The holoproj flowered in a multicolored flow of words and symbols as the program, stored on Galac-Net, downloaded itself into the local system node.

"Honey, I'm home!" a deeply masculine voice said. "Did you miss me?"

Jasmine grinned at the AI-gram's comment. It wasn't really sentient, but it had some funny combinations it sometimes put together.

She subvoked her commands as her fingers did their independent dances, left, right, left, twist, twirl, bend . . .

Here was the magic in using a trimode—you could up- and download tremendous amounts of information in a short time, much faster than any human or sentient alien could do in a single mode. In the space of three seconds, Jasmine brought up three more stored programs. They had long code names, but she thought of them as Cracker, Finder, and Writer.

Cracker broke into systems, opening a door so that Finder could slip in and locate the information she wanted. That done, Writer could alter the information to whatever she needed it to say. Auto system-hounds wouldn't catch it, and only the best organic ops could, and they'd have to be looking right at her when she did it ninety-nine times out of a hundred to catch her. A major codesweep would find the doctored docs, of course, but nobody wanted to shut down a multitera-byte system every time they *thought* somebody *might* have gone in and rascaled it. Especially for something piddly.

Generally, big systems went off-line every six months or so for debugging; some only once a year. Once that happened, they'd spot her alterations and the new material would be deleted, but by then it wouldn't matter. She would choose her targets accordingly, and cross-reference those so there would be coverage even if somebody shut down a system or three immediately. It wasn't perfect, but it was as much as they needed and then some.

She sliced Cracker into a half-dozen breakbots and sent them out into the net. Alliance records were actually the easiest; there was so much access to those that it was impossible to protect them all the time. Corporate security was harder. Planetary records varied from world to world. News orgs were so-so.

Hackerweb was the hardest. It was full of geeks with nothing better to do than worry about being snooped, and they were constantly shifting their routines. And there were some military securities that were hard . . .

The first breakbot came back, flashing on the holoproj screen. She waggled her hands and sent a locatebot that way.

Another breakbot reported in. She dispatched a second locator.

As more of the harder systems were breached, she followed up.

Pretty soon, the locatebots started to log back, and she started overwriting the files they found, using Writer's editbots. She had already composed the files she wanted to install, with Joe's help, so that was just a matter of cut-and-paste, and making sure the joins were smooth, and that the backdate showed the material had been there for months or years.

Coming and going, coming and going . . .

All over the galaxy, from news reports to police files to corporate records, a history began to assemble itself. The members of Star Risk were changed into pirates. Blurry images of them showed up. Reports of their actions. Suspicions of their activities. Anybody looking to run a background check on the new identities would find them perfectly valid.

Each overwrite had a worm built in, and a backdoor to reach it, connected to a single launch site. At any time, Jasmine could walk to any computer terminal hooked into the net and, with a few keystrokes or a coded phrase, wake up the worms, which would then eat the fake files. That was necessary, because after this caper was done, they did *not* want to be busted as pirates, so all that had to go away.

Bots reported, more were dispatched, touch-up editing was done on the fly. Jasmine lost track of the time. In single mode, it would have taken days to do what she wanted. In trimode, it went much faster . . .

The *betydelse* system chimed, and the female vox said, "Session terminated. Thank you for using Intergalactic Business Systems and please consider us for your future ventures."

Jasmine blinked as she came out of the trance. She looked at the chronometer on the desk. Two hours. Not bad. Not bad at all. She did feel a little sweaty, and probably a little more fragrant with that perspiration, but that was how it went.

Behind her, leaning against the wall, Joe said, "Wow. You're good. You make my accountant look like a primary kid's first built-a-robot kit."

She smiled. "Thank you. I can't imagine it was that interesting to watch."

"Oh, it's always a pleasure to see an expert work, Miz King."

"Call me Jasmine," she said.

He liked that, she could tell. "So, we're good to go?"

"The pirates have come to town to buy themselves a casino and wash their dirty credits. We are as good as a hovervan full of platinum ingots."

They both smiled.

Goodnight touched his ear, and the tiny comm implant therein chirped and shut off.

Next to him, Grok raised an eyebrow.

"We o-ficially beez piretz, Bozz," Goodnight said. "Letz go get us something to drink, hey?"

"Now that you mention it, I am a bit dehydrated. You have a place in mind?"

"Local LEOs answered twelve calls on three shifts last week at a pub named My Brother's, near the port in the district they call Rat Town. I thought we might see how the beer there was."

"My Brother's?"

"Yeah, like when your wife calls and asks you, you say, 'Where am I? Why, I'm over at my brother's.'"

"Sounds like our kind of pub."

"It does, doesn't it? Sometimes I really love this job."

Grok grinned, and if it was larger and more wolfish than Goodnight's expression, it was pretty much a match for intent.

My Brother's hadn't spent a great deal of time or money on the decor. No ferns overflowing hanging pots, no holovid showing sports, no lovely wooden tables with ornate seats. No music, either. The place had a plastcrete floor with a slight slope toward a large grated drain in the middle of the room. The tables were expanded metal and bolted down, as were the stools. The bar along one wall was constructed of the same materials, and the liquor racks behind it were protected by a heavy-mesh durasteel screen. Once the place was empty, you could stand on the bar with a fire hose and clean it, and Goodnight wouldn't be surprised if that's how they did it.

If the various kinds of smoke were any thicker, you'd have to cut your way through it to move. People came here to get blasted and that's what most of them seemed to be doing. A working being's pub, no frills.

The waiters and waitresses were not remotely attractive unless you were *really* stoned, and they went for bottled, given the look of the place. The guy who had brought them their first beers—well, he had a face that would scare a nest of puke-snakes back into their hole.

The waitress who brought the second round made the waiter look like a beauty contest winner. Her body was hard, her face was hard, both were scarred, as far as they were visible, and she had black-chrome teeth, most of which came to sharp points when she smiled, Goodnight noticed. That expression that did not engender any great warmth. She could take off a couple of fingers in a single bite, easily.

Goodnight didn't think he could smoke or drink enough to make *that* waitress seem attractive, not without passing out. He shuddered when she walked away.

Grok looked at him. "What?"

"Did you get a look at our waitress?"

"You fancy her?"

"Good gods, have you developed no sense of what is attractive in humans after all this time?"

Grok shrugged. "You all look so much alike to me. Sorry. I liked her teeth, though. Very functional."

Halfway through the second beer, a very large and very drunk fellow, bigger than Goodnight but considerably smaller than Grok, stumbled to their table.

"What'n the seven hells're you?" he said.

Goodnight looked at his pinky chrono. "Eight minutes. Is that a new record?"

Grok said, "I believe it is, friend Chas."

"Hey!" the drunk said. "I'm talkin' here!"

Grok turned his head very slowly to observe the drunk. "You are addressing *me*?"

"Yeah, furball, who'n crapland you think?"

"I," Grok said, "am the Tooth Fairy." He smiled. The guy was not so drunk that he didn't catch the display of sharp white enamel gleaming in Grok's mouth.

"Whoa! You do got some choppers, don'tcha? Ugly, ugly!"

Grok turned back to look at Goodnight. "Did he just call me 'ugly'?"

"Technically, I don't believe he did. He observed that you had teeth, which is certainly true, and then he said that word, but I am not certain as to his precise meaning. Maybe he didn't mean *you* were ugly."

"Hmm," Grok said. "Perhaps he will clarify it for us." Grok looked at the drunk. "When you said 'ugly,' were you referring to me?"

The drunk laughed. "You? Why . . . no, I was talkin' about your alien-loving pal here! The guy who was leering at my girlfriend!" He nodded at Goodnight.

The *waitress* was this guy's girlfriend? Man . . .

"Ah, friend Chas, it seems that you are correct. Good that I did not react violently. Since he was not insulting *me,* that would have been against the rules."

"I am glad you realize that." Goodnight shifted his butt on the metal stool a little. Still seated, he reached out with his left foot, hooked his boot's instep behind the man's ankle, and, as he tugged, hard, snapped his right knee to his chest suddenly and then thrust-kicked. He thumped his boot heel into the man's sternum, nice and solidly, with good opposite leverage—

The drunk went backward, sailed two meters through the air in a back racing dive, and smacked into the hard floor, his head and shoulders slightly ahead of his back. He hit hard enough to shake the floor. Sounded like somebody dropping a large block of wood.

He was not going to be getting up on his own anytime soon.

Goodnight sipped at his beer. "Called *me* ugly? Guy needs to have his *vision* checked, given his taste in women."

"Mayhap after his other medical conditions are attended to, he will consider it."

"Damn well should."

Three men at a nearby table were already on their feet and heading toward Goodnight and Grok.

"It would appear that our nearsighted friend has companions," Grok observed, sipping at his own beer. The size of his hand made the bottle look tiny.

"Don't they always? Can I have one?"

"No, you had yours. The rule says it's my turn."

Goodnight nodded, accepting this, but not happy. "All right. But the next ones after those are mine."

"That would be proper."

As the three men stormed toward them, Grok stood. Which action gave them pause, to be sure. One of them uttered a word that indicated somebody in the area must have had an incestuous relationship with his female parent.

As it turned out, both Goodnight and Grok got several more turns before the sound of approaching sirens indicated that they should leave . . .

# TWENTY

The casino was called the Lucky Moon, and von Baldur and Riss sat in the manager's office across from the owners, a pair of almost comedic-looking characters. The place was not what one would call busy. Now and then, a slot machine would pay off with a cascade of tokens and musical tones, although the sound was muted through the closed door. Von Baldur estimated the number of patrons playing games of chance or sitting at the bar at maybe one-tenth the place's capacity, if that.

They couldn't be making enough profit to pay the power bill.

One of the owners was tall and thin, with a hangdog face, the other short and tubby and looking puzzled, and they *really* wanted to deal, but there were certain niceties to be observed. While the laws were flexible in this city, the planet, and the whole system, breaking them with impunity required, as Joe had carefully detailed, care in selecting the right people to bribe to look elsewhere when you did so.

Von Baldur and Riss weren't making it easy for

Hangdog and Puzzled here, because, as Joe had also pointed out, that would create suspicion and, as a matter of course, suspicion cost more to fix . . .

"So, ah, Mr. Jones—" Hangdog began.

"No, I'm Jones," Riss cut in. "He's *Smith*."

"Ah," Hangdog said. "Of course, of course. My fault, sorry."

Both the Star Risk ops smiled large. All experienced beings of the galaxy here.

"Then, Mr., um, Smith, where did you say your funding was coming from?"

"I don't recall that I said," von Baldur said. "Does it matter?"

"Well," Puzzled said, "technically, there are some, ah, *restrictions* as to who may hold a gaming license."

"Is that so?" Riss said. She smiled. Butter wouldn't melt in her mouth, she was so cool.

"Yes," Hangdog said. "No one with a felony criminal record, say, or with relatives on the Gaming Council, can run a casino."

"We have no relatives on the Gaming Council, I can assure you," von Baldur said. "And neither Jones nor Smith, nor any of our partners—Mr. Doe, Miz Roe, or Mr. Moe—have any criminal records anywhere. Not," he said, smiling again, "even a parking ticket."

Hangdog and Puzzled exchanged glances. You didn't need to be an astrophysicist to know which way those solar winds blew. "Oh, well, that settles that, then," Puzzled said. "Now as to the matter of price . . . ?"

Von Baldur kept his face neutral. Joe had told them the casino was worth, at most, two million. He reckoned that the owners would start out greedy and ask for twice that. The Star Risk team should haggle and get the price to two and a half—the owners would be thrilled at that, and while it would mark the new owners as maybe not the hottest traders in the spiral arm, they wouldn't be thought fools, either. The assumption would be that the credits they offered were stolen in some manner anyhow, certainly after the background checks came back, which would have happened before the dickering began. These two knew—they thought— with whom they were dealing, and it didn't seem any kind of impediment that von Baldur could tell . . .

"What did you have in mind?" Riss asked.

"We couldn't reasonably allow it to go for less than five million," Hangdog said.

Von Baldur laughed. They were more than just greedy, they were downright venal. "Really? Is it situated over buried treasure? A hidden opal mine? Please, gentlemen, do we look like we just dropped off the soybean truck from the outback co-op? It will take more than the place is worth to get it up to a condition that will attract paying customers. We were thinking more along the lines of a million five."

The owners exchanged quick looks. Puzzled took the lead. "Well, yes, we will stipulate that there are some minor repairs that need to be done. We could drop the price to reflect those. Call it . . . four million . . ."

Riss shook her head. "New machines, new paint, new carpets, and ridding the hotel floors of rats alone will cost a small fortune. We'll have to hire staff who can actually deal cards and do simple arithmetic in their heads. Cooks, waiters, entertainers, guards, bean counters . . . Considering all that, it would be generous if we bump our offer to two million."

From here on out, Hangdog and Puzzled were in gravy, and they knew it.

It showed on their faces. Von Baldur would have loved to have had a chance to play cards against these two. They had so many "tells" that he could read them as if they were babbling at him aloud.

"We do want to get out of the business," Puzzled said, "but not if we have to take a cold bath to do it. Three million would satisfy our investors, though they wouldn't be happy about it."

Since they had no investors, von Baldur wasn't too impressed with this sortie, but he had a role to play. "Okay, let's skip the appetizers and get to the main course here. The place is worth two. We'll give you two and half. Take it or leave it."

"We'll take it," the two said as one. Quickly, before he could change his mind.

"Pleasure to do business with you," von Baldur said. "How would you like the funds? We can do a certified bank transfer chip. Or we can pay you in cash—credit certificates or platinum ingots."

"A certified chip would be fine," Puzzled said.

They were pretty sure they had von Baldur and Riss's number—even without the background checks, anybody who offered to pay in currency or ingots was either very eccentric or as crooked as a mountain-switchback road. Like, say, pirates and smugglers.

"We have engaged the services of a local law firm," Riss said. "Doorine, Fill, Margo, Lin, and Associates."

"First-class firm," Hangdog allowed.

"So we have heard," von Baldur said. "Have your

legals contact them; they'll have a contract ready by this afternoon. We'll get together—with our other partners. We'll all sign on the dotted lines, tender the price, and that will be that."

"There is the, uh, matter of the gaming licenses. An application for an investigation will be necessary," Puzzled said.

Riss said, "I'm sure there must be some way to get such an application, ah . . . *expedited*. Why don't we add another, say, hundred thousand to the purchase price as a fee for your service, and you take care of that for us. Is that doable?"

Puzzled almost drooled at his sudden windfall. The Commission's investigator locally could be bought for a quarter of that, and Star Risk knew that because that investigator was already in Joe's pocket. They could have had him for free, but that wasn't the point. What these two needed to know was that Smith, Jones, Doe, Roe, and Moe had money and would spend it on whatever they thought necessary. Word would get around fast enough.

"Why, uh, yes, I think we could handle that."

Hangdog nodded. "Oh, I'm sure we can."

Puzzled said, "We, uh, also know some contractors who are quite reasonable for any improvements you might like to make."

"That is most kind of you," von Baldur said. "But I think we have that covered, don't we, Miz Smith?"

"I'm Jones. *You* are Smith," she said.

"Ah. Right. How silly of me. Local gravity must be making me forgetful after my time in space."

Everybody smiled. Money made for happiness now and again, when you had a lot of it heading toward your pocket. Who cared about a name? Certainly not these two fellows . . .

And come this afternoon, Star Risk was going to own the Lucky Moon casino. Ratty and rundown, and it wouldn't really belong to them, but at least they had a place where they could legitimately hang out and have a reason to be there.

Things were going along nicely.

# TWENTY-ONE

Susa—if he had another name, Makko had never heard it—was so quiet that Makko was afraid the man might have had a stroke or something. Sitting there on Makko's couch, that would be bad. Everybody would assume that Makko had poisoned Susa or some such, and he'd have instant enemies because of it. Instant friends, too.

A stroke didn't seem likely; Susa was a big guy, but not fat, into working out and eating healthy foods. He could lift ungodly amounts of weight, pump an Exercycle the equivalent of going up and down a mountain, and knew enough martial arts to smash a small army flat. The picture of fitness. Normally, he was affable, easygoing, and smiled a lot. When he got quiet and still, that was not a good sign. Bad things tended to happen when Susa got quiet. Terrible things . . .

"You killed him," he finally said.

Makko wasn't sure what Susa was getting at here, but he couldn't see how that would be a problem. "Yeah. He hired somebody to come in and screw with us. All that crap on the shipping stations? That was him; the preacher was behind it."

"And so you killed him." It wasn't a question.

"I didn't really mean to, it just kind of . . . happened. Besides that, he had Neves taken out. I had no choice but to deal with him. You can't let stuff like that pass."

Susa shook his head. He sighed. "I suppose it's my own fault. Sometimes I keep things to myself that would be better shared."

Makko didn't much like the direction this conversation was going. The preacher had been a thorn in his foot, he had pulled him out and gotten rid of him; what was the problem here? Susa didn't have any moral scruples against killing; he had done plenty of that himself.

"Let me explain. Do you recall a small problem that Uhnal had on Abesse a while back? Having to do with some mercenaries he rented out?"

"I heard some things," Makko admitted.

"What did you hear?"

Makko said, "Well, I never got the whole story, but word was, Uhnal leased some merc ships to somebody who hit an Alliance transport for some valuable cargo."

"And . . . ?"

"And they got it, but, somehow, they lost it."

"And do you know what *it* was?"

Makko understood as well as anybody that knowledge was power, but Susa must already know as much as he did, and more. Susa was his boss, and he was the elected chairman of the Board, the most powerful man in the system, not to mention the richest. Whatever power Makko might gain from keeping something from him wasn't going to even be a drop in Susa's bucket.

He said, "I heard it was currency chips for the Mid-Galactic Mint. Credit plates."

"Your information is valid. Twenties and fifties. At my direction, Uhnal sent the mercs to hit the transport. His troops collected the plates and returned to the system. Unfortunately, the commander of his merc troop was, unbeknownst to him, in the process of undergoing a religious conversion. He saw the light, as it were, and came to repent his evil, thieving ways."

"Uh-huh . . . ?"

"Thus the commander of the mission did *not* deliver the plates to Uhnal. He disappeared with them."

"Oh, man."

"Exactly. The largest prize anybody in this system ever scored, and we lost it."

"I take it you didn't find him?"

"Actually, we did, only a few weeks later. Quite by accident—literally. The commander's personal hovercar blew a repeller and he slammed into the side of an office building in Tufa City at speed. Killed instantly. Gone to join his Maker, it would seem."

"And the plates . . . ?"

"Nowhere to be found. However—and this is part you will find interesting—eventually, we found out that the man who helped the late commander find his way from sin into redemption was none other than the Reverend Josiah Williams."

"Ah," Makko said.

Susa saw him get it. "Yes. If you were repenting your past sins and somebody brought you into a state of grace, as it were, mightn't you be disposed to share the important things in your life with that person?"

Makko offered an obscene two-word invitation to sexual intercourse. Rhetorical, of course.

"Precisely. If there was somebody who our late commander would have trusted with the knowledge of those plates—even the plates themselves—it would have been his spiritual counselor. And that advisor won't be telling us where they are, now, will he?"

"I—I—"

"Yes, I understand. You didn't know. Wouldn't have had any way of knowing. I blame myself. I was working my way around to dealing with the reverend. I wasn't in a hurry, it had been years since the theft— if he indeed had the chips, they weren't going anywhere. And such things have to be done delicately. Religious fanatics don't behave like normal people. They are hard to frighten and they are willing to suffer much because where they go from here is a better place. Death is nothing to a man who believes he is going to sit at God's right hand when he dies."

"Um."

"Which leaves the matter of the missing chips unresolved."

"Maybe I can . . . poke around some. Talk to some of Williams's associates."

"Less harshly than you spoke to him, I assume?"

"Yeah, I—"

"Keven, let me be perfectly clear. We are talking about a monstrous fortune here—the ability to print notes that will pass muster anywhere. Millions, even billions. I already have the formula for credit-note rag paper; all it would take would be a production mill and a few weeks' work to come up with bales of the stuff. I have the formula for the ink. I have access to the best presses. With those chips, in a week or two, I could fill a freighter with twenty- and fifty-credit notes that would pass an experienced teller's examination at any bank in the galaxy. All the holograms, watermarks, security threads—the serial numbers would even be sequenced. It wouldn't just look like real money, it would, for normal intents and purposes, *be* real money."

Makko felt his throat go dry at the thought. If he could get his hands on those chips . . . Susa wasn't the only one who could use them. It was hard to even think about how valuable they would be. You could buy your own country. Maybe even your own planet . . .

"You won't be the only one looking for them," Susa continued. "The Alliance is quietly offering a ten-million-credit reward for their return. There are bounty hunters who have gotten a whiff of this and who are out pounding the plastcrete looking. Private security systems, police, military, you name it. Our advantage is that we know who took them and what happened to him. Nobody else has that link."

"Right—"

"Even though you can't really be blamed because you didn't know, you did kill the man who most likely had them, or knew where they were. And now that you know, you will step more lightly and with great care, yes?"

"Uh, yes."

"Good. If you find them, you will become a lot richer than you are now, and so will I. But if you screw this up?" He shook his head.

There was no need for him to say any more. Makko could well imagine what would happen to him if he screwed it up.

Goodnight looked around the main floor of the Lucky Moon, empty now. As soon as they had signed the purchase papers, von Baldur had shut the place down. Pretty soon there was going to be an army of workers here; builders and painters, revamping the casino and upgrading everything in it.

"I've been in worse places," Goodnight said.

"As have we all," von Baldur said. "That's the tour. Top floor will be our apartments; high rollers will be one level down from us. Below that, the restaurant, then the hotel—mostly as comps for the big spenders—and then the main level here is for the riffraff."

Joe wasn't there, but he had cruised the place, and his estimates to make the casino into a big draw ran to about the same as it had cost. Once that was done, he'd said, it would be worth three times what they had in it, and gaining value by the day.

Riss was going to be the general contractor, and she was already soliciting bids from subcontractors—most of whom Joe would supply in a backhanded and sub rosa manner. He knew who the best people were, and he'd make sure they came round.

Goodnight and Grok were to be the coheads of security, which suited them. They had already trashed three pubs, and had enough of a reputation from that so word would get around that they weren't to be messed with—if you wanted to stay out of the emergency medical units.

Von Baldur would be in charge of gaming—he'd hire the dealers and croupiers and machine-riggers, the pit bosses, and Joe would steer competent people their way.

Jasmine, in addition to buying information, would hire and deal with the rest of the staff—the waiters and waitresses, the bartenders, entertainers, maintenance, the tellers and accountants, like that. While much of gambling money was electronic these days, there were always those who wanted to feel the crisp bills, or even coins, in their hands, and some who wanted it that way to avoid having records that would be available to the tax collectors. A wallet full of cash was portable and left no trail, and while technically casinos had to report big winners to the government, sometimes certain . . . accommodations could be reached. Instead of one player walking out with a hundred thousand credits, say, a dozen players might each leave the building with less than ten thousand each, which piddly amount did not have to be reported to the tax folks. If they all gave it to one man once they left, that was not the casino's business. Not legal, but on a planet like this, it was just one more way of doing biz . . .

Ostensibly, the Star Risk crew were pirates come to turn their ill-gotten loot into legitimate money, but von Baldur reckoned that within a few months they could make back what the casino had cost to buy and improve, and be making a tidy profit. Not that they'd be here that long, all things going well, but you never knew. Once they caught and punished Josiah's killer, they'd have a nice chunk of change, and Joe would have another jewel in his chain-of-casinos crown, so it was a win-win for everybody.

"So, what shall we call it?" Grok asked. "The casino."

Riss looked at him. "It's already got a name."

"Pardon my ignorance, but isn't it unwise to keep the name of an unsuccessful venture? Would it not be better to start with a, how do you say, clean page?"

"Big hairy there has a point," Goodnight said.

Jasmine said, "Something that connotes good fortune for the potential patrons, I'd think."

"Why not just 'Winners?'" von Baldur said. "Winners Casino."

"It has a nice ring," Riss said.

"I concur," Grok said. "Friend Chas?"

Goodnight shrugged. "Fine by me. You can call it 'We Just Got Your Rent Payment, Sucker' for all I care. We get to drink, eat, and gamble on the house, right?"

"I believe there might be some limits there," von Baldur said. "Eat and drink all you want, but casino employees aren't permitted to play in their own establishment."

"But *you* get to do it?"

"I represent the house," von Baldur said. "That's legal."

"Well, hell, there goes half the fun of having it," Goodnight said. "Can we at least hit on the waitresses?"

Grok said, "I recall a waitress that you seemed enamored with recently, in the pub called My Brother's.

Black-chrome teeth, she had. Perhaps we can hire her especially for Chas?"

Goodnight indicated that Grok should perform an obscene and physically impossible act upon his own person.

Grok's laugh sounded like somebody tearing heavy canvas.

"Laugh it up, hairball," Goodnight said.

"What?" Riss said. "What is funny here?"

"I'll tell you later," Grok said. "It is a most amusing story."

# TWENTY-TWO

Jasmine had a problem. Not a major, caper-killing, professional problem, just a small, personal one, but she hadn't decided how she was going to handle it yet.

She had the hots for Joe.

They were in a so-so hotel room in a bedroom suburb on the western outskirts of Malid, only a few kilometers from the sea. It was clean, if not a first-class place, and while she sat in a chair next to a cheap table, Joe perched on the edge of the large and quite comfortable-looking bed a meter or so away.

It took little imagination on her part to imagine him reclining upon that bed—and with fewer clothes on, too . . .

He was smart, good-looking, and, more importantly, he seemed to respect her for her mind and not just her body, which went a long way in her book toward making a man attractive. Their meetings about the caper had to be kept clandestine, of course, to make sure he wasn't connected to them publicly, which meant sneaking in and out of rooms like this, usually one at a time. They met in rented houses or offices, spots where nobody was apt to know either of them, and they were never where they would be seen together. During one of those earlier meetings, regarding the care and feeding of a casino—things about which she and the other Star Risk crew were becoming familiar, if not actually adept at, he had offhandedly made a remark when talking about another casino owner that she had found intriguing. The woman, he had said, was brilliant, and that he found smart women incredibly attractive . . .

So there it was. Definitely a potential there. And it had been a while since Jasmine had found time to play those kinds of games. Her standards were, she had to admit, hard for most men to meet. She set the bar at championship levels, and if a man couldn't clear it, the match never began. But Joe had already demonstrated more than enough qualifications: smart, rich, handsome, and the kind of guy who liked a woman for her *mind* . . .

Means, motive, and opportunity, the classic triad of a crime, and she had them all. The question was, was she going to act on her feelings?

All this went through her mind as she was half listening to Joe offer advice on staffing the casino, which was already undergoing major construction and renovation. The whir of power tools droned through the place all day and all night—they had three shifts working round the clock, and even on the top floor where they had taken over the living suites for their own apartments, the sounds filtered through, if not so loudly as to disturb their sleep. M'chel was doing a great job getting Winners into shape, again in no small part due to help from the handsome fellow sitting there on the bed, close enough that she could lean over and run her hand through his thick, dark hair . . .

*Focus, girl!* Getting involved with clients was a bad idea, generally. Not that it didn't happen—she remembered that hemp farmer who'd hired them to keep a competitor at bay, and who been incredibly sexy and tender. Too bad he was married, but even so, it had been fun while it lasted.

Joe was unattached, and unless her radar was wrong, he was offering subtle signals that he wouldn't slam a door in her face if push came to poke . . .

"—so I'd say you might as well go ahead and get the union in on things now, before you start hiring. A little grease on the wheels now will save you a lot of trouble in the long run. The steward for the local is a very reasonable man. I'm sure that he'll be happy to accommodate you. What do you think?"

Oh, what the hell. In for a tenth, in for a credit.

She leaned over slowly, and kissed him gently on the lips. "I think it's time to stop talking the talk and start walking the walk."

He grinned as he put his arms around her. "Yes, ma'am," he said.

After that, nobody talked for quite a while.

Riss was conferring with the man who was going to tile the freshers. The tiles were no problem—they were hardcast with slickcoat, so anything short of a diamond-tipped chisel wouldn't leave graffiti on the surface—but she was trying to make certain that he knew the grout she wanted him to use needed to be nonporous and waterproof. If all you had to do was wipe the surface with a cloth to keep it clean, that was good. If you had to use a fungicide in the cracks every few days to keep mold from growing there, that meant paying somebody to do it. With a dozen freshers on the casino level alone, that extra effort could lead to either a lot of overtime or more maintenance workers, and neither of those helped keep costs down. Yeah, the best-quality grout cost more up front, but it would pay for itself in a hurry.

"No problem," the guy finally said, once he realized she wasn't trying to do the job as cheaply as possible. "What color you want?"

Riss looked up as Jasmine strolled into the room. She looked like the cat who had just dined on prime parakeet.

The tile guy left and Jasmine ambled over in a walk that was, in a word, lazy. Satisfied. A guess-what-I-just-did look . . .

"No," Riss said. "You didn't!"

Jasmine smiled. "Well, actually, yeah, I did."

Riss shook her head. "And . . . ?"

"You don't think I would kiss and tell, do you?"

Riss laughed. "Come on. How was he?"

She beamed. "Terrific! Very, um, adept. Tender. I believe he could tie a figure-eight knot in a cherry stem using just his tongue."

Riss said, "My, my." She paused. "You do know it's a bad idea, right?"

"Uh-huh."

"But you are going to do it again anyhow?"

"Oh, yeah. Soon. As often as possible."

Riss laughed once more. "Freddy'll be pissed if he finds out."

"And how is that going to happen?"

"It shows."

"To you, it shows. The rest of the crew are men—they won't notice. They never have before."

"That's true."

A design subcontractor, Rouweez, flounced up, bearing swatches of fabric. "M'chel, you simply *must* give me your decision on the color scheme for the foyer! I can't go forward without knowing that! Is it to be 'sunrise' or 'mood'?" He waved the two color swatches at her as if sending semaphore signals.

To Jasmine, Riss said, "Sorry, I have to get back to work."

Rouweez gave Jasmine a speculative glance. "Oh, my, look at you. Been naughty, haven't you?"

Riss chuckled. "You were saying about the crew not noticing?"

Jasmine shook her head. "Spare me. None of them have Rouweez's sensitivity."

The man smiled, revealing deep dimples.

"Go away and gloat," Riss said to Jasmine. "If I don't pick a color, Mr. Sensitive here is going to have to be treated for hysterics."

Jasmine left, and the just-laid look was just as obvious to Riss from behind, too.

*Must be nice,* she thought.

"Muh-shelll," Rouweez said, drawing out her name. He cut his gaze to the ceiling, then fastened it on her again. "Can we *focus* here, please?" He waved the swatches.

"Mood," she said.

" 'Mood'? Are you *serious*? '*Mood*'?!"

Riss laughed yet again. This was turning out to be quite the entertaining day. "You ever think about doing stand-up comedy, Rouweez? I think you'd kill at it."

Who would have thought that running a casino would be so, well, daunting?

Neither Goodnight nor Grok were the beings to be telling security guards to take it easy, but von Baldur had made it quite plain that the purpose of uniformed guards in the casino was to reassure the patrons. They were to be polite, well mannered, and even if they were escorting somebody who did not want to leave out of the building, there were to smile and make it seem as if they were old friends.

"You mean they aren't supposed to stomp a loud-mouthed drunk who takes a swing at them into a puddle of goo," Goodnight said.

"That is exactly what I mean. The plainclothes guards are the real security force, and that loud-mouthed drunk might still have five hundred credits burning a hole in his pocket, and we want his money before he leaves. As long as he doesn't create too much of a disturbance, he should be handled as though he's as fragile as a tower made of spun sugar."

"Where is the fun in that?" Goodnight said.

Grok nodded.

Von Baldur sighed. Like talking to overexcited little boys at times, dealing with these two. "The fun is in doing this caper and going home with millions of credits in our pockets."

"Yeah, well, there is that."

"If a gang of armed robbers charges in, you and Grok can turn them into barbecue sauce—as long as you don't splash it on the paying customers. What we want here is quiet, low-key, pleasant. A place where you could take your granny for fun and relaxation without her getting upset by guards beating on some fool who just lost the children's college fund at the card table."

Goodnight shook his head. "Dull."

"That's exactly what we want. We are supposed to be pirates who want nothing more than to clean our dirty money. No muss, no fuss. Are we clear about this?"

"Yeah, I suppose."

"We are, friend Freddie."

"Good. So when you pick the guards who will be in uniform, pick some with pleasant demeanors, who don't look as if they have been stitched together from spare parts. Somebody you wouldn't mind your dear old granny talking to if she needed to know the way to the ladies' fresher."

"Well, *my* dear old granny was a long-haul trucker who could fry the paint off a wall with her cursing," Goodnight said, "so maybe that's not—"

"Chas," von Baldur cut in, shaking his head again. "You know perfectly well what I mean."

Goodnight grinned. "Yeah. I hear you. C'mon, Groko, let's go find us some pretty boys to dress in their new uniforms."

Von Baldur watched the two leave. None of them had ever run a business like this before; glitches had to be expected. It was going surprisingly well, all things considered. The renovations were proceeding quickly, given the three shifts laboring on them. The hiring of staff, from dealers to cashiers to maintenance workers, was also on track. Already, Jasmine had a string of informants feeding her information. It was a bit early to start too directly down the road to finding Josiah's killers, but sooner or later, Jasmine would cultivate the right person, and those leads would be forthcoming. Subtlety was important here, especially since they had no way of knowing with whom they were dealing.

The whole process was, he reflected, quite stimulating, in a way different from the standard kick-ass-and-take-names caper that was their bread and butter. Different challenges, different feelings of accomplishment when you met and overcame one. Who could have known that hiring away a top-grade pit boss from another casino could be so satisfying . . . ?

# TWENTY-THREE

Sitting along in his sumptuous office, Makko was more than a little frustrated. The dear, departed preacher didn't seem to have any close friends or family, and the people his operatives had spoken to had not been forthcoming with useful information—they didn't have any.

Nett had proved adept enough, and since Makko liked to promote from within, he was the logical choice to replace Neves. With somebody who was already a member of your organization, you didn't have to bring them up to speed on the little matters, like who was dead and why.

"Boss?"

Well, think of the Devil and he appears. "Yeah?"

"We might have something."

"Empires have fallen because of that word. What *might* we have?"

"The preacher was in the military a while back."

"I already knew that."

"But while he was, he had a dependent listed on his insurance."

"Oh?"

"A spouse."

"Ah, that is interesting."

"She died about ten years ago."

Makko glared at his underling. "Why is this 'something'? If the woman was dead when the preacher got involved in our business, how do you figure that helps us? You think he hid what we want in her coffin?"

"Nope, she was cremated."

"Nett, don't make me sorry I raised you up."

"Sorry, Boss. What it is, is, somebody got into the system and planetary records and did some cutting and pasting. Our computer guy found that much. Though he couldn't bring most of the original files back, he knows they were messed with."

"And . . . ?"

"Turns out there is a reference on the Josiah Williams biography, just a line in the middle of a background file, a passing reference the hacker must have missed."

"Tell me what it is or I will kill you, right now."

"A kid. Josiah Williams had a child. No ID, name, not even the sex—that's all been deleted—but we know he at least had one thirty-some-odd years ago."

That got Makko's full attention. Offspring? And erased from official records? As if somebody were trying to hide him—or her. Ah, that was news. At least it was a place to start looking.

"Go find out about this kid," Makko said. "Who he or she is, where they live, if there's any chance that the old man might have been in contact with them in the last couple of years."

"I'm on it, boss."

After Nett left, Makko felt a little better. At least they had a starting point now. Something.

He looked at his computer screen. He had a pretty full social calendar. Tonight, the new owners of the old Lucky Moon casino were having a grand re-opening bash, renaming the place "Winners."

He laughed. He was pretty sure the new owners, a bunch of pirates gone semistraight according to his sources, didn't mean the players but the house when they used that term. Well. He would probably drop around, check it out. He didn't get a piece of the casino action—that was Susa's rake-off—but it was on his planet and in his city, and knowledge was always useful. Might as well check out the new guys in town.

The Star Risk team sat in von Baldur's office on the new mezzanine overlooking the casino's main floor, one of three offices Freddie had for different functions.

Jasmine had called the meeting, and they all looked at her.

"Jas?" von Baldur said.

"I have some scut from one of my informants," she said. "We are going to get a visit from a local street gang looking for protection baksheesh."

Goodnight and Grok both perked up at that. "When?" Goodnight asked.

"Tonight," Jasmine said. "During our opening. The gang reasons that we don't want any trouble, nothing to mar our coming-out party, so they figure we'll be more tractable about meeting their terms."

"Good thinking," von Baldur said. "That's how I would play it. Do we know what the terms are?"

"According to my source, they want one percent of our action to make sure that we don't have any accidents or street rowdies stopping by and causing problems."

"And do we know the name of this gang?" Grok asked. "And where they might be found?"

"We do," Jasmine said. "They go by the name 'Mamas Boyz,' and they have a clubhouse in the warehouse district, a couple of kilometers from here."

"Ah, well, that's convenient," Goodnight said. "Neighborhood extortion—so much better than having to deal with some out-of-town stranger."

"Needless to say, we do not need this irritation at this time," Jasmine said.

"Or any time," Riss put in.

"And," von Baldur added, "we probably don't want to start out with a reputation as people who allow ourselves to be pushed around, given who we are supposed to be."

"Oh, I agree completely," Goodnight said.

Von Baldur looked at Jasmine. "Do we know what kind of associations these 'Mamas Boyz' have? Who their patrons are?"

"They are loosely linked to one of the two Board members who run this planet," she said. "Fellow named 'Susa.' But apparently he is not concerned with their day-to-day operations, as long as he gets his percentage of whatever business revenues the gang generates. He is already getting a piece of what we make; it comes out as a dealer's tax or some such. Plus he gets a cut of the contractor's gross, and undoubtedly the food and liquor supply businesses. Got fingers in a lot of our pies."

"Ah. Well, the question is, would this fellow Susa be overly displeased with us if we were to, um, deal with the Mamas Boyz on our terms?"

Jasmine shook her head. "Hard to say. From what I have gathered so far, you are either a wolf or a sheep in these parts. The predators don't have much respect for the prey."

Goodnight said, "Well, I'm looking around and I don't see anybody who could pass as a sheep. I say we make that real clear."

Von Baldur nodded. "Discussion?"

Riss shrugged. Jasmine said nothing. Von Baldur said, "Well, that's it then. We'll leave it to Chas and Grok to . . . deliver a message as to what kind of creatures we are, agreed?"

They all nodded.

Von Baldur looked at the chronometer inset into his desk's top, a lovely antique Volstok analog that probably set them back a couple of thousand credits. Amazing what you could do when you had a fat bank account full of somebody else's money to spend. He said, "Our soiree officially begins in six hours; best it is done quickly."

Goodnight came to his feet, grinning. "C'mon, Grok, let's you and me go have a meeting and discuss this with the Mamas Boyz. Where's this clubhouse, Jas?"

Grok also rose, a small and fur-covered mountain with teeth that in no way could have ever developed in any family of sheep.

Von Baldur allowed himself to smile. These people had no idea with whom they were messing. How sad for them . . .

\* \* \*

The Mamas Boyz had a block-shaped building at the edge of a warehouse complex in a rundown part of the district. Good-sized, but nothing to look at from outside; standard castplast construction, not many windows, three entrances.

Sitting in a hovervan with a sign that identified it as belonging to a fictitious plumbing supply company, Grok and Goodnight looked at the building.

"Hypothetically speaking, Grok, how would you run this extortion if you were the leader of the Mamas Boyz?"

"I would not attempt it," Grok said. "I would have done my research and determined that people such as ourselves were better left alone."

Goodnight laughed. "Yeah, you would have. But obviously these clowns are not in your league when it comes to strategic and tactical thinking. Try and dumb down your thought process to their level and give it a go."

Grok considered it. "I would gather a sufficient force to be both noticeable and a viable threat. I would arrive at the target establishment with this force made apparent to the victims, so that they would not think I was bluffing. I would make my offer and if it was refused, I would have my underlings break a few things to make sure the victims knew I was not bluffing. If they didn't agree to pay up, I would trash the place. Not enough to destroy it, but to make my point. I would then leave with a promise to return for another round of perhaps harsher negotiations in the near future."

Goodnight nodded. "Yeah, that's how I see it.

Which probably means that most of the gang is in there right now, mounting up for this evening's festivities."

"One would expect so."

"And our best strategy?"

Grok gave him that sparkling, sharp-toothed grin. "We should go and negotiate with them before they leave."

Goodnight smiled and slapped Grok on the shoulder. It was like hitting a carpet-covered concrete statue. "My thoughts exactly."

The main entrance to the Mamas Boyz building had a security cam over the door. Goodnight pressed the admittance buzzer, and a speaker popped on. "Yeah?"

"We are representatives of a new business venture," Goodnight said. "And we understand that you offer certain security services to such ventures."

"Yeah?"

"We would like to negotiate the terms of such an agreement on behalf of our establishment."

"What establishment would that be?"

"Winners Casino. We thought we would save you a trip."

While Grok was a formidable-looking being, neither he nor Goodnight had weapons showing, and there were only two of them.

After a moment, wherein the speaker probably consulted with a higher-up, the electronic lock clicked.

"Come on in," the voice said.

Both Goodnight and Grok refrained from grinning. No point in making the Boyz wonder why they were smiling . . .

The guards inside the door had blasters out and pointed in their direction. "You need to leave your hardware here," one of them said.

"No problem," Goodnight offered. He and Grok carefully removed their blasters and set them on the desk. Grok also removed a pair of knives from somewhere and added those. Goodnight knew that Grok didn't really need those, but he sometimes liked to keep his claws from getting gory.

"Nice," the other guard said, examining Goodnight's sidearm. "Military-issue thrummer. Hard to come by."

Goodnight smiled. "Going to carry, might as well carry something with some punch."

"Step through the weapons detector."

They did, and as they had no more hidden weapons, the device remained silent. Goodnight's internal units were bionic, and the batteries and such didn't set gunfinders off, a useful trick.

One of the guards led them down the hall to a large, unfurnished room. In it were eighteen, no, nineteen men. They were all young, most of them wearing glowing facial tattoos, and all of them sporting weapons small enough to hide under a jacket.

One of the young men, a tall fellow with a tattoo done in shades of green and blue and black that made his face look like a giant bruise at a distance, sauntered over toward them.

"You are?"

"Two of the owners of Winners," Goodnight said. "We understand that your organization intends to pay the casino a visit later this evening to discuss a business arrangement."

"How do you know that?"

Goodnight smiled. "We didn't come down with yesterday's rain."

"Why are you here?"

"Truth be known, we'd rather not have any kind of disturbance at the casino tonight. Better to deal with our biz here."

Bruise laughed. "You got balls, got to give you that."

"So," Goodnight continued. "What is the deal you are offering?"

Bruise looked around. He was surrounded by eighteen armed men, and both his visitors had been disarmed at the door. He obviously wasn't worried. He said, "We take one point of your gross off the top, and for that, nobody bothers you."

Goodnight appeared to consider that. "And how will you know how much we are making?"

"You hire one of the boys as an accountant, and he keeps tabs."

"Well, that sounds simple enough. One percent, which probably will work out to hundreds of thousands of credits a year, and nobody busts up the place?"

"That's the deal."

"Any wiggle room? Negotiating points?"

"Nope. Take it or leave it, and you really want to take it."

Goodnight looked at Grok. Then he looked back at Bruise. He rubbed at his chin, as if considering the offer. Tapped his chin and triggered bester-mode.

"I think we'll leave it," he said. He smiled.

# TWENTY-FOUR

Bruise snaked his hand down to his holstered blaster, but to a man in bester-time, Bruise was moving in slow motion. Goodnight had time to step in, grab the man's arm, break it, catch the blaster as he let it go, shoot the man in the face, and turn toward the nearest of the Mamas Boyz before that one could clear his weapon's muzzle from the holster—

Grok roared, and even though he wasn't as fast as Goodnight, he was a lot faster than these thugs. He extruded his claws, leaped, and had already slashed a pair of the startled gangsters into spewing bleeders before his feet touched the ground again—

Goodnight jinked to his left, fired three times, and each bolt skewered a different man, none of whom had managed to get a blaster aimed in his direction—

Another of the thugs had his pistol up and working, but the shot went wide as Grok grabbed him, picked him up like a doll, and threw him at three others, knocking them all down into a heap—

Goodnight trigged the blaster twice more and its charge ran dry on the last round. He threw it, bouncing it off the nose of another attacker, and stepped in to smash a fist into the man's throat. The guy went down, gargling his own blood—

Grok dived, rolled, and came up as a beam sizzled over him, missing by centimeters. The shooter didn't get a second shot as Grok plowed into him and ripped *his* throat out with a single claw in passing—

And fifteen seconds later, they were almost done. Goodnight shut down his bester-mode, reached to the ground and picked up a fallen blaster, and turned to the hallway as the two guards who had frisked them at the door came running. He emptied the blaster into the surprised pair before either could fire.

The party was over.

"You are showing off," Grok said. He was busy wiping his claws on the shirt of one of the dead gangsters.

"Not really. You could grow trees waiting for those two bozos to get here. Normal speed was all I needed."

Grok grinned. Goodnight returned it.

"I think there is going to be a fire here," Goodnight said. "A terrible tragedy that cost these fine young men their lives."

"Such will not fool a forensic investigator for ten seconds."

"It won't have to. The local LEOs will assume a rival gang was responsible."

"Possibly," Grok allowed.

"Oh, certainly. Our friend Joe has a connection in the arson investigator's office, which is why I brought it up."

"Ah. It is good to have friends in low places."

"Yep. Oh, my, look at the time. We'll have to get

back to the casino and get cleaned up and dressed. No dallying here. Come on, let's have a barbecue."

"Can we eat them?"

"No. It was just a figure of speech."

"Ah. Too bad. It's been so long since I had human."

Goodnight looked at his friend.

"Just joking. Got you, did I not?"

"No way. I knew you were kidding."

"Sure you did."

Riss was nervous. Even though this was just a necessary part of the caper—not as if they were really casino owners—the press of people crowding in for the grand reopening of Winners was impressive.

They had sent out invitations to a couple of thousand of the movers and shakers in-system, and it looked as though most of them had chosen to show up, along with their hired muscle. Since it was invitation-only, there were guards checking people in at the door, and so far there didn't seem to be many attempts at gate-crashing.

The susurrus of the crowd waxed and waned, voices blending into a *walla-walla* sound from which only snippets of conversation were understandable. Drinks and food were on the house, and Joe figured it would cost a couple of hundred thousand credits for this party before it was done. He was supposed to be here somewhere, just another guest.

Freddie was the most public face of the new cabal, glad-handing people, introducing himself, smiling and playing the happy owner.

Goodnight drifted over, looking sharp in a custom-made suit.

"Nice turnout," he said, sipping at something bubbly in an electric green glass flute.

"It is," she said. "How did the *negotiation* go this afternoon?"

"No problems at all."

"Good to hear. Where's Grok?"

Goodnight shrugged, and took another sip of his drink. "I believe he is in the library upstairs, probably breaking into somebody's computer network. Big parties are not his thing."

Riss nodded. Yes, she knew that.

"Well, I believe I will circulate and make friends. There's a striking brunette over there, wearing what appears to be a thin coat of paint, who looks like she needs company."

"Careful, Chas. She's either somebody important or attached to somebody important. Don't step on any toes."

"Me? Perish the thought. Besides, I am a man of substance, right? Part owner of this place. Between that and my staggering good looks, how can I go wrong?" He drifted away, angling toward the spectacular brunette—and while her sheath surely wasn't a coat of paint but an expensive silk garment, it *was* very snug. She either spent a lot of time in the gym or had an expensive plastic surgeon. Maybe both.

"Hey," Jasmine said.

"Hey, yourself. Your boyfriend make it yet?"

"Ten o'clock, standing by the bar."

"Who is that redhead with him?"

"I dunno, his mother?"

Riss laughed. "Looks more like she's of an age to

be his daughter. Younger sister, maybe. Gorgeous, too.

"Cover, that's all," Jasmine said. "Arm-candy."

"Well, don't go and punch her out, or drool on him."

"I will be very circumspect."

"I'm sure you will."

Jasmine moved off.

Freddie circled past and paused. "Seems to be going well, eh, M'chel?"

"It does."

"Ah, look who just arrived."

Riss knew better than to be obvious in doing so. "That Makko?"

"It is. I need to go and say hello."

"Is that wise?"

"We've never met, and I don't look like that bird-watcher anymore."

"How many bodyguards does he have with him?"

"Eight."

Riss scanned the crowd. Frowned. "I can only spot seven."

"That's the official number he included on his invitation. But there is another. Look again."

Riss's frown deepened. "The place is filthy with armed muscle, but I still only see seven orbiting Makko . . . wait."

Freddie grinned.

"The waiter carrying the tray of drinks, behind him and to his left?" She paused.

"Good catch."

"Shouldn't he work for us?"

"Our employee called in sick. The agency sent this one as a temporary replacement."

"Ah. Smart."

"Makko isn't entirely stupid. Nor is he the only one with the same idea. A few of the other staff seemed to develop sudden illnesses, to be replaced with last-minute substitutes."

"They are careful around these parts."

"Indeed, and we will all do well to keep that in mind. I'm off."

"Have fun."

"I almost always do."


Makko looked around at the renovated casino. Nice work, compared to when he'd seen the place last. That had been a while; it had been a dump for a long time, and he didn't frequent dumps.

An older man headed in his direction. The body-guards tensed, but Makko signaled them to stay calm. Guy looked familiar.

"Mr. Makko, pleased to meet you. My name is Smith. I'm one of the casino's new owners."

Makko nodded. "Have we met? You look familiar."

"I don't believe so. My associates and I are only recently arrived on this world. We aren't from around this system."

Makko nodded again. His security people had run a check on this crew, as part of his preparation for coming here. A bunch of pirates looking to do a little money-laundering, come in from the cold of space. Probably they'd get bored pretty quickly—guys who liked action tended to want to get back into it eventually, in his experience. If the place did well—and no reason why it shouldn't—they could sell it for a nice profit in a year or two and head out. Whatever, they'd fit right in, as long as they didn't get too ambitious and paid the proper baksheesh. That would be Susa's worry. If they had whores working for them, that would be the responsibility of the second member of the Board onplanet, Reese—he ran prostitution.

"Well, enjoy, Mr. Makko. If you want to get into a game, the high rollers are uplevel. The private elevators are programmed to admit you and any guests you have."

"Thoughtful of you," Makko said. "I don't indulge in risky ventures like gambling."

The man gave him a slow military bow. "You are a wise man, sir. Pleasure to make your acquaintance."

He left, and Makko caught the attention of his sub rosa guard, posing as a waiter. The man brought his tray of drinks over and Makko took one. Champagne, and not the cheap stuff, either.

These guys would do all right. They were smart enough to recognize who the big dogs around here were, and seemed to be setting up to run a first-class operation.

A kind of hush fell over the room around him, and Makko turned to see Susa walking in his direction. The man radiated fitness, practically bounding as he moved. He wore black silks that probably cost as much as a good hovercar, and cloned-lizardskin slippers that had been grown on lasts made from molds of his feet; slippers that were easily worth a middle-class family's yearly income. First-class all the way. Life was too short to be cheap, he liked to say.

Makko smiled.

Susa arrived, and Makko nodded at his waiter, who offered his tray. Susa looked at the waiter, then back at Makko.

"One of mine," Makko said.

"I know," Susa said. "Which glass is the carrot juice?"

Makko shook his head. Of course. That's why Susa was where he was. He didn't miss much.

Susa took the indicated glass. He would hold it but he wouldn't drink from it, even though Makko vouched for it. Another reason he was still alive—he didn't trust anybody. Makko had eight guards with him—Susa had three times that many, and probably a couple of his were on staff, too . . .

"Nice operation," Makko observed.

"It is. They should do well. Have you met the manager?"

"Yep. Older guy, there, in the maroon silks. Smooth, for a pirate."

"You know what they say. There are old pirates and there are stupid pirates, but no old, stupid pirates . . ."

Makko nodded again, and sipped at his champagne.

"I think this crew will be an asset to the city," Susa said. "They are resourceful. You know about the Mamas Boyz?"

"Clubhouse burned down and everybody in it at the time got cooked," Makko said. "A few hours ago. Somebody hit them."

"Know who did it?"

"Probably the Abbos, they—" He stopped, as Susa grinned.

"*These* guys?"

"The Boyz were gearing up to pay the casino a visit.

Be kind of a coincidence if they got wiped out by another gang just as they were ready to leave, don't you think?"

Makko shook his head. "Means they got some serious muscle."

"So it would seem."

"Good to know."

"Indeed." Susa glanced up. "I must go rescue my date. Some big guy seems to be trying really hard to entertain her."

Makko looked around, and spotted the most gorgeous woman guest in the room. "The brunette?"

"None other. We'll speak later."

He was gone.

Makko sipped at his drink, finishing it. The waiter took the empty glass. "Another, sir?"

"No, one is enough. A man needs to keep his wits about him."

"Yes, sir," the waiter said.

Time to find a woman of his own, Makko decided. There was a tall blonde over there eyeing the crowd. Maybe she was lonely . . .

# TWENTY-FIVE

Jasmine, deep in her role of information buyer, was very careful when she asked follow-up questions. The data she needed, in theory, was anything that would concern a bunch of ex-pirates trying to lie low on a backrocket world in a corrupt stellar system to avoid Alliance notice. Everything began there.

She leaned back in her chair, steepled her fingers, and looked thoughtful. It was a hot day, and the air cooling system was purring along, keeping her office at the perfect comfort level. For Jasmine, anyway.

The woman sitting across from her seemed rather plain at first glance. Not young, not old, not fat, not thin, brown hair, brown eyes, brown skin. Her clothes were not expensive, but neither were they shabby, nor cheap. As with any source who showed up with information to sell, Jasmine started from the idea that this one could be a double agent. She had the perfect look for it; she could blend in anywhere. A little makeup, some nice clothes, and she'd be a new woman. She could work for the government—local, planetary, system, or the Alliance. She might be in the employ of a rival casino, one of the local ganglords, or the high-level crime bosses. She might work for any or all of them. Anything she had to say was suspect until it could be verified by at least one other source, preferably two, and even then her reasons for offering it might be anywhere from benign to malevolent.

They had face-recognition software installed in the casino, and the database included not only the commercial casino imagery, with known cheats and those who somehow always mysteriously won, but also the planetary LEO's criminal-records imagery. This latter was courtesy of Grok, who had hacked the police computer net and downloaded the files.

This woman, holographed as she walked in through the casino's delivery entrance, was not in either rogues gallery. Which didn't mean much by itself.

Jasmine said, "So, Miz, uh, Brown, why would I care about an accident involving a mercenary from another world?"

The woman calling herself Brown smiled slightly. "You wouldn't, not by itself. But the Alliance seems to care, and *them* you might want to keep track of."

This was on the edge of what Jasmine wanted, but she had to keep this woman off balance by playing it cool. "The Alliance is concerned about a lot of things, many of which do not worry us."

"Tell you what. I'll lay out what I have. If you think it is worth something to you, you pay me. If not, no charge."

Jasmine pretended to consider it. "All right."

"A while back, some merc pirates hit an Alliance delivery vessel. It was running undercover and it had something very valuable on it. What it was doesn't matter, only that the Alliance is offering big bucks to get it back."

As a former pirate, Jasmine would naturally be interested in such material, and she had to assume that Brown, here, knew her fabricated background. "You have my attention."

"There's a connection to this system. The guy who ran the pirate ship took off with the prize. A lot of people went looking for him. He got killed in an accident."

"And . . . ?"

"And what he stole didn't get recovered."

"That it?"

"Well, no. See, the merc, he got religion before he croaked. And the preacher who saved his soul, or whatever, he also got killed recently. On purpose."

Jasmine fought to keep her face calm. She feigned a lack of interest. "So? People get killed. Too bad, but not my concern."

"But here's the thing. Some powers that be have made a connection between the dead merc pirate and the dead preacher. They think maybe the merc told the preacher where he stashed the prize."

"Well, if the preacher is dead, probably they found out where it was, otherwise, better he stayed alive."

"And maybe they didn't find out. The Alliance is still looking. And, since the preacher got himself offed only a few kilometers from here, this world, this city, *this* is where they are probably going to be turning over rocks, soon as they find out about the merc-preacher connection."

"If they find out."

"Oh, they will." She grinned. "There's a big reward

for recovery of this prize. Big. Somebody will put a bug in somebody's ear, you can book it."

Jasmine pretended to chew on that. "Well. Yes. That could be of interest to the people I represent."

"I thought it might."

"Five hundred credits."

Brown smiled. "That'll make my morning brighter."

"I'll give you a chip. Take it to the tellers and they'll give you the cash."

"Pleasure to do business with you."

Jasmine pulled a chip-encoder from her desk, tapped in the amount, and waited for the chip to eject. The machine whirred.

"You're sure the Alliance is still looking?"

"Oh, yes. *Every*body is looking—including the guy who killed the preacher, so the prize is still out there."

Although she already knew, Jasmine also knew it would be in character to ask. "I don't supposed you want to tell me what this prize is?"

"Got another thousand credits?"

She smiled. "Never mind. We aren't treasure hunters."

The woman returned her smile. "Never hurts to offer."

Jasmine removed the chip from the coder. Here was the crux of the matter. She had to do this very carefully. She handed the chip to Brown. "There you go. Thanks." She paused. As offhandedly as she could, she said, "This guy who killed the preacher—he wouldn't be likely to cause us any trouble?"

"Nah. He's a strong-arm, named Nett. Works for Keven Makko—Makko is into nightclubs, not casinos."

*    *    *

Von Baldur's office was the biggest—naturally—and that's where the team met. After Jasmine laid it out, Goodnight said, "Well, that's it. We scoop up this Nett guy and it's game over."

"Not really," Riss said. "Nett is muscle. Not likely he would kill Josiah on his own, so we have to figure that Makko is involved. And since Freddie had some dealings with his people, we know that killing people is no big deal for him.

"The question is, how far up the chain does it go? Who does Makko answer to?"

"Susa," Grok said. "There are two members of what they call the Board on this world, and Susa is the more powerful of the two. Other guy is named Reese. All operations of any size must be cleared through one or the other of them. Such as the late and unlamented Mamas Boyz, if you recall."

Jasmine said, "So the question is, does it stop at Makko or go higher up? If it's Susa, who does he answer to?"

"He's chairman of the Board," Grok said. "He answers to no one, not directly. Board members run their own planets. Except this one, which is divvied up."

"So we grab up Makko and squeeze him, and find out if it was his idea or if Susa told him to do it."

Von Baldur looked at Goodnight. "That might not be a good idea. Susa commands an army of thugs, has access to the local police and politicos, also has more money than God, and some of his people are almost certainly better than dull-witted blaster fodder. He'll protect his own. We don't have the organization to start a stand-up war. If Makko had Josiah killed on

Susa's order, then we have to figure out a way to come at him other than directly."

"Guerrilla tactics," Riss said.

"Yes, and not just with guns and steel, but with other tools. Financial, political, like that. Utilizing our brains as well as our brawn."

"Why are you looking at me?" Goodnight said. "I got brains."

"Where do you keep them?" Riss asked. She smiled sweetly. "Below your belt?"

The moment passed without a comeback, and Riss chalked up the point to herself. When Chas finally started to speak, Riss waved him off. "Too late," she said.

He shut up. He was smart enough to know she'd gotten that one.

"What about Joe?" Jasmine asked.

"What about him?" von Baldur asked.

"Do we tell him what we know?"

"Not yet, I don't think," von Baldur said. "First, we need to see if we can determine who was responsible. Joe doesn't just want the triggerman; he wants the man who gave the order. If it's Makko, then it stops there. If it is Susa, it takes a little more effort. He doesn't just want the man dead; Joe wants to bring his organization down, remember. But at least we have a starting point now, a place to stick our pry bar and start levering things open."

The others nodded.

"Let's see if we can come up with some strategy and tactics to move us along . . ."

# TWENTY-SIX

Aside from his occasional flashes of brilliance, Nett was turning out to be merely adequate. A man in Makko's position needed not just a strong right arm, but a smart brain to move it, and Nett didn't seem to have all the necessary gear. Already Makko had been carefully looking around in his organization for some young and smart up-and-comer he might bring along. He couldn't be too smart or too hungry; those were dangerous qualities. At some point, a sharp player might decide that the old man at the top wasn't up to the task of running things properly, and that maybe he should retire—one way or the other.

Nett was loyal, and that counted for a lot. And he wasn't stupid, but "not stupid" wasn't the same as smart. It was something to which Makko needed to attend . . .

All these thoughts drifted through Makko's mind as he lay facedown on a padded biogel table with a pair of massage techs working his muscles, pounding, kneading, leaning on their elbows, digging in, and finding sore spots he hadn't known he'd had. They were attractive women—he preferred women to men when it came to massage—but the reason he had two of them wasn't for fun and games, but because he was big enough so that one would wear out before he was satisfied. It took a couple of hours to get his muscles as loose as he liked. Let Susa spend that time in the gym moving heavy weights about; a good, all-over body massage was much more pleasant as far as he was concerned.

Once or twice a week was enough for him. It took several days for the press of work to tighten him up so that his back got stiff and he started to have head-aches. He could slap on a myoderm or pain patch, of course, but he preferred the more natural methods of relaxation. Sex was easy; he had all kinds of talent on call for that—a woman a day kept the doctor away, he liked to joke—but a good massage took real skill. . . .

One of the techs—he could never tell which was which once he lay down and closed his eyes—put a lot of weight onto her elbow and found a tender spot just under his left shoulder blade. Ah: It hurt, but in a good way . . .

He was forty-five minutes into it and they were working on his butt and legs, when his com started playing Pachelbel's *Canon in D*.

Everybody in his allowed-to-call-his-private-comm list had their own tune, and there weren't so many that Makko couldn't remember them all.

The classical piece was Nett's song.

Makko frowned. His people knew better than to bother him while he was on the table. He'd fired people for it. So if Nett was calling, he thought it was important enough to interrupt Makko's massage, which was ranked one notch above sex.

"Give me the comm," Makko said.

One of the women handed him the unit. Moving only his arm, he put the comm to his ear. "What?"

"We found the preacher's kid," Nett said. "You aren't gonna believe who it is."

An hour later, dressed and in his office after his abbreviated massage, Makko sat behind his desk and looked at Nett, who lolled on the couch.

"You are certain?"

"As death and taxes."

Makko didn't pay taxes, but he understood the saying. "Tell me." He wanted to hear the longer version, to be sure.

"We threw out everybody on the planet who wasn't in the right age range, thirty plus or minus five years, to be safe. That narrowed it down to less than a hundred million people.

"We ran known family ties and racial stuff, medical records, and threw those out. Narrowed it down more, to under ten million.

"We got the preacher's DNA, and we ran that, and that eliminated *every*body alive who had DNA on file, so then we were down to a couple of hundred who, for one reason or another, didn't have DNA records. I sent ops out who got DNA samples of everybody they could find. That dropped it to twelve."

"Really?"

"It's an information society, boss."

Makko revised his opinion of Nett back up again.

Enough of these leaps and maybe he would average out to bright enough over time.

"Checked those backgrounds. Nine of them we couldn't find. Could be dead, could have moved, whatever. Came up with three. Got DNA samples from two without them knowing. Found junior by the process of elimination. He doesn't use that name in public, but it turns out that, buried under a bunch of shells, that's who he is: Josiah Williams II. Not the name you know him under, but him."

"Son of a bitch. I've been bumping into him for years—he's a player, with all those casinos and more than a few under-the-table businesses. I would never have guessed it."

"So you figure he's got what we are after?"

Makko shrugged. In truth, he doubted it. If a player had his hands on the plates, chances were he'd be long gone. But you never knew—maybe he was waiting for something before he moved. "No way to tell until we talk to him."

"Won't be as easy as snatching up his old man. He's got a pretty good guard team. That's why we couldn't get his DNA."

"I'm sure we can hire enough guns. Still, that is a point. We don't want to send guys in blasting. He might get killed and then we'd be back where we were. We are going to grab him; we'll have to do it carefully."

"I have some ideas."

"Do tell."

As Nett began to lay out his thoughts, Makko found himself nodding. He had, he decided, been hasty in deciding that Nett didn't have enough on the ball to be his lieutenant. The man had potential, no doubt about it. A bit erratic, maybe, but over time that could be smoothed out.

In the end, it was a simple plan. If a man is guarded by a bunch of shooters and you want to be sure he doesn't get accidentally hit in a blaster battle, then the best thing is to make sure nobody starts firing. They needed to get junior away from his protection, and there were situations in which a bevy of armed guards was not considered polite. If you went to see the planet's heavy hitters, you didn't bring your gunners into their houses, you relied on their soldiers to protect you. Junior wouldn't come to see Makko that way—Makko didn't have the clout to demand that.

But Susa did. Everybody on this planet answered to Susa, one way or another . . .

Lying in bed next to Joe, Jasmine suddenly propped herself up on her elbow and said, "What?"

"I said, I've been invited to a meeting with Susa. Apparently he wants to discuss a business venture with me."

"What kind of business venture?"

"I won't know that until I talk to him."

She frowned.

"Something?" he asked.

Jasmine chewed at her lip. She hadn't told Joe what they had found out. She had told herself she was waiting for confirmation on the report she had gotten. Could this overture from Susa be coincidental? She didn't trust that while on a caper. Coincidence could get you killed.

"What?"

She considered her options, and made a decision. She'd explain it to the others. They were equal partners, right?

She told Joe what the informant had told her.

After she was done, they were both sitting up and he was nodding, intent, focused.

"I wanted to say something, but I wanted to be sure first. One report wasn't enough to verify it as true."

He nodded. "I understand. Why did you tell me now?"

"Nothing we know about Susa indicates that he is dull. Either he or his man Makko is beating the bushes hard, looking for those missing chips, and that would explain why your father was killed."

"Yeah, that would."

"What if they have made the connection? What if they know who you are?"

Joe considered that for a moment. "It's pretty well hidden."

"People like this have access to the same kind of information flow that we have. You have to assume they can hire talent as clever as anybody. We're good at what we do, maybe as good as anybody out there, but we aren't the only ones who know how to look."

He nodded again. "You think they might be setting me up?"

"If I were them and I figured out who you were, that's how I'd play it. They killed your father and didn't find what they wanted. You're the logical next step."

"But I don't have what they want."

"They don't know that. You walk into Susa's arms, they collect you, and they take their time finding out what you know or don't know."

He nodded again. "Yeah, makes sense. If they have uncovered the relationship."

"You want to risk your ass that they haven't?"

He considered that.

Makko was with his lady of the day when his comm started playing that contrapuntal canon again. He shook his head and looked at his naked partner. "Hold that thought a moment," he said. He disengaged.

"Now what?" he said into the comm.

"We got Junior out on his own, no guards!"

"What?"

"Sneaked off. He's with a woman, at a hotel in the Garden District."

"Yeah, some of us like to get laid now and then. So what?"

"I can grab him, boss. We can collect him without having to involve Susa!"

Makko frowned. "Maybe that's not a good idea, Nett."

"No, no problem. He's in there with his pants down, we shoulder the door; we have him!"

"Hold up a second—"

"Oh, crap, the door's opening, he's coming out! I gotta go, boss. I'll call you back!"

"Nett! Don't—!"

Too late.

Makko said "Call Nett" into his comm. The screen

flashed and reached for the connection, but Nett didn't answer. He'd shut it off, the bastard!

Makko sat up.

"Hon, what is it?"

He blinked at the woman. He'd forgotten all about her. He said, "We're done here." He stood, and began putting his clothes back on.

# TWENTY-SEVEN

There were four of them, Jasmine saw, eight meters away and coming in fast, all holding handguns. Joe spotted them at the same time, and he must have had the same thought she did: If these guys wanted them dead, they'd already be shooting. Since they weren't, they had a chance.

Jasmine did a fast draw, snatching her blaster from its waistband holster behind her right hip, and she was aware that Joe was pulling his own piece as she moved, but she didn't have time to track him.

One of the four fired, and the bolt seared into her, digging a shallow furrow along her left side, low, under her ribs—

"Don't shoot him!" one of the attackers yelled—

By then she had her own weapon up and was leaping to the side as a second bolt sizzled the air, barely missing her—

She point-shot the guy who had grazed her, a bolt to center of mass, then dropped low and locked onto the second target, fired—

Joe got off a triplet from his weapon, the *thrum-thrumthrum!* of a spring pistol firing flechettes—

—one of the attackers fell, but got off a bolt as he hit the floor—

—the last attacker pointed his weapon at her, but the spring pistol's *thrum*! came again, and the attacker slapped his throat with his free hand and collapsed—

Time slowed back to normal. The four shooters were all down: two with blaster burns to the heart, two with bleeding dart wounds. From their skin color, the darts were poisoned, full of shocktox. None of these guys were going to make it.

Joe was also down.

Jasmine dropped to her knees, her weapon still held ready.

"Joe!"

He looked up at her. "We get 'em all?"

"Yes."

"Good. You okay?"

"They grazed me."

He managed a tight smile. "Good. Listen Jas, I—"

She was looking into his eyes as his pupils dilated.

He was gone.

Jasmine felt a pang of loss, sharp, cold, and deep. But she looked around. Down the hall, doors were opening, residents peeping out. There were five dead men piled up and nothing she could do to help Joe now.

*Time to leave.*

She stood. The bolt burn on her side had mostly cauterized itself, so she wasn't bleeding much. She put the blaster away, turned, and walked quickly down the hall.

Damn. Damn, damn, *damn*!

# TWENTY-EIGHT

There was no need, nor any desire, to involve medics.
The team went to the casino's infirmary, and shooed
the doctors and nurses out for an early lunch. All of
the Star Risk team had plenty of experience with first
aid for blaster wounds. Riss finished dressing Jasmine's injury with a second layer of plastic flesh that
sealed to her skin. "Nothing," she said, smiling. "The
scar will give you character."

Jasmine put a clean shirt on, and pulled it down to
cover the bandage. She didn't return M'chel's smile.

"I'm sorry about Joe," Riss said.

"It was my fault," Jasmine said.

"No, it wasn't," Goodnight said. "Man left his bodyguards at home. He should have had them all over
that hotel, outside the door, covering his ass."

"Chas is right," Grok said. "You did not shoot
our client."

"If he hadn't been with me, he wouldn't have died."

"If there wasn't any gravity, then bird crap wouldn't
fall out of the trees," Goodnight said.

Von Baldur shook his head. "It is regrettable, but

there is nothing to be done for it. Once again, we find ourselves without a client. The opposition has proved to be better than we thought. We underestimated them. We are lucky it was not worse."

"Client got killed, that's bad enough. I was just getting used to this place," Goodnight said. "Food, drinks, waitresses, a little exercise now and then."

Von Baldur said, "Yes, it is a shame. But from the police reports, we know that one of the men involved in the shooting was almost certainly the triggerman who killed Josiah, so there has been some measure of justice."

"Not much," Jasmine said.

"Better than none," von Baldur offered.

"So what now?" Riss said.

Goodnight said, "The party is over. Dead clients don't pay."

Von Baldur's comm chirped. He frowned at it. "Smith here," he said. "Yes? Yes? Really?"

Goodnight raised an eyebrow at Freddie, who held up a hand. *Wait* . . .

"I see. Right. Well, thank you for the call. We'll be in touch."

He broke the connection.

"What?" Goodnight said.

"That was Margo, our lawyer. It seems that our late client left instructions that, in the event of his death, the firm was to contact us immediately."

"And . . . ?" that from Jasmine.

"His will must be properly probated, but it seems he has left us this casino—provided we complete the service for which we were contracted."

"Holy crap!" Goodnight said. "This place has been

pulling in money by the truckload. It's worth millions *and* is a license to steal! He left it to us?"

"It would seem that dead clients do sometimes pay. And in this case, exceedingly well," von Baldur said. "It seems we still have a job."

Nobody said anything for a moment.

"When we get the guy responsible," Jasmine said, "he's mine."

"Of course," von Baldur said.

And nobody argued with that, either.

# TWENTY-NINE

Makko was, not to put too fine a point on it, royally pissed off. If Nett was still alive, he would have killed him himself. Once again, they were back to square zero. It was as if some bored god had decided to take a hand in keeping those plates away from him; every time he got a lead, it wound up dead.

Yes, he could blame himself, since it was his man who had wiped out both father and son, but it just didn't seem *fair* that it had come down that way.

He looked out through the polarized one-way window of his limo. Susa had summoned him, he was on the way to see him, and that was another problem with which Makko was going to have to deal. First, because he had used Susa's name to lure the departed Junior into his hands, and not bothered to pass that along. Second, because Nett's stupidity in trying to capture Junior on his own had ended so badly, Susa would almost certainly be displeased—especially after he had made a special point of telling Makko not to screw up again.

Makko sighed. It was always something. People just kept getting in his way.

He could placate Susa, he was sure. Junior had been with a woman, and she would be another lead to be followed, once his people figured out who she was. Not that he expected much from that. She was probably somebody's wife—otherwise, why would Junior be sneaking around in a low-rent hotel to bang her?

Unless, of course, he wasn't there for sex, but for something else? Like, perhaps, she had the missing chips . . . ?

Makko shook his head at his own thoughts. Wheels within wheels, too many to interface and keep track of, it seemed.

And if he couldn't explain things satisfactorily to Susa, then what?

Maybe it was time to consider some options in that area. If he could find those missing chips, he would vault from rich to very rich. With enough money, he could buy influence, troops, guns, whatever. With enough power, a seat on the Board was not beyond the realm of possibility . . .

Then again, with a billion credits in his pocket, why would he need the hassle? He could move to a more pleasant world, live a life of total luxury, have his every whim catered to for as long as he could possibly live. The superrich were different—they had way more money . . .

Yes, he could do that. But how boring would that get? Here, he was a player, still on the way up. If he did it right, he could climb to the top of the heap and then really dance the dance. That was a lot more appealing. No point in having a big stick if you didn't whack somebody with it now and then, just for fun.

So, he would see Susa, he would kiss his ring, offer to make amends, and then he would get his ass into high gear. Take care of business. That was what a man did. He took care of business . . .

"We still have a million or so in the operating account," von Baldur said. "Plus a nice profit rolling in every day."

The rest of the team waited to hear what else he had to say.

"We are pretty sure that Makko is in it, and if I had to guess, I'd say Susa is involved, too. So maybe we need to get back to our basic ways of doing business."

Goodnight said, "Like, shake everything like hell and see what falls out?"

"Now and then, even a blind pig finds an acorn," von Baldur said, smiling at Goodnight.

"What is a pig?" Grok asked. "And an acorn?"

"It's an old Terran saying," Jasmine said. "In this case, it means that even Chas gets it right once in a while."

"Ah."

"What it means is, we hit Keven Makko and we hit Susa, and we keep hitting them until something useful happens."

"What might that be?" Grok asked.

"We'll know it when we see it," Riss said.

"And the best place to start, I think," von Baldur said, "is where it hurts the most. In the wallet. As for strategy in general, I think 'divide and conquer' is still as valid as it ever was."

The others nodded. They'd been down that road before. There were all kinds of new theories on how to wage war, but the old stuff mostly still worked just fine. Sun Tzu and Miyamoto Musashi would be as home in a modern dustup as they were back in the days when a bunch of men with sharp steel ruled mankind's only world. The only difference was that the weapons were better, and since a knife would kill somebody as dead as a bomb, that didn't matter much, either . . .

So it was Grok who threw out the first pitch, and, despite his appearance, it was a subtle and clever one, bespeaking his not so easily recognized talents.

For Grok, getting into the building that housed the World Lottery had been a piece of—what was the phrase humans used?—a piece of pastry?

Electronic surveillance and computer-operated alarms and cameras were prey to attack, and Grok knew all the ways to hit them. Sensor confounders, scramblers, double-backs, worms, viruses, smartbot subroutines—Grok was like an orchestra-conducting maestro; he could wave his hands and make music, and he did so.

The main game of the lottery was called the Mark Six, and was, according to the advertising, the "most honest and fair" lottery in the system. The prizes were based on percentages of the total jackpot rather than arbitrary standard amounts. During the game six numbers were drawn from an antiquated mechanical machine filled with small balls, each with a number on it. Picking all six numbers would result in winning—or sharing—thirty-five percent of the jackpot. Beings who scored five numbers would share twenty percent, as would people who scored four numbers, and twenty-five percent of the money would be added to a special drawing that occurred one every five draws. Nothing special here, just different ways of dividing the pie.

This meant that there were more rich winners—which was why Mark Six was such a popular game. What people didn't know however, was that the lottery commission hid a fairly high overhead, one which concealed largish salaries for its operators.

For every hundred million credits in a jackpot, there were at least two hundred million credits taken in. Not that anyone knew this, of course, but Grok had hacked into their system and looked at the books before planning his caper.

Exposing the high overhead wouldn't really be news on Una, where a portion of every credit spent seemed to wind its way into the corrupt pockets of the elite—but if the *game* itself was rigged, why, *that* might upset the applecart a bit, von Baldur had said.

Another fascinating phrase whose genesis he wished he knew. Had there ever been carts capable of emotions on humanity's homeworld? Was an applecart actually yet another metaphor lost in the mists of time?

Humans had many sayings like these, and yet they often had no knowledge of their history or even their meaning. Strange.

Grok moved into the room where the number selection machines were kept and began examining them. Even with his not-inconsiderable skills, these were about as tamperproof as could be engineered. The machineries themselves were sealed—with only a hopper at the top for the balls, and a chute at the bottom where selected balls came out. There was no way to get inside to mess with the actuator arms, the air blowers, and anyone who tried would damage seals, both active and passive, on the machine, triggering alarms. Even Grok.

So he had to find another way.

He created a variety of nanite that could be put on the balls that went into the machine. When active, they would assemble themselves into large-scale nanostructures that would control the movement of the balls. Which would insure that only the balls that Grok wanted would go into the exit chute. In theory, anyhow. Experimental nanites sometimes took a wrong turn, and there was always a possibility that they could just turn whatever they happened to fasten upon into gray goo—the balls, the machines, the people in the room, the building.

Ah, well, life was not without risk, and he was certainly willing to take this one.

When he went to load one of the boxes of lotto balls with the nanites, however, Grok made an interesting discovery.

Someone else had beaten him to it.

A cruder version of the nano he'd created was already on the orbs.

The lotto was *already* rigged.

He grinned. Wonderful. That actually made it easier.

He fired up his nanite farm and did some reprogramming. In a few minutes a modified variant was ready.

He put it into the box of balls.

To anyone without a nanoreader, nothing would seem to have happened. And whoever had rigged the system would make sure there weren't any nanoreaders around, he was certain.

A war was waged. The nanites already on the ball were tough. Thousands upon thousands of submicroscopic robotic warriors met, grappled, and died, all invisible to any watcher.

In the end, Grok's little fighters were tougher. Within ten or so minutes the enemy had been eliminated—and he had prisoners.

Grok extended a sampler to the surface of a ball with the number eight on it and waited a few seconds. When his machine lit up green, he started the analysis.

Well. Here were the next six big lottery winners.

He reprogrammed his nanites and released them. It wouldn't do to *not* have things roll out as planned. However, in addition to the winners planned by whoever had installed the original nanites, he added several of his own—a five-number winner, and a six. All of his nanites were set to self-destruct after the sequence of winners was completed—no point in leaving evidence, since, as he had learned, it had a nasty tendency to point where you didn't want it to.

Once he was done, he distributed nanites to all the other boxes of balls in the room, just in case they chose one at random.

He rascaled his way into the lotto number system

and implanted a virus that would alert him when one of the winning sequences was entered.

He was set.

The next day he received several messages from the virus he'd planted, telling him that the numbers had been chosen for the next game. Apparently two distant relatives of current city council members were about to become winners. Clever, but hardly beyond Grok's ability to suss out.

That afternoon he went to a local shop, called an EZ mart, one of a large chain of such places. The clerk behind the counter looked a bit concerned when Grok entered the store, but calmed down when he saw him head toward the lotto machine.

Apparently a gambling-addicted monster wasn't quite so frightening.

Grok tapped the numbers into the lotto machine and then pressed a button. Within seconds the machine spat out a richly printed plastic ticket. He was now entered in the evening drawing for the Mark Six. Unlike most everyone else, however, he was sure he was going to win.

As predicted, his system worked. As a five-number winner he earned several thousands of credits, which he had put into a cashier's draft. Von Baldur would be pleased.

He used a public comm to send a message to the local newstat, to a reporter whose byline he'd picked earlier. In it he mentioned the two city councilmen who had won the day before, and listed the winning numbers for the next day—the six he'd programmed into the machine.

"I know you'll know what to do with the information," he wrote, and then sent the message, date-stamping it, and assigning it a high urgency.

That evening he turned on the local news channel to watch the drawing.

The first ball came up, the number one.

Followed by two.

And three.

Four.

Then five and, finally, six.

Statistically, this was almost impossible.

*That should give them something to think about.*

He turned off the channel and went to bed.


When he awoke, the story was all over the network—*Planetary Lottery Rigged! Government Workers Involved in Fraud!*

*Ah, heads will roll over this—at least figuratively speaking. Excellent!*

When you couldn't crush them directly, sowing dissent among one's enemies was the next best thing . . .

# THIRTY

Riss and King were alone in Riss's office at the casino, comparing notes.

M'chel said, "So we know Susa is the big dog locally and system-wide, when you total up the score, but there is a second player on Una of some note: Reese. He is a member of the Board, but not nearly as powerful as Susa. Apparently content to be second banana, not ambitious beyond where he is now, smart, but not brilliant."

Jasmine nodded. "Yeah?"

"I was wondering why there are two Board members on this planet and only one on each of the others."

Jasmine said, "This was the first world settled in-system. Still the most populated, the richest. Probably happened back in the early days."

"That makes sense. But it could be a point of friction. Reese is apparently easygoing and content with his lot. He handles the drug trade, prostitution, some of the sports gambling, while Susa runs casinos, clubs, a lot of trade unions, and politics, the last of which is where the real money is. Construction contracts are worth a lot more than whores and dope."

"Right. So?"

M'chel said, "So Reese's piece of the pie is a lot smaller than Susa's."

Jasmine said, "And? If he's happy with that, how do we exploit it to our benefit?"

"He doesn't have to *be* a threat. Susa only has to *think* he is a threat. And vice versa."

Jasmine said, "I must be getting stupid in my old age. Of course."

"And if Reese suddenly finds himself under attack by Susa's people—"

"—or somebody he *thinks* belongs to Susa . . ." Jasmine finished.

"Exactly. If Susa and Reese are hammering at each other, neither will likely be paying the kind of attention he should be paying to other biz."

"What did you have in mind?" Jasmine said.

"Well, to start with, something right up our alley," M'chel said. "Us being pirates and all . . ."

Since Reese ran the drug trade on Una, and since a lot of what people wanted to snort, toke, or derm wasn't produced locally, that is to say, in the system, it had to be imported. Some chems were so convoluted that it took a master labsmith to concoct them without creating nasty side effects, and since killing customers was bad for business, it was cheaper to pay for the good stuff and have it shipped in than it was to risk making it yourself. Successful criminals had to take the long-term view; quick profits for a load of bad dope couldn't pay off anywhere near what a year-in, year-out biz would for quality product.

Reese's operation was not unusual in this regard,

which was why Goodnight, Riss, and Grok were in their still-reeking ship, cloaked and waiting in deep space outside the patrolled lanes near Una.

"Here it comes," Spada said. "Right on schedule."

"No escort?" Goodnight asked.

"All by herself."

"Stupid," Goodnight said. "Good for us, but c'mon."

"Reese is the second most powerful man on the planet," Riss said. "That's all the escort he has ever needed. Screw with one of his dope ships, you get all kinds of heat; everybody local knows that."

"Yeah, I suppose."

"And he won't be able to connect it to us," Grok said, because there will be no motive, and thus no trail leading to us."

"I still disagree with that," Goodnight said. "A ship full of illegal chem worth millions? We don't have to try and move it in this system. We could just park it somewhere, and—"

"No, we discussed this and agreed, Chas," Riss said. "You lost the vote, four to one, remember?"

"Yeah, I remember. But it is such a waste!"

"No, it is part of the plan."

"Yeah, well, I still—"

"You would fill school yards with the most addictive and nasty drugs around if you could make a profit on it," Riss said.

"Hey, kids have parents—it's not my job to take care of them."

"Forget it."

Goodnight just shook his head.

"In range," Spada said.

"Send the hail," Riss said.

Spada touched a control, and a recorded radio-sig lanced out from their cloaked vessel to the drug ship. All the hail said was, essentially, "Halt or we shoot!"

What was important was that the sig was coded, and that the frequency was a tactical channel used by the drug ships. Nobody outside of Reese's organization was supposed to have either the freq or the code, which got changed every trip, and that meant that whoever had sent the hail had to have inside knowledge. It had taken both Jasmine and Grok most of two days to get the information, but it would be worth it.

The drug runner was armed, but he couldn't see a target, them being effectively invisible.

"Cook 'em, Spada," Goodnight said.

The pilot lifted the cover of the firing stud. He thumbed the button.

A powerful charged-particle beam streaked invisibly across the kilometers of empty space and drilled the drug ship's main engine. The engines blew apart, shattering the rear of the vessel, slewing it off course and into a series of slow spins.

Already in their vac suits, Grok, Riss, and Goodnight headed for the hold where their scooters were charging. The ship wasn't going anywhere, and the we've-been-attacked distress signal would take a while to get to the planet. Help would be coming, but by the time it got there, Star Risk would be finished and long gone.

The next part was central to their plan. Any competitor would simply salvage the ship; either tow it or unload it. But that wasn't going to happen, and what they planned seemed, as Chas had put it, a waste.

So the question would be: Who would *do* such a thing?

Even as the three mounted their cycles to finish the job, Jasmine was working her computer magic to lay some well-hidden clues pointing at somebody who knew nothing about it: Susa.

Sooner or later, Reese's people would find those clues. It would take work, enough so nobody would think they were plants, but they'd eventually uncover them.

Then things would start to get interesting.

At the wounded ship, the crew—mostly robotic, with a couple of humans, as they had learned—didn't seem in any hurry to take to the life pods.

As Goodnight and Grok jetted up and down the length of the craft, using puffs of air to shove the scooters along, and merrily slapping remora charges every few meters, Riss toggled her short-range op-chan on, using vox-shift so that she sounded like a basso profundo. "Hello, the drug-smuggling ship. Your engines are trash and we are about to turn your vessel into incandescent dust. If you don't want to be part of that, I suggest you pod up and hit vac. We aren't interested in you, but your ship and cargo are going to undergo radical alteration in form. Up to you."

The hatch sliding up to her left caught Riss's attention. No sound, of course, but she didn't need that. A man in a vac suit appeared in the hatchway and pointed a sidearm at her. She tapped her starboard jet control and got shoved the opposite way as the guy fired. Without any air to ionize, she couldn't see the bolt, but she did catch the glow at the blaster's muzzle.

*Son of a bitch! The stupid bastard shot at me!*

Riss's reactions were quick, and she reached for her own strapped weapon, but before she could draw it, the shooter's suit blew out over his chest, a mix of air and blood spewing into the cold and freezing into sparkly crystals. The reaction knocked him back into the hold.

Goodnight's vox over the suit radio said, "And after we gave them such a nice warning and a chance to get away and all? How stupid are they?"

Riss nodded to herself. "You about done?"

"Last one," Grok said. His vox-shift gave him a high, girlish voice that made her smile.

Back in their ship, they looked at the drug smuggler via cam as they moved off.

Spada said, "Safe distance."

"Any of the pods eject?" Riss asked.

"Not that I see."

She shrugged. "Too bad. Hit it."

"Let me," Goodnight said. "I love fireworks." He reached out and touched the remora remote.

The drug ship vanished in a brilliant, silent flash.

"Think the black box recorder survived?" Goodnight said.

Spada nodded. "Yep. Got the locator-sig yelling loud and clear."

"All that money," Goodnight said. He shook his head.

"*That's* the point, Chas. Who would just throw that away?

Only somebody who didn't really need it, who had other reasons to blow it up."

"Yeah, okay, right."

"I think our work here is done," Riss said. "Now what was that other thing you found? Some kind of art-smuggling ship? Let's go find that one . . ."

# THIRTY-ONE

Von Baldur loved to meddle in politics. Fiddling with mostly honest systems was fun, but messing around in crooked ones was a pure delight, since it was so much easier. Honest officials—and despite what the news-statters would have you believe, there were plenty of those—were a problem, because they weren't open to bribery. God save you from an upright man if you tried to make him party to an illegal or immoral deal. Yes, you certainly could cheat an honest man, he had done so many times, but you had to work harder at it than you did against one whose scruples were more flexible.

Money and power, and what they represented, were the two driving forces for officials who were out for their own and not the public's good. There were a lot of different ways these two manifested, of course. One man might be delighted at the idea of a nineteen-year-old girl in a limo with a half kilo of cocaine, while a second would have you arrested for daring to make such an offer. Then again, the second might drool at the prospect of acquiring a certain rare, five-hundred-year-old violin, and if you had one, he would trade you his mother for it.

The question when approaching the venal and corrupt was not whether they were bribable, but only what they wanted. Sometimes this was easy, sometimes not. It was all part of the game.

Von Baldur, wearing another disguise, this time a very well-made fatsuit that made him both heavier and darker-skinned, sat in a booth at a very high-class restaurant in a coastal resort a hundred kilometers away from the capital. He glanced at his chronometer. His appointment should be showing up in a few minutes. The man, an election official, had chosen this place because he was sure he wouldn't be seen by anybody he knew here. Nobody in his salary range could afford to eat in such a restaurant. Given the prices—a hundred credits for a lunch entree, five times that for a decent bottle of wine—that was understandable. But since von Baldur would be picking up the tab, it was a good place to hide. . . .

The host approached, immaculate in a full-dress suit, leading a somewhat dowdy-looking middle-aged fellow behind him. Even in a place far from home where nobody would know him, the man also wore a disguise, and it was—professionally speaking—pretty sad. A fake mustache and wig, and what looked to be fake eyebrows and dabs of bioflesh on the ears that didn't quite match his own skin color.

Sad.

"Good afternoon, Mr. . . . ah . . . ?"

"Mohammad," the dowdy man said.

Von Baldur nodded. Smith, Jones, Mohammad; common as dirt, those.

He offered up his latest op-nom. "Ah, yes, pleased to meet you. I am Arwee Eenakord."

"Mr. Eenakord."

"Try some of the wine. It is a passable vintage."

Mohammad took up the expensive crystal glass after von Baldur poured, made a pretense at sniffing the wine, and took a big sip. "Not bad," he said.

Von Baldur wanted to laugh. Nine hundred credits a bottle, an exquisite nine-year-old Cabernet Sauvignon from the best the local vineyards could produce, and this man called it "not bad"? No doubt he would rather be drinking beer . . .

"You had a proposition," Mohammad said.

"Cut right to the chase, eh? I like a man who doesn't dillydally around. Yes, sir, I do. Very well, then. To cases. The upcoming election on Una features a race between Tarlo Rutgie and Guita Movise, for the Planetary Senate."

"Yes."

"Movise is ahead in the polls?"

"Movise will sweep it. Rutgie has not the slightest chance of winning. Three to one, perhaps a greater margin. Movise could drop dead the day before the election and still win." Mohammad sipped at his wine again. His hand shook. "You can't want me to rig it so Rutgie wins?"

"Oh, no, of course not. Nobody would believe that, would they?"

Mohammad seemed to relax a bit. "No, they wouldn't. Even Rutgie's handlers wouldn't buy it."

"What I want you to do is skew things just a bit. Instead of winning by three to one, what if Movise took the election by, say, two to one?"

Mohammad blinked. "What would be the point of that? Rutgie loses huge or he just loses big?"

Von Baldur smiled, and the fatsuit dutifully copied the expression perfectly. "Well, hypothetically speaking, suppose somebody placed a large wager that the margin of victory was two to one instead of three to one? The odds against that would be passing long, would they not?"

Mohammad nodded. Ah. He got it.

"Such a result would still be almost impossible," he said. "There are limits to what can be done."

Von Baldur's faux face went serious. Here was the crux. The man calling himself Mohammad was not greedy, but he did have a daughter upon whom he doted, the light of his life after his wife died in a skiing accident. "I understand that there is a young man of rather exalted station by the name of Omar Murov who attends the same university as your daughter," he said.

That startled the man. "How do you know this?"

"I work for a man who is very highly placed. I will not mention his name, but let us just say that he is a member of a certain . . . *board* of which I am sure you have heard."

Mohammad swallowed dryly. He'd have to have been an idiot to have missed that one. Nothing subtle about it.

In case somebody ever got around to asking, best that this was on record. Since there were but two members of the Board on this planet, and since the one who might come asking would know it wasn't *him* the fat man had been talking about, that would narrow things down . . .

Von Baldur continued; "It is also my understanding that this young man has been pledged in marriage to a woman that he has never met. A financial and political arrangement?"

Mohammad nodded, his face suddenly grim. "This is so."

"And that if this young man was not thus encumbered, he would be free to choose a mate for whom he had . . . deeper feelings? A young woman who also feels much love for him."

Mohammad nodded again.

"Suppose, for the sake of argument, that this young man's potential in-laws decided that such a match was not in their daughter's best interests? Called it off?"

"You could *do* that?"

All men had their prices; the trick was in figuring out what they were and if you could afford them.

"Let's say my employer could. If young Omar were free to choose his spouse, and that happened to be somebody whose father had scrimped and saved enough to throw a very lavish wedding for his daughter, how might that affect the shading of an election in which the man who was going to win still wins, but by a smaller margin than expected? Harming no one in the process?"

Mohammad drained the rest of his wine in two gulps. Such a waste of fine cab. "Voters are fickle," he finally said. "Sometimes they tell pollsters one thing, then vote a different way."

"Such has been my experience," von Baldur said.

"How would such an . . . arrangement be manifested?"

"Well, a certain young man would have to call upon

a certain young woman and tell her the happy news, of course. And there might be a stock account, which, upon examination—should anybody ever have reason to do so, which would be unlikely—would appear to be twenty years old, with small deposits being made into it every few months. The stocks in this account would have done rather well in two decades, and the account would have grown to a nice value. Say . . . a quarter-million credits. Enough to throw a very nice wedding, and to make a down payment on a new house for the bride and groom."

Mohammad said, "I believe I might have a splash more of this wine, if that's all right?"

"Oh, certainly." Von Baldur picked up the bottle.

When his glass was filled, Mohammad lifted it, and von Baldur raised his to join the toast. "To marriage, Mr. Eenakord."

"Indeed, Mr. Mohammad. To marriage."

After Mohammad was gone, von Baldur sat long enough to finish the bottle of wine—no point whatsoever in wasting it. In a day or two, a young woman who did not want to get married to a man she had never met was going to come into enough money to catch a fast ship to another system, where she would have enough to party high for months, and whereupon her father would have to renege on the marriage arrangement he had made for her. Children. They broke your heart, but you still had to love them anyway . . .

And a member of the Board was going to lose a small fortune covering the spread on planetary politics when he took what seemed like a sure bet at long odds and had to pay off. Maybe they'd get it sorted out eventually, but von Baldur didn't care. If they got to Mohammad and he told all, that was so much the better—they'd sting their target for the money *and* sow discord.

Eventually, the universe would run down and entropy would rule all. What happened between then and now was what mattered.

This really was good wine. He wondered what a case of it might run.

# THIRTY-TWO

Jasmine's next move was more direct than her usual computer skullduggery.

She meant to pay a visit to Susa's hunting lodge.

Susa didn't go there to hunt. There weren't any large animals on Una worth the effort for any real sportsman, but a rustic place in the woods—and the word "mansion" was closer to the truth than "lodge"—was a place where the boys could get together and party and pretend to be roughing it.

Since she didn't want to drive a vehicle where it might be spotted by Susa's security—and she had to assume they had the roads watched—she decided to hike in from the nearest town, about fifteen kilometers away. And because that was her cover—she was a hiker—she didn't want to be carrying anything that might immediately give the lie to that if she was stopped. Thus her backpack contained water, food, a comm, emergency supplies, a film-blanket, a GPS-locator she could trigger if she got lost, binocular-cam, a windup flashlight, things like that. No blaster, though she did have her knife on a belt sheath out in the open, and a walking staff. This last was an expandable titanium-and-steel device with a snake-spike on one end and a wooden knob and strap on the other. In the hands of an adept, it made a good close-quarters weapon. A hard jab from a fifteen-centimeter-long needle-pointed steel spike in the belly would probably encourage a frisky attacker to think twice about his actions . . .

She could get away with clothes that wouldn't glow in the forest—a dark green shirt and mottled brown-and-green silk cargo pants, hiking boots—but an electronic camosuit like the one Freddie had was out of the question. A sensor confounder built into her water bottle's vacuum pump was about as much as she could risk on that front, and that was easy enough to turn off so it wouldn't rascal something when she didn't want it to. Like if a guard was running a scanner up and down her, checking for just such a device.

While she believed that Susa likely knew that Makko had been responsible for the deaths of Josiah and Joe, she didn't have any proof that he had personally ordered the killings; still, that didn't really matter. Susa was as dirty as a double shift of coal miners, and if he hadn't ordered Makko to delete the father and son, he had certainly done worse. You didn't get to be the top crime boss on a planet without crushing a few eggs . . .

The temperate rain forest was beautiful: a lot of very tall, old-growth firlike trees reaching up a hundred meters, moss growing on some of them, a rooflike canopy throwing plenty of shade down onto the humus-thick ground. Not a lot of undergrowth, probably kept down by the needles and lack of direct sunlight. Even though it was a warm summer day, the forest was much cooler, and even a few breezes made the hike pleasant. The walk was refreshing—she got to work her muscles, and it was so quiet that she could hear her own heartbeat when she paused to rest.

There were also small creatures who lived here—the local equivalents of squirrels and rabbits and all manner of birds, plus some deerlike creatures the size of large dogs that, over the years, had worn narrow trails throughout the forest.

Susa wasn't at the lodge, which was good, because in that case, even with a confounder, security would be too tight to allow her to walk right up to the building. She had memorized the images of the structures she had found, and she had forest service maps of the woods, which stretched for thirty kilometers around the lodge.

She could maintain a fairly brisk pace in the forest, and she did, so the first fourteen kilometers took her just under three hours. She was sweating, even in the coolness, but it wasn't yet midday when she got within stalking range.

The last klick took forty-five minutes, because she moved very carefully. She didn't spot any tripwires or hardwired sensors, and she armed the confounder to rascal Doppler, radar, or infrared motion detectors. Walking quietly should keep her from being picked up on any listening devices—they couldn't set the level too low on those, or else every bird that cheeped or smeerp that farted would blow out the microphone circuits.

It was afternoon when she got to a point where,

hidden in the trees, she could see the main part of the compound.

There was the lodge, which was huge, and several smaller outbuildings: garage, storage shed, generator shack, and a guard kiosk on the only road leading in.

There was a guard in the kiosk who appeared to be watching a vid on a small holoprojector; another guard walked patrol. Both were men, and the walker was armed with a blaster carbine.

A trio of gardeners worked the area, mowing grass, trimming bushes, weeding flower beds.

A carpenter worked on one corner of the lodge, itself a natural wood structure, likely built of local timbers.

She unlimbered her binoculars and scanned the compound in detail, noting the distances on the range finder and memorizing them, but not recording holos. She examined the workers. Probably there were domestics inside—maids, cooks, whatnot—but she couldn't see them.

She worked her way around the perimeter. There wasn't a fence, which was good, and after another hour she had fixed the setup in her mind. Now all she had to do was wait.

Jasmine eased a little deeper into the forest, found a smooth-boled tree, sat so it supported her back, and became invisible.

She had to smile at that thought. When she'd been younger, she had spent a year working as a game warden on a world where hunters came to play. The taking of game was strictly limited and enforced, the fines if one was caught poaching were astronomical, and, for some of the rarer animals, shooting one out of season or without a license was worth a year in jail. Even so, there were those who thought they could beat the system, and who took to the mountains or forests with illegal intent.

As a warden, it was Jasmine's job to catch such hunters.

Since she didn't have any experience in the field, she was paired with a grizzled old man named McClain. Mac was as tough as boot plastic, couldn't utter a sentence without obscene expletives in it, and knew more about moving in the woods than any man she had ever met, before or since. He had taught her how to become invisible.

"First thing," he'd said, "you don't wear any moth-erfreakin' clothes that stand out. Pulse-glo orange hats and vests are great if you don't want to get shot by another hunter, but anything with color vision will see it four klicks away and that's no motherfreakin' good. You want to look like the forest or the field or the rocks, and you sure as feces better dress that way, copy?"

She had nodded.

"Second, you don't freakin' move when somethin' might be freakin' lookin' at you. Any critter that's gonna eat or get eaten tracks motion. Step into the kitchen and a deelybug on the counter sees you, it takes off for the nearest cover. Big cats looking for prey look for something runnin' from 'em. Prey looks for big cats comin' in on 'em. Don't freakin' move. Park your ass somewhere and sit motherfreakin' still, copy?"

She nodded.

"Third, make the crystal fountain."

"Huh?"

Mac grinned. "You imagine you have a fountain coming out of the top of your motherfreakin' head. Shoots up a few centimeters, and then spills down over you, covering you. But it's not water, it's freakin' crystal, like little bits of quartz or diamond. Once it covers you, you reflect the light back, nobody can see you."

"Bullcrap."

He had laughed, a rough, raucous cackle. "Sounds like it, don't it? But it works. Ninja stuff, snipers, spookers, they all have their own variations of the fountain. What you are trying to do is be something other than a freakin' human being sittin' in the bushes. Not with your mind workin' ten klicks a minute. There are animals—some humans, too—who can somehow sense people thinkin' too hard. So you don't think. But since that's freakin' impossible to do for long, the crystal fountain is your focus point. Like a mantra. You aren't freakin' gonna really be invisible, but if you've picked a place where nobody is expectin' to see anybody, if you are freakin' sitting still, and if you aren't putting out any mental static, people—and some animals—just won't see you, even if they look right at you."

"How do you watch for somebody and keep this, um, fountain going?"

"That's the tricky part. You have to have just enough consciousness to be aware of what's goin' on around you without being *too* aware."

She had shaken her head. It had seemed to her at the time that the old man's mumbo jumbo was drivel.

Oh, she could see the right-clothing, right-spot, keep-still stuff was useful, but the make-the-crystal-fountain? Please.

And yet, over the course of the next few months, while sitting surveillance or tracking poachers and out-of-season hunters, she had, for the sake of argument, tried it. Sometimes, she would do all the other stuff and skip the fountain business. Other times, she would add that in. She felt silly doing it, but she did it.

And it worked.

When she did everything but the fountain, she was spotted maybe one time in three or four, which was pretty good.

When she concentrated on the visualization, she had *never* been spotted by her quarry.

Being pragmatic, Jasmine shrugged. If it worked, it worked. Why was not as important. Chalk one up to Mac, wherever he might be.

So now, she relaxed against the tree, brought up the crystal fountain, and sank into a more or less mind-less state.

When she came out of the reverie, night had fallen.

The rest of it shouldn't be that hard. There were lights in the compound, the guards still patrolled, but there were plenty of deep shadows. Jasmine didn't stand out in her dark clothing. She took her time, moved slowly and carefully, and in half an hour had made her way to a spot only a couple of meters away from the back wall. Hidden in the night, she opened her backpack and removed three packets of trail mix.

To anybody looking, the mix of dried grapes, nuts, crackers, and berries was standard enough—basic

GORP hiking food, high in nutrition, low in fat, tasty, if you liked that kind of thing.

But this mix was different. The dark, round bits that looked like dried greenberry weren't fruits at all, but sonically triggered thermo-putty. She removed those from the bags and mashed them together into three blobs, each the size of her last thumb joint. To each of these, she added a drop of what was supposed to be binocular lens cleaner and worked it in. This was the catalyst, without which the putty would not function. Now armed, each blob was a miniature firebomb. When triggered, they would ignite and burn with a temperature sufficient to eventually melt durasteel. Adding water to them wouldn't do anything to quench them—nothing short of class-one firefoam would even slow them down, and that wasn't what a standard fire extinguisher carried.

She took out one of the two water bottles in her backpack. Half of what was in it was indeed water, perfectly good to drink. A membrane halfway down the inside of the bottle separated the water from a chemical that, once mixed with water, made an accelerant—fast-burning and hot, but odorless. The stuff would appear to dry in minutes, but remain flammable for six hours.

She used her knife to puncture the seal. The two fluids mixed.

She waited until the roaming guard was on the other side of the building, then darted to the wall. She mashed one of the putty balls into the wood at the base of the wall, then squirted a third of the accelerant onto the wood above it.

She repeated the action twice more. Then she removed her finger chronometer and laid it on the ground next to the last charge, worked it down into the grass out of sight, and then hurried away back into the shadows. The chronometer's alarm was set to go off in five hours, and the frequency of its tone was the same as that needed to ignite the thermo-putty. All three blobs would go up together, *whoof!*

In five hours, when the alarm went off, this back wall of the lodge was going to erupt into a sheet of fire, and somebody hurrying to use the water hose conveniently lying right there would only make the situation worse, spreading the flames faster.

Maybe it would take down the whole place, maybe not. The amount of damage was less important than the act. Somebody had sneaked in here and set Susa's lodge on fire, and that was going to irritate him big-time . . .

As she was slipping back toward the cover of the forest, feeling pretty clever and pleased with herself, Jasmine almost ran over one of the guards. She saw him as he rounded one of the outbuildings, the storage shed. What was he doing there? That wasn't his patrol pattern!

Maybe he needed to take a leak. Or maybe he'd heard something.

That didn't matter. What mattered was, he was five meters away and, while he hadn't seen her yet, he would, even if she stood still and tried to make herself invisible. There were limits to that trick.

She had to take the initiative before he saw her. She took two more steps, closing the distance.

"Excuse me?" she said.

He spun, spooked by the voice in the night, his

blaster carbine coming off his shoulder and into a targeting hold.

"Can you help me, please? I seem to have gotten lost."

"Who the freak are you?" he said. "Don't move!" He lifted one hand up to trigger his comm, worn over one ear.

Jasmine already had the hiking staff in a spear-throwing grip. She raised her hands as if frightened. "Don't shoot me, please!"

The staff was positioned where she wanted it.

"Your sister is a parakeet, isn't she?"

The guard blinked. "What—?"

She threw the staff like a javelin. She didn't need to put as much shoulder into it as she did, though. The point took him in the left eye and sank to the base. He collapsed, the carbine falling from his spasming hand. Effectively brain-dead before he landed.

She grabbed the staff, jerked it free, and considered her options. She bent, grabbed the guard's ankles, and started to drag him toward the woods. A dead guard would certainly raise an alarm. One who just vanished would, too, but that would take longer. They'd have to go look for him, and nobody would likely get twitchy, since they wouldn't see any signs of trouble. The nicely cropped lawn shouldn't even show any drag marks.

With any luck, they wouldn't find the body for a few hours. She planned to be back at her vehicle before that happened. It would be tricky in the dark, but the windup flashlight should be enough to show her the way.

# THIRTY-THREE

Another summons from Susa, this time a polite invitation to a sporting event—the local bashball team, the Sharks, hosted the current system champs, the Jets, for a preseason match. The game was carried on the entcom's sports channel, of course, but there was a stadium for those people who liked to attend such things in person.

Makko was not a particular fan of bashball. He didn't mind the violence, but the vagaries of the scoring system were entirely too esoteric for his taste. Two teams, seven players each, strived to throw, kick, or carry a hard plastic sphere the size of a man's head through a constantly shifting playing field to deposit it in a bin at the apex of the field. This had to be done while the other team attacked them with stylized boxing and wrestling moves. Different numbers of points were awarded to both teams by a panel of referees for knocking an opponent down with a strike, a kick, or a full body slam. Additional points were given for the style of the attack or defense, and for taking down more than one opponent. There were time penalties, penalties for continuing to attack a fallen player once his back or chest touched the ground, and half a dozen other things. Either or both teams could thus make points on every play.

All the players wore padded plastic body armor, gauntlets, and helmets, but injuries were frequent and required a time-out to attend to the downed player. The game was divided into four twenty-minute quarters, and tended to be high-scoring—eighty or a hundred points over the course of play for both teams were not unusual.

Susa had a private cube, and a bird's-eye view of the field from the middle. The cube had climate control, a giant armored and polarized glass window that was proof against small arms' fire up to 20mm AP, and all the comforts of home: a well-stocked bar, refrigerator, and the services of a bartender, waiter, or hostess, if desired. You could, if you wanted, have a woman sitting on your lap stark naked and nobody could see you from without—you could watch the game and *play* games at the same time, though that was unlikely in Susa's case. He didn't care for such vulgar behavior.

In the cube, Susa sat at the window, watching the game. There were two holoproj units, one to either side, on which one could watch recorded replays for the finer details of play. Three bodyguards sat behind Susa, with another scanning the crowd with binoculars, looking for potential trouble. Makko left his own bodyguard team outside in the hall with Susa's main force.

"What's the score?" Makko asked as he sat next to Susa.

"Sixty-eight to twenty-four, middle of the second quarter."

"Sharks ahead?"

Susa looked at Makko and laughed. "Right. Our boys are getting the crap kicked out of them. The Jets are in a league of their own."

Makko nodded. He wasn't a big fan, but he knew that much.

On the field, the Sharks had the ball. They launched a complicated feint-and-rush, then tried to move the ball around the portside of the Main Path.

It was not complicated enough. The Jets read the play and were there en masse to fall upon the attacking team. Sharks dropped like skittle pins.

"You heard that somebody blew up Reese's drug ship." It was not a question.

"Yeah. Doesn't make any sense. You were going to hijack a ship like that, you wouldn't turn it into glowing frags."

Susa watched the Sharks and the Jets line up again. "Me?"

"I was talking in general," Makko said. "Not about you specifically." Makko frowned. What brought *that* up?

The Sharks charged. The Jets stomped them flat again. It was like watching grown men go against boys.

"Going to be an after-play penalty against the Sharks' central smashback," Susa said. "Watch."

Sure enough, the closest field ref, impossible to miss in his neon yellow coveralls, flashed a red light on his belt, pointed at the Sharks player, and made the announcement: "Personal foul after play, number four, third team foul, minus six points."

"Sharks are getting frustrated. They keep playing like that, they are gonna wind up in minus figures."

Makko nodded.

"Whoever blew up the drug ship, they knew the route, and they had the opchan frequencies and the hailing codes."

Makko watched as the two teams shifted positions, once, twice, three times, before the Sharks launched the next play. This time, the ball carrier's defense team wedged open a gap in the Jets' attack, and the left smashback shot into the hole and ran thirty meters before the right lastditch hit him with a flying sidekick, nearly knocking the ball loose.

The local fans roared. That play was worth ten, eleven points for the home team, easy.

"So it was an inside job," Makko said, stating the obvious.

"Of course. But Reese says he has vetted all of his people—Truth scans, and everybody passed."

Makko looked at his boss. "Must have a pathological liar somewhere who can beat the scan."

"He says not."

Makko chewed on that for a few seconds. "What's his point?"

"His point is, what kind of idiot would blow up millions of credits worth of tax-free dope when they could just take it? Whoever it was holed the engines, they had a stealth ship, and they had to go out of their way using hand-placed charges to make sure the cargo wasn't going be recoverable."

"Some kind of antidrug fanatics? Or somebody trying to ding Reese for some reason. Revenge, maybe?"

The Sharks had achieved momentum. The next play, the central smashback knocked over two defenders—one with an elegant backfist to a poorly protected neck—and made it all the way to the scoring bin, where he dumped the ball and then danced around in triumph.

The crowd went wild.

The dance was short-lived, as one of the Jets plowed into him from behind after the play had been honked to a stop. That would cost the Jets ten points, but then, they had plenty to spare. Even with the score, the Jets would still be ahead by twenty, and they would then get the sphere.

Susa said, "Maybe. Reese doesn't seem to think so."

"What does he think?"

"He hasn't said exactly, but I think he thinks I was responsible."

"You? Why would *you* do that?"

"Precisely. I wouldn't."

Makko shook his head. Reese was easygoing, but pretty sharp. If he thought Susa had anything to do with the destruction of his ship, he'd have to have a reason. Makko would like to know what that was.

"You hear about my lodge?"

Makko looked at his boss. "Your lodge?"

"Early this morning, somebody set it on fire. Killed one of my guards; looked like he'd been stabbed in the eye."

"Damn," Makko said. "How bad was the fire?"

"Not too much. One wall was scorched pretty good, some smoke damage. Whoever did it must not have known about the upgraded fire-suppressors in the walls."

Makko shook his head.

"The arson team found a pretty sophisticated ignition system—thermo-putty, accelerant, a sonic driver.

I don't believe for a second this was done by some loon who likes to watch things burn."

"You think it was Reese? Getting back at you because he thinks you totaled his ship?"

"I think somebody would like me to believe that. What I think is, somebody is screwing with us—the Board."

"Who would be that stupid?"

"That's the question, isn't it? I have my best snoops on it, and I want you to put out the word to your people. Finding out who is our number one priority, as of yesterday. Everything else comes second, you understand?"

"Yeah, sure."

"I want whoever did this to be found and squashed, whoever they are, whatever their reasons."

"I understand."

"Good. You want to stay and watch the rest of the game?"

"Maybe not. I ought to get on this."

"I knew I could count on you, Keven."

As Makko left, his guards falling into position, he considered what Susa had just told him. Somebody trying to dick with the Board? That was more than passing stupid, that was suicidal. Why? And more importantly, who?

There was a lot of clout to be made here if he was the one who figured it out. Susa squashed his enemies, but he rewarded his friends.

The times had become interesting, no doubt of it . . .

# THIRTY-FOUR

Goodnight and Riss hung in the cold darkness of space, waiting.

The view was interesting. Abesse was a ringed planet; it had a thin, multilayered circle around its terminator, and sunlight glinted off the ice and other high-albedo debris that comprised it. Beyond the ringed world was Ica, one of the largest moons in the system. From their vantage point Ica was just a crescent, the majority of its surface covered by Abesse's shadow. It was a view that astronomers would kill for.

Not why they came, though.

They were between their stealth ship and a freighter that had just lifted and was gearing up for warp. They had followed it up from Abesse when it launched, matching speed while keeping far enough back not to be caught in its wake. Once it was in a parking orbit, they had moved closer, and now they were only about twenty or thirty meters away.

One of the tidbits of information they had been buying had paid off. Apparently there was a ship that didn't exist, which made frequent trips to and from various worlds in the Artegal System, all very hush-hush.

Intrigued, Goodnight had investigated.

It was true. About once a week a ship with no registry, no official ID, and no record of its passing arrived at the port. After a day or so, it took off; again, no records.

Even more intrigued, Goodnight and Spada had trailed it to each of the other planets in the system.

The ship held stolen goods, and that was no surprise—but of a very specialized nature. It contained one-of-a-kind boodle: paintings, jewelry, art, and precious metals, all in unique, recognizable forms. As a former jewel thief, Goodnight knew that valuables like this were hard to move—unless you had an off-world conduit.

After all, while there were few things which were truly world famous, there were fewer that were system famous, and fewer still apt to be recognized in another part of the galaxy. A gold sculpture from Terzo could appear on Una and never be recognized; a system-famous painting in a stellar system near the Rim, or far out on one spiral arm, would not raise eyebrows here.

It was, Goodnight reckoned, a private treasure ship. The members of the council trafficked in special objets d'art, and traded these unique items among themselves.

Which of course made such a ship the perfect target. Goodnight had encountered similar schemes, but nothing quite to this degree. These people had corruption and graft *down*. It was admirable, from a crook's point of view.

\* \* \*

They triggered small compressed-air jets on their suits to propel themselves toward the freighter.

Between them, they hauled a P38—a portable emergency air lock. Rather than trying to diddle the controls on the main air locks of their target, they'd brought their own. The device was a large tube that had two hatches. On one end of the tube were two concentric strips running around the edge—one strip was a two-part thermosetting adhesive, and the other was a shaped det-cord charge. When activated, the device quickly and permanently bonded itself to a target ship, and when the shaped charge was set off, it popped a hole in the ship. Voila! Instant air lock.

They had sprayed it with signal-damping paint, to prevent their target from picking them up on sensors. If the ship was going to land in atmosphere, the P38 would have to be jettisoned and the hole patched, otherwise it would probably melt off during reentry and open a big hole in the side of the ship as it did so.

Based on their reconnaissance, there were eight guards on the ship, plus pilots.

The plan was that the guards and the pilots would be left to tell tales, which was why they were wearing skinmasks under their helmets.

The idea was to sell most of the stock back to insurance companies. Most of the valuables were unique enough to warrant insurance policies, if not to require them. Some of the money from this would then be dumped into one of the Board members' accounts. This would clearly point a finger in a way that was sure to cause concern. The key word there was *some*. After all, Star Risk was going to make a profit on this every way it could. Some of the money was going to wind up in *their* accounts.

To mix things up a bit more, some of the swag would be delivered to a few of the other members. This was sure to stir things up even more.

Divide and conquer . . .

They reached the other ship.

Carefully, Riss and Goodnight lowered the P38 to the hull, aligning it to a central hub they had figured would give them the closest access point to the ship's bridge.

Riss triggered the glue strip and there was a slight discoloration as the thermoplastic bubbled and sealed itself to the hull. When it turned green, the two of them moved to the sides and she activated the cut-through.

Both outer and inner doors opened, and the shaped charge fired.

Abruptly the ship was shoved to one side. Air rushed out, crystallizing in the intense cold.

Riss used a remote, sealed the inner door, and Goodnight climbed in.

Riss sealed the outer door, then opened the inner—

Goodnight triggered bester and went through—

From the blur of bester, the inside of the ship was a blast of stop-motion detail. There were two guards waiting—

Scratch that—one was waiting, one was dead. Must've had the misfortune to be directly under the bulkhead they had blown in.

*Nasty.*

But the former Alliance commando couldn't stop to

feel sorry for the guard; the survivor swung a blaster around and fired—

Goodnight had time to widen his eyes and roll out of the way, bester-quick.

*What an idiot! That's not a safe weapon for a ship—*

The muffled roar of the weapon could be heard faintly though his helmet.

Goodnight dove toward a corner and snapped off a shot with *his* ship-safe weapon—a dart thrower with a particularly fast anesthetic dart.

The dart hit the guy right between the eyes, which rolled up and showed white almost instantly.

Scratch one more guard.

But here came some more . . .

Riss was supposed to be in here by now, and everyone was reacting much faster than they should.

Further, the people in the ship were not wearing space suits. He was only two or three times as fast bundled up in his suit.

*Not good.*

He fired another dart, caught a guard on the chin—

One of the remaining guards raised a shoulder-mounted *plasma cannon*—

*Holy crap! What a* moron!

He was going to blow the ship up—but worse, he was going to blow up Mama Goodnight's little boy—

Chas used his bester-powered muscles to jump back to the new entrance chamber really fast. Inside, he threw the killsafe switch, slamming open both hatches. He launched himself into space, and hoped that Riss wasn't in his way—

The sudden loss of pressure became a real problem

for the guys in the hall who weren't wearing space suits, and who were suddenly being sucked into the room by the now gale-force winds rushing toward the new air lock.

The lock became clogged with bodies, weapons, and other crap rushing out to space, and Goodnight was able to shoot the remaining guards who still had enough air to breath.

He waved at Riss as he floated past her.

So the guards got dead instead of just knocked out. Too bad, but they'd made the call. Idiots who started firing inside of their own ship with plasma cannons and blasters did not meet the basic criteria for being smart enough to live.

At least that was how he reasoned it.

Besides, now it would be easier to deal with witnesses.

He and Riss moved in, cautiously. He shut bester down, and they closed the inner hatch.

Nobody alive in the corridor. They double-checked the rest of the ship but only found one pilot, hiding in a fresher. They knocked him out. One witness was plenty.

Once they were sure they were safe, Goodnight contacted Spada and had him move the stealthed ship closer.

They had goods to steal . . .

"Once again, let's review, shall we? Who wants to start?" von Baldur said. "Jasmine?"

Star Risk had gathered in Freddie's office, and since the new soundproofing and antisnoop devices had been installed, the room was very quiet, despite the noisy—and nearly full—casino racket outside the door. The room smelled nice, as if somebody had been burning incense or the like.

"My intel was a little old," Jasmine said. "I didn't know about the upgraded fire-suppressors Susa had installed in his lodge. But the point was made, I think." She was pleased with herself, she had to admit.

"Reese's people have been buzzing around like mad hornets after the drug ship we blew apart," Riss said, "and we're pretty sure they've uncovered the pointers we left for them."

Von Baldur nodded. "And come the local election, Susa is going to be out between six and eight million credits, depending on the last-minute shift of the odds when a sure-thing candidate wins by somewhat less than the spread. I have some thoughts as to things we might do for the system-wide election, too. I'd say we are moving along well."

Riss said, "The art ship thing went fine. Most of the stuff is on its way back to where it was stolen. Jasmine made the deposits where they were supposed to go. We'll make some good money ourselves."

Goodnight said, "I know our standard procedure is to rattle cages and see what hits the bars snarling, but I still think that grabbing up Makko and asking him pointed questions would get us there faster. Grok and I could hire a few guns, take down his guards, and snatch him, no problem."

Grok nodded, obviously eager to engage in such an action.

Von Baldur looked around and apparently saw that nobody else wanted to leap on that one, so he took it. "Actually, there are several potential problems there, Chas.

"First, a guy like Makko probably has a neural-cutout installed, and since he can afford a first-class impress, chances are we won't get anything out of him if we grab him and hold his feet to the fire.

"Second, even if he doesn't have a block, torture doesn't really work that well, since at some point the guy you are prodding will say anything he thinks you want to hear to make you stop. He figures he's going to die, so he's looking for the least painful way to get there.

"Third, if you go charging in there like gangbusters and there are blasters and spring guns and needlers going off hither and yon, there's a chance your target could catch a round between the eyes, and that's the end of the dance. Sure, you and Grok can shoot straight, but can you be certain any help you hire won't put a stray round into the target? Or that one of his guards doesn't trip over his own boots and blow the back of his boss's head off?"

Goodnight made a face and shrugged.

"That's what I thought," von Baldur said. "It's a high-risk, low-yield operation, no matter how you stack it. And to forestall your next suggestion, the same logic applies to Susa. We need to find evidence, a link, something that we can be sure of."

Goodnight said, "Susa is guilty of a whole lot of illegal crap, so why not just take him down anyhow? Everybody in the nest is a viper; let's fry 'em all."

Riss laughed. "That's funny, coming from a guy who doesn't go to the fresher unless he knows who is paying for his time."

Goodnight offered Riss a filthy proposition involving her mouth and one of his intimate body parts, a suggestion that she had refused more than a few times.

"You wish. Listen, it's not our mission to make the whole galaxy safe for children and old folks," Riss continued. "Our job, as specified by our late employer, is to find who gave the order to kill his father, and take him and his organization apart. If we start along the highway of righting wrongs because we can, there is no end to it."

"Or her," Grok said.

Riss looked at him as if he had just turned into an electric pink squid. "What?"

"It is conceivable that the person who gave the order is female, is it not?"

Riss sighed. "Yes, Mr. Politically Correct, it is *conceivable* that the deed was done by a woman. We haven't come across any women in our efforts who would be in a position to do that, but I will grant you the possibility."

Grok nodded. "Thank you. I shouldn't need to tell *you* the violence of which human females are capable."

She shook her head. "My idea of hell would be to have to spend eternity cooped up in a room with you two."

"I am wounded," Grok said, his voice grave.

"Yeah, me too," Goodnight said. "You're hurting our feelings here, M'chel. We're sensitive guys, me 'n' Grok."

If looks could kill, both Grok and Goodnight would have become radioactive smears on the carpet under Riss's gaze. But since looks didn't damage them, both of them smiled. Point each for them, Jasmine figured.

Von Baldur laughed. "Children, children, let's play nice. I have a new thought I would share with you."

They all looked at him.

Given that it was his idea, von Baldur thought he was the one to implement it.

The target was an office building, owned by a shell company that was in turn owned by a dummy corporation that was owned by Susa. The building was five stories tall, and the top floor was reserved for Susa's use. This was where the powers that were in this system—the Board—met from time to time to make decisions on how things would be run.

There was to be such a meeting soon, a day or so in the future, von Baldur had learned, to select the next prime minister for the stellar system. Not directly, of course, only the candidate who would then go on to win, but the effect was the same. People in this planetary group knew which way the wind blew, and they knew better than to go against the Board . . .

Susa's security did not want to make it easy for somebody to just pop in and disrupt such meetings, and after the fire at his hunting lodge, the wards had been increased.

It would have been difficult to break into this particular building, even with the tools of a gifted burglar, and the top floor exceedingly hard to manage—security was simply too tight for a late-night sneak-in. The place was alarmed, and even the alarms were alarmed—any attempt to shut down power, break a hardwired circuit, or rascal an electronic sensor would trigger a backup. There were half a dozen guards patrolling the top floor, probably all itching for a chance to shoot somebody, plus the guards in the lobby and on the other floors, and while it might have been possible, it was beyond anything von Baldur could manage to figure out in the time allotted.

So, when you couldn't sneak in, then an alternative was to just stroll in like you owned the place, in front of everybody . . .

Von Baldur temporarily became a sales rep calling on an import business on the fourth floor of the building. He arrived, dressed for the part and suitably disguised, was scanned and admitted, and he took the elevator to the fourth floor. There, he was checked against a list, and allowed to enter the office of the company. He met the buyer, made his pitch, and, as expected, found little interest in his theoretical service. But as he was leaving, he stopped at the receptionist's kiosk.

"There a fresher nearby?"

The young woman nodded. "Just down the hall, third door to the left."

"I need an admit code?"

"No, it's not locked."

"Thanks."

Von Baldur proceeded to the fresher. It held three toilet stalls. Nobody else was inside, and no surveillance cams were evident. Bad form to put them in such places, not to mention illegal on most worlds.

Quickly, von Baldur entered one of the stalls, climbed up on the pipe and flush apparatus inset into the wall, lifted a loose ceiling panel, and put a hand-sized device disguised as part of his briefcase into the drop ceiling. He shoved it next to an electrical junction box. It was a little popper that would make a flame, but he didn't really expect it to start much of a fire—the suppressors in this building were first-rate and would extinguish it pretty quickly. But the device had a wonderfully effective smoke bomb built into it, and it would create billowing clouds of dark, sooty smoke. Way more than needed to set off the detectors and trigger the automatic call to the local fire department.

It was an old trick, but it still worked. When your building seems about to burn down, you don't stop the firefighters at the front door . . .

That night, when the timer set the fire- and smoke bomb off, von Baldur was seated in a dark hovervan in a parking lot across the street. He checked his chronometer as the building alarms, audible across the road, started screaming. This being Susa's building, he didn't think it would take long for the firefighters to arrive.

He was right. The first truck fanned up within three minutes. The big, bright yellow vehicle settled to the ground, maybe a bit harder than it should, and firefighters started piling out and running for the building.

A fire department thopter zoomed in from overhead, and police sirens Dopplered in as the local LEOs began to arrive. Night-shift people started to come out of other buildings to see what all the fuss was about.

Freddie von Baldur, now wearing full-turnout gear, including a Nomex hood and air bottle, and carrying an ax, hurried across the street to join the other firefighters. The gear was regulation, and he was effectively faceless, just another firefighter among dozens more.

It was dark, and a lot of people were milling about, shouting and hooking up water hoses. Already the smell of smoke had drifted down an air or elevator shaft and into the night.

Von Baldur had a working radio inset into his helmet, set to the opchan the firefighters were using. He could hear the lieutenant and captain on-site issuing orders:

"—thopter One, the roof door locks are being opened, get your crew into the stairwell—"

"—H and L, soon as you get here, get a ladder up to the top floor and next to the hall fire exit—"

"—Alpha Team, get your lights and fans going, I repeat, lights and fans!"

Von Baldur started up the south stairs behind a team of firefighters. Five floors in full turnout was a bitch. Had to admire these guys and gals who could do it on a routine basis. He kept meaning to work out more . . .

Winded, and his legs burning, he made it to the fifth floor landing. If only getting into good shape wasn't so much work . . .

The hall was filled with smoke and jets of suppressor foam and water from the building's sprinklers, but von Baldur wasn't worried about any real danger—the structure's extinguishers would have handled the little fire by themselves, and there'd be more smoke and way more water damage than anything else.

He clicked on his IR viewer and made his way down the hall, able to see well enough with the heads-up augmented visual aid, even in the smoke.

He found the conference room, opened the door—automatically unlocked by the outgoing fire alarm call—and shut it behind him. He looked around. He assumed there might a security cam somewhere, though he didn't see it, so he kept his hood down and walked to the conference table, a large, oval piece of rich, dark brown Zabrillion Rosewood, full of purple and orange swirls and hand-rubbed with at least a dozen coats of expensive raluba wax to bring out the grain. Fifteen, twenty thousand credits worth of furniture, the table alone, easy. He kneeled, and twisted the head of the ax. The head came off. He removed a patch of double-stick tape from his jacket pocket, peeled the protective cover off one side and stuck it to the ax head. Then he peeled the other cover off, crawled under the table, and pressed the ax head against the wood. The tape, which would hold the weight of a heavy man, adhered to the bottom of the table.

It wasn't an ax head, of course. It was a fragmentation grenade, with a passive electronic sensor set to pick up heat. If more than three humans sat around the perimeter of this table, the sensor would, in a couple of minutes, be kicked on by their ambient body heat. That would start a timer. Five minutes later, the grenade would go off, and anybody within ten meters would be having shrapnel for lunch, which would be their last meal. . . .

The grenade in place, von Baldur crawled out from under the table, stood, dusted off his hands, and headed for the door.

*Not bad,* he thought. *Not bad at all . . .*

# THIRTY-FIVE

Riss and Jasmine had gotten tired of using the ultrahigh-class treadmill at the casino's gym. Boring just to run in place, no matter how good the holograms were. You missed the smells—such as they were—the feel of real night air, the sounds and sights of a living city.

Jasmine suggested they go out. There was a jogging trail at the local park; why not go there?

They wore the latest in exercise thinskins, tight, form-hugging fabric so breathable that it virtually sweated for them, complete with thin channels for perspiration disguised as racing stripes. They had to carry their weapons in small pouches worn around their waists, because the thinskins were *very* thin and there wasn't room for anything else. They wore the latest in footwear—padded, flexible racing soles that adhered directly to their feet with molecular grippers. The soles effectively had no tops save for sweat-soaks, which made them very comfortable.

"I'd still rather be wearing combat boots when the feces hits the fan," Riss said. "Nothing like a solid boot attached to your foot to crack heads and cave ribs."

"But not so much fun to run in," Jasmine said.

"Point taken."

They created quite a stir as they left, with men and women turning heads to stare at the two athletic supermodels in their midst. *Hey, you got it, flaunt it.*

Outside in the Una night, they quickly made it to the park. By the time they had reached the central trail hub, they had worked up a good sweat, but it was wicked away pretty well.

They began a steady, loping run. Apparently the park wasn't that popular for such endeavors at night—they went half a klick or so without seeing any other runners.

The paths were lit by dim amber lamps, obviously designed to help keep their night vision unaffected.

Riss saw something ahead first. "Heads up," she said, easing off the trail.

Jasmine followed and they moved out of the light, skirting the pathway. In their black matte skins they were nearly invisible.

"It would appear to be a drug buy," Jasmine said.

"Pickings might be a little lean since that freighter got blown up," Riss said. They smiled at each other.

They moved closer. Sure enough, it was a buy. Nothing huge. One guy dealing, another buying. Money was exchanged, hands were shaken, and the deal was done.

Jasmine motioned to Riss, indicating the drug dealer.

*Let's follow him, okay?*

Riss shrugged. *Sure.*

Their target waited several minutes for the buyer to leave before carefully easing his way off the path and toward the opposite side of the park.

They followed him out of the park, to a neighborhood not represented in any of the tourist must-see literature.

The two Star Risk ops tensed as they reached the edge of the park. If the dealer had a car, he was going to get away.

Fortunately, he didn't have a vehicle.

They trailed him into an even seedier area.

This was not a neighborhood in which anyone with any brains would travel unarmed.

Jasmine took it all in. She'd only brought one extra magazine for her blaster. This was really a three-magazine area . . .

Their target moved to a large, blockish, single-story building that had seen better decades. He pulled a key out, looked around, opened the door quickly, and slipped inside.

The two of them walked around to the side of the building, eyeballing the windows.

When they reached the back of the structure they found a locked door. Riss reached into her pouch and pulled out a lockpick kit. Part of the kit was a tiny electrical probe which she pointed at the door, moving it up and down along the edges.

"Not wired."

The lock, an old key-type, took a little longer than an electronic one would have. Riss worked at it for several minutes, carefully working a rake across the pins, keeping tension on the cylinder.

"Damn," she said. "I'm getting out of practice."

And on the last syllable the lock gave a slight *snick* and popped open. "Back in the old days, I'd have done that in half the time."

"Back in your old days, did they have locks? Doors? Didn't you grow up in a tree? Or was it a cave?"

Riss chuckled. "Funny."

They moved quietly, sliding the door open ever so slowly. Their plan would only work if their target didn't know they were here—and never suspected they had been here.

Inside, the room was like a thousand other abandoned warehouses. Old boxes and discarded equipment ate up space in the corners of the room, with the rest of the floor mostly empty.

They crept. Lights lit up a living area that had been put together in the middle of the room. A few sofas, an old holotank, and a few cabinets.

Behind one of the sofas was a large steel security cage, and inside the cage . . .

"Ah," Riss whispered.

"Yeah."

Large white packages were stacked to about waist height inside the cage. Firearms and credits lay next to the drugs.

Their drug dealer lay on the sofa, watching a holovid, a smile on his face. Not asleep.

They slid closer, and Riss pulled out the probe.

The cage was alarmed to the eyeballs.

Jasmine looked at the drugs and did some mental arithmetic.

She nodded at Riss, who had been studying the alarms, and made a gesture.

*Got enough?*

Riss nodded, and they slithered away.

When they were back outside again, they both let out long breaths. "You think?" Jasmine said.

"Sure, why not? I'll go back to the casino and get the gear we need for the alarms."

"I'll go find the other stuff."

Riss headed toward the casino, going over what she'd need to disable the alarms.

*Let's see—sensor probe, variable transmitter, quantum number generator—*

She stopped when she realized she had company.

*Cristo, Riss, you're slipping.*

She'd been so busy thinking that she'd almost missed the telltales. Three of what passed for street punks on this backwater had come out of an alley on her left. They were dressed in what could be described as urban junk—one wore studded leather with lots of chrome on it; one wore dark skins with an oversized belt; and the third wore what looked like a large plastic garbage bag. Lord.

"Hey, hey, sweets," Studs said. "Nice night, ain't it?"

"Yeah," added Belt, "but kind of warm, ayuh?"

*Wait for it . . .*

And sure enough, Trashbag came in: "Maybe you'd like to, uh, get out of those hot clothes, get a little more comfortable?"

She shook her head. What, did these guys all get up every day and go buy copies of the same script? Head over to central casting and get issued their daily doses of stupidity?

Why was it that dirtbags never seemed to have an original line?

"Hmm, no," she said, "I'm busy. Got to go pick up some gear. Another time."

Studs grinned. "I've got some gear you might like."

The other two sniggered.

"Back off, kid," she said. She didn't have time for this, but she knew what was next. She sighed.

Yep, here he came, the direct approach—he stepped toward her and reached out . . .

She moved in, almost slowly, since she knew what he was going to do. She put her foot just behind his, then she shoved with both hands, hard, tripping him—

Studs stumbled backward toward Belt, who hurried to get out of his way, but didn't make it. Studs slammed into Belt, and then both of them fell and hit the plastcrete—

Trashbag tried to step around his two buddies toward her—

She swept his ankle, caught it just before he put his foot down. The effect was instant—he stepped, but there was no support there. He pinwheeled down to land on top of his buddies.

"Ow!"

"Hey, get your ass off my face!"

"Stupid prick! Get your face off my ass!"

She was already thinking about her equipment again.

*Laser redirector? Maybe a PROM debugger?*

His pride wounded, Studs came up. He pulled a knife.

Only paying half her attention, Riss was still a parsec ahead of him. She already had her pouch blaster in hand.

The three looked at the gun.

"Oh, crap," Trashbag said. "What'd you get us into?"

"Go bother somebody else, boys. Or I can just cook you where you stand. You decide."

The only reason she gave them the choice was that she didn't need the bodies cluttering up the sidewalk until she and Jas got their business done. Which made them lucky, these three low-rent buffoons . . .

Even they weren't that stupid. They took off in a hurry.


Jasmine had seen the shop while they were trailing the drug dealer, and it had provided the inspiration for her plan.

She went inside and saw a clerk behind the counter. He was thin, young, and bored. Until he saw her.

"How can I help you?" the kid behind the counter said, getting to his feet.

"Hi," Jasmine said, and told him what she was looking for.

"Huh. Yeah, I think we have that much."


They met back at the warehouse. By the time Jasmine arrived towing a small cart with her supplies, Riss was waiting by the back door.

"Took you long enough."

"*You* didn't have to carry as much," Jasmine said.

Riss pulled the back door open.

"I already narcogassed our buddy. He's having a long nap."

They went into the warehouse, pulling the cart, and parked it next to the drug cage. The gate was already open.

The drugs packed in here were, in their refined state, a pale yellow powder; some kind of narcotic. Oddly enough this looked almost exactly like a popular energy booster powder stirred into a drink called MuscleGroGo.

They spent more time repackaging the stuff to look like the dope than they had finding it, and it was nearly dawn by the time they finished replacing the drugs with the health food.

But the thought of what was going to happen to all of the drug suppliers when their users realized they'd been sold a natural high was worth it.

Boy, there were gonna be some pissed-off dopers. This dealer was going to be in big trouble PDQ.

Okay, okay, so it wasn't exactly a major sortie against the forces of evil, but every little bit helped. More fun than jogging, anyhow.

Just another night's work for the women of Star Risk . . .

# THIRTY-SIX

Makko looked over his organization and came up with a suitable candidate to replace the late and unlamented Nett. This time, he decided to go with a woman. Not that they were always smarter than men, but at least women tended to be a bit less reckless, in his experience. And, as it happened, he had a qualified one.

The new assistant, one Balantch Doobwa, ran security for one of his strip clubs, the Pink Pearl, in Chiba City. The club made good money, and there weren't a lot of problems with it—LEO reports were few and far between, the skim wasn't cutting too much into profits, and that meant that security was doing its job. Makko put in a call.

The woman's image swirled to life in the air over the comm. She was a natural redhead, hair cut tight and short, and her pleasant, handsome face didn't seem to go with her ability to kick ass and take names. She looked like somebody's nice sister, as though she ought to be married, with a couple of kids, and going to school meetings and ball games. That would be a help in her biz. If people underestimated you, so much the better.

"Boss. What can I do for you?"

"Pack your clothes case. You're coming to work for me."

"When do you need me?"

"Yesterday."

"Be there in . . . two hours."

Since it was a ninety-minute run by express maglev train from Chiba City to Sarcid, that was pretty impressive. Makko smiled into the comm. When do you need me? I'm there—that's what he wanted to hear. He liked her already.

He shut the comm off, and before he could even lean back, the incoming-call tone started playing Franz Liszt's *Les Preludes*:

Susa.

Makko waved the comm back to life.

"Get over here," Susa said. No preliminaries, and, from his tone, he was not a happy man.

"On my way," Makko said.


Makko and Susa were alone in the conference room. Upon the large table next to which they stood was what appeared to be the head of a fire ax.

"A grenade?"

"With a heat detector and a timer. My bomb guys have deactivated it."

"Who would—"

"That's the question, isn't it? Who wanted to send us a message?"

"Killing the Board would be a hell of a message."

Susa waved that off impatiently. "They didn't mean to kill anybody. They knew enough to figure out a way in here past my security to plant this, they know we do routine sweeps every week and an intensive search before every meeting. We have the guy who did it on the security cam. There was a fire last night. They seem to like that tactic. Guy came in big as you friggin' please, disguised as a firefighter. No way our people would have missed this." He nodded at the grenade. "He might as well have left a message telling us where it was."

"But it was armed?"

"Oh, yeah. It could have gone off if we had been complete morons. And he is seriously pulling our chain. He could have carried a regular frag grenade in here and used that. He made it look like a fireman's ax head just to show us he could."

Makko shook his head. "Doesn't make any sense."

"Somebody is really ticking me off," Susa said. "You know that the art ship was taken down?"

"I heard some things." His next thought was, *Why tell me?*

"And you are thinking, why tell you? Because, Keven, there are only a few guys in my organization I can trust to take care of business without me looking over their shoulders, and you are one of them. One, maybe more, of the others might be getting ambitious." He looked at the fake ax head. "Could be it came from one of the other Board members, but I don't think any of them are gearing up to take a run at me. Or it could be that it's one of their people trying to make *them* nervous. I don't know. But I *will* know, and you just became the point man to get me that information.

"Find out who it is. If it is somebody in my organization who is trying to move up, then what is his becomes yours when you nail him. If it is a lieutenant of one of the other members of the Board, same deal. I can guarantee that planet's runner will pay the toll.

"And if it is one of the Board members himself? I have the votes to thumb up or down one of their replacements, and if you can show me proof it's one of them—you get his world."

Makko blinked at the size of that offer.

"Whatever other business you have on the table, you get somebody to handle that—this is your new, full-time, better-get-it-done job. Any problems with that?"

"No, sir, no problems with that at all."

It was a serious situation, but it was all Makko could do to keep from grinning his ass off. There had just been a major power shift in the stellar system, and if he handled it right, he was about to become one of the heaviest of heavyweights. Talk about opportunity knocking? Keven Makko was on his way to open the door and let her in. Man, what a jewel to have fallen right into his lap!

He had better not fumble this one.

# THIRTY-SEVEN

"Coin flip?" Riss asked.

Jasmine nodded. "My coin, I toss it, you get to call it."

Riss smiled. "What, you don't trust me?"

"I remember cutting the cards to see who had to deal with that Morokian toad that time."

Riss laughed. "You never proved the deck was rigged."

"I couldn't figure out how you did until later. Freddie showed me."

"Why, that's against the Magician's Guild rules, to reveal how a trick is done."

"I flip, you call it." Jasmine held up a half-credit coin and showed Riss both sides.

"Go."

Jasmine thumbed the coin into the air.

"Tails," Riss said.

The half credit fell onto the desktop, bounced, then rolled and rattled to a stop.

"Heads," Jasmine said. "I win. So he's yours."

Riss shook her head. "Well. At least he's better-looking than the Morokian."

Both women laughed.

D'tum Pree was rich, not really bad-looking, middle-aged, with enough gray in his hair to look distinguished. He wore expensive suits that were tailored to cover the beginnings of a pretty good paunch. He had a pleasant laugh, was passing intelligent, and could talk the ears off a bronze park statue. He was oily as an olive press and smoother than a sheet of flexiglas covered in lube.

He was, in short, a politician. And very successful.

Riss watched him from across the restaurant as Pree entertained a table full of well-to-do businessmen. He told a funny story, and they all laughed when they were supposed to laugh, and doubtless considered themselves lucky to be in his company.

Pree, after all, was going to be the next prime minister of the Artegal System. It was all but a done deal.

Like a lot of stellar systems, the five planets that made up Artegal's inhabited worlds had a variety of governments. Local, state, planetary, and systemic. All were elected democracies, but some favored a unicameral system, some bicameral. There were houses, senates, diets, parliaments, or variations thereof.

The system government was a single chamber—a Senex—with several parties that shared the power. The majority party chose and fielded the prime minister, and passed out the other ministerial posts; the minority parties, sometimes called back benchers, ate the crumbs from the table and worked for the day when they could change places with the majority.

This was typical throughout the galaxy, and not unusual here.

The majority party of Artegal, the Social Republocrats, had been in power for six years. They were, as most of the effective politicians in-system were, as crooked as pigs' penises. They made way more money from bribes and kickbacks than they could possibly make as servants of the people; that was the way of things, and everybody knew it.

Pree, who was the minister of finance, made more baksheesh than most. And he was about to do better, since it had been decided by the real power in the system, the Board, that Pree was going to become the next prime minister of the System Senex.

Freddie had gotten the scat about all this, and thus Riss's next move had come to be. Had Jasmine lost the coin toss, it would have been hers . . .

The current PM would retire and go off to become a gentleman of leisure, or to write his memoirs or some such, and Pree would be elevated. That he was in bed with the Board was a given, else he would never be considered for the job.

Another candidate would be put forth for consideration, of course—it was pro forma that such happen—and in a sop to the more liberal minority parties, a do-little reformer was selected. He had not a prayer of winning, but for the sake of their constituents, the Senexers had to at least *pretend* that the process was legitimate . . .

Riss watched, and when, a few minutes later, Pree

stood and headed in the direction of the fresher, she stood and headed that way herself.

She was dressed to make an impression on a normal heterosexual human: She wore an expensive silk blouse colored a delicate sea-foam green. It covered her from throat to wrists to waist, and the drape was such that it revealed her form without showing any skin. Her skirt was short enough to show plenty of leg, but not so much so as to seem tawdry. Her slippers were four-thousand-credit-the-pair Orachi handmades, and she had a single piece of jewelry, a mauve diamond in an emerald cut inset into a white-gold nugget on a platinum chain that hung in the center of her chest. Big enough to be impressive; not so big as to be gaudy. She'd had her hair done, and wore a hundred fifty credits' worth of personalized Hergama perfume, blended with her own pheromones.

She looked wealthy, she looked good, she *smelled* good, and she knew it.

She reached the unisex fresher's door at the same time that one of Pree's bodyguard's did. The man looked at his client, who smiled broadly, revealing expensive dental implants. "Please," he said, waving at the door.

The restaurant was a classy one, and had unobtrusive weapon scanners built into the entrances. Riss could have beaten those, but she hadn't—she wasn't carrying anything, not even a little knife. The reason for that was because of what the bodyguard—there were three of them here with Pree, and two more pretending to be lunch patrons in the dining room— was doing with his right hand inside his jacket pocket:

Using a scanner to see if the tall blond woman was armed.

Riss smiled back at Pree, acknowledging his courtesy, and entered the fresher.

Entering one of the six stalls and closing its door unlocked the fresher's entrance behind her, and she sat as if she meant to use the facilities as she heard that door open behind her. She'd bet a thousand credits to a bent demi-cred that Pree had come in alone and left the muscle in the hall.

She waited until she heard his stall door close, then flushed the toilet and exited her own stall, and was leisurely washing her hands when he emerged to stand next to her at the sink.

"Ah, good afternoon," he said, running his hands under the ultrasonics.

"Minister Pree," she said. Of course she would know who he was.

"I am afraid you have the advantage of me," he said.

"Suleel Cawtcha," she said. She smiled at him, offering her freshly cleaned hand.

"Suleel," he said, bending to touch his lips to her hand. "What a delightful name. That's Terzonian, isn't it?"

"You have a good ear," she said. "Yes, I am from Bunkko, on the Middle Island."

"Ah, yes, the MI, a delightful place. I vacationed there once, at the Belecaste."

"West Resort or South?"

He smiled again. "South."

"You must have swum the Singing Coral Cove."

"Indeed I did. Fantastic experience." Convinced

that she was native to, or at least acquainted with, the planet Terzo, from which she claimed to be, he said, "What brings you to Una?"

"Shopping, actually," she said. "The Ritamon Apparel premiere. I thought I might pick up a few fall suits."

She watched that register. Whether he was into clothes or not, everybody who was anybody knew who the designer Todd Tiel Ritamon was. And that you couldn't touch one of his outfits for under fifty thousand credits. Even the knockoffs were expensive. Right away, that put her into a whole different class of well-off. A woman who could afford such things and who casually tossed out the notion that she might pick up a few suits? Either richer than God or married to somebody who was.

"Traveling with your spouse . . . ?" he said, raising an eyebrow.

She smiled, to show that she understood what the question really meant. "Actually, he doesn't much care for travel. Likes to keep a low profile. He stayed home."

He grinned, and she could read his thoughts like a child's primer: A gorgeous woman, married to a rich man—and thus cautious—on her own on a planet far away from home? How perfect was that?

As it happened, there was a rich man named "Cawtcha" back on Terzo, though his sexual preferences did not seem to extend to women. No matter. If anybody bothered to check, the name would show up. Pree here wouldn't dig any deeper than that; he had no reason to do so.

He said, "What a shame that you are all alone. As

it happens, my wife is visiting her relatives, so I find myself at loose ends, as well. Perhaps we might . . . ah . . . get together and have dinner, or something?"

"Why, that sounds like a grand thought," she said. It had to be his idea, of course. But once he bit, she could set the hook. "But we would have to be discreet. We wouldn't want anyone to get the wrong impression."

His grin got bigger. "I have a townhouse here. As it happens, my evening is open, and I have an excellent cook."

"That sounds even better, Minister Pree."

"Please, call me 'D'tum.' "

"Deedum. And you must call me 'Suleel.' I'm sure we will have ever such a good time."

She thought he was going to drool on his expensive shirt. Mentally, he already had her naked with her hair spread on a pillow. "Shall we say . . . eighteen hundred?" he said.

"Let's."

After he left, Riss smiled at herself in the mirror, adjusting her necklace and hair. This was going to be like shooting stoned civets in a small cage . . .

# THIRTY-EIGHT

Pree's townhouse was tastefully done, but positively reeked of money in the details. Riss, now dressed in a flowing, translucent black gown over a black silk catsuit with spray-on slippers, knew enough about the trappings to see how artfully it had been arranged.

That small painting in the foyer was a Bodé original; the Tavanese pitar leaning against the wall in the corner of the main receiving room was a handmade instrument whose label bore the maker's name and the number one; the couch was spun caterpillar websilk over biogel cushions. But it was all offhand, and Riss knew that if she asked about any of the objets d'art, Pree would shrug and downplay them. He had been born to wealth; he was not a self-made man, and second- or third- or fifth-generation rich took such things for granted.

*Must be nice,* she thought.

In her role as rich woman come to drop a couple of hundred thousand on her wardrobe, she was not to be impressed with such things as would occupy a townhouse, so her comment was, "A nice place, Pree."

"A drink?"

"Yes. But—allow me."

She glided to the bar set against the far wall. "What can I make for you?"

A proper rich man's wife would, of course, be able to mix drinks for guests. That Riss had learned how to do so in a sleazy pesthole of a pub whose worth was less than the pictures hanging on the walls around her instead of a high-class finishing school? That didn't matter to the game.

Pree, who was in a red silks and a maroon lounging jacket, moved to stand in front of her as she stepped behind the bar. "Can you make a Sweetwater Sling?"

"Of course. Dark rum or light?"

"Dark, please." He smiled.

She selected the bottles—all the best and most expensive varieties and brands, naturally—and set them on the bar's top. She poured the ingredients into a shaker and triggered the $CO_2$ cooler to chill the mix. It had to be shaken and not stirred.

The freezer under the bar held icy highball glasses. She collected a pair of those—good, leaded crystal, no doubt—waited for them to frost properly, and poured the frothy bluish-green drinks into them.

Pree was only a meter or so away from her as she worked, watching and smiling, but anybody who thought you couldn't slip something into a drink right under somebody's nose had obviously never seen a decent street magician. Any hack could make an elephant disappear on stage; that was a gimmick, a commercially-available illusion available to anybody with the credits to buy it. It was by-the-numbers legerdemain; do this, then that, then *this*, presto, the elephant vanished!

Real skill was being able to do a sleight-of-hand move with somebody close enough to touch looking right at you. Riss remembered a story about a famous stage magician who was approached by robbers on the street one night. The man managed to turn his pockets inside out to show the robbers that he had left his wallet and passport in his hotel, when, in fact, he had palmed them right in front of the robbers and kept them hidden. Now, that had been a command performance, grace under pressure . . .

Adding a colorless and odorless drug to a drink with somebody standing right there? That was nothing.

Drinks in hand, they moved to the couch. Pree sipped at his.

"Ah, excellent! You have a talent as a mixologist!"

Riss smiled and sipped at her drink. That was true. Working undercover in a pesthole where the patrons would throw their drinks at you if they didn't like the way you made them tended to help you get it right.

Five minutes later, and mostly done with their drinks, Riss said, "I need to make a run to the fresher, Deedum. Why don't you slip out of those clothes while I am gone and I'll do the same and be back in a minute?"

His grin practically covered his face. She had no trouble reading his mind: Get right to it, no need to do a long and complicated mating dance, hey? Good . . .

Riss stood and gave him a good view of her muscular backside as she did a stripper's stroll out of the room.

Inside the fresher, she pulled a throwaway comm from her purse. "Two minutes," she said.

"Gotcha," Goodnight's voice came from the little speaker.

Across the street, half a block down from Minister Pree's townhouse, Goodnight and Jasmine sat in a rented car. "Showtime," he said.

The two of them were only lightly disguised: different hair colors—he had black hair, she was a brunette—plus a little skin tone to make them darker.

"Let's do it. And, uh, watch where you put your hands, Chas, if you want to keep them."

"You wound me, woman. I'm a pro here."

"Right."

They alighted from the vehicle and started walking down the sidewalk, side by side, but a little bit apart. They were supposed to be a couple, but at the moment, they weren't happy with each other. Simmering in their own angers.

Seated in a hovercar in front of Pree's townhouse were two of his bodyguards. There were two more in back, but they were out of sight and not part of the play.

As Goodnight and Jasmine drew closer to the townhouse, they started talking, and raising their voices slightly with each exchange.

"Well, if you had been freakin' paying *attention,* you would have seen it!" Goodnight said, glaring at her.

"I wasn't the one with *my* gaze glued to that slut's chest!"

"I told you, I wasn't looking at her tits, I was looking at the scar on her shoulder!"

"Right! You're a hound, that's what you are! You'd stick it in a knothole in a tree if you thought there might be a squirrel in there!"

"Stupid twat!"

By that time, they were directly across the street from the bodyguards, both of whom were watching them and grinning. Chas's last comment was practically a yell.

Jasmine stopped and turned to face him. "What?!"

"You heard me!"

She whipped her hand back and slapped him in the face, and she didn't pull it. The smack felt solid, and you could hear it across the street, she was sure. Oh, she enjoyed that . . .

Chas used the "C" word, and she reared back for another slap.

He caught her swing, and they began to grapple, swearing loudly at each other. "Ready?" he said in a whisper.

"Yep."

He threw her to the plastcrete. She landed on her back. He kicked her in the ribs, making it look a lot harder than it was.

"I'll kill you!" he screamed. "You lying bitch!"

When Riss got back to the living room, Pree was half-undressed and fully unconscious, sprawled on the couch.

She went to the security console, opened it, and wiped the security cam's recording for the last two hours. She shut the cams and perimeter alarms off, then went back to Pree. No record of her coming, none of her leaving.

She squatted next to him, got his arm, and hoisted him over her shoulder into a fireman's carry.

Ugh. He was heavier than she had thought.

She stood and headed for the front door. Good thing she worked out, otherwise she'd never be able to carry him.

The bodyguards had come out of their car and started across the street as Goodnight kept kicking the downed Jasmine, who jerked and yelled and pretended her ribs were breaking.

"Hey, pal, hey!" one of the guards said. "Knock it off!"

Goodnight looked up at the pair. Big men who probably had some training, but they wouldn't have a prayer against him even in normal mode, Jasmine knew, much less bester. But he wasn't going to play it that way.

"Mind your own damned business, butthead!" Chas said.

"Butthead? Who you callin' 'butthead'?!"

The guards glanced at each other and obviously decided that this guy needed a lesson.

The two moved in. Chas backed off a little, but doubled his fists. "Come on, I'll kick your asses!"

The door to the townhouse opened. Jasmine saw M'chel come out, Pree slung over her shoulder. She staggered to the bodyguards' vehicle, managed to get the door open, and rolled the unconscious man onto the rear passenger seat.

Chas punched wildly at the guards, but his blows were mostly ineffectual. At the same time, he somehow managed to keep their best attacks from connecting solidly. Even so, he was taking some punishment.

Riss slipped into the driver's seat of the car.

"Leave him alone!" Jasmine yelled at the two guards, drawing attention away from the car's engine cranking.

Jasmine stood as Goodnight backed away from the guards, saying, "Okay, okay, I'm done! You win! Stop!"

Jasmine ran to him, standing between him and the guards. "Quit hitting him!"

The two guards exchanged pissed-off looks.

One of them said, "You two got serious issues! You need to see a freakin' counselor!"

"Yeah, yeah," Goodnight said. "C'mon, Mari, let's get outta here."

They turned and started walking quickly in the direction of their vehicle. Five seconds along, they started running.

They were thirty meters away and going at speed when they heard one of the guards say, "Where's the mothermilkin' *car*?"

Jasmine grinned. By the time the guards started in their direction, she had the hovercar cranked, fans blasting, and they slid away on an invisible cushion, leaving the guards pounding along the walk after them, cursing loudly.

Star Risk rides again . . .

# THIRTY-NINE

**SENEX MINISTER ARRESTED!**
Interplanetary News Bureau
Dateline: Sarcid, Una

Netted in a predawn police raid this morning was D'tum Pree, Senex Minister of Finance, and a longtime member of the majority Social Republocrat Party.

The raid in the Fornica District of Sarcid early this morning resulted in the arrest of more than a score of people on assorted felony charges including prostitution, pandering, possession of drugs with intent to distribute, possession of illegal weapons, and contributing to the delinquency of minors, law enforcement officials said.

"The finance minister was arrested and charged with alien miscegenation," LEO Captain Ed "Bobbe" Munds said, "along with illegal possession of Class II narcotics, and resisting arrest."

Munds refused to amplify his comments,

but sources close to the investigation have revealed that Minister Pree was allegedly found sans clothing in a hash parlor engaged in illicit congress with a male alien of the *Drong Groys* species. When confronted by police officers, he allegedly became combative and had to be restrained.

Alien miscegenation is a class-B felony punishable by a twenty-thousand-credit fine and up to forty months in jail. Possession of Class II narcotics is also a class-B felony, and resisting lawful arrest is a class-C offense. If convicted on all charges, the minister could face as much as a fifty-thousand-credit fine and nine years in prison.

Released on his own recognizance, Minister Pree refused to speak to reporters. A written statement from his office says, "The charges are totally without merit, and the minister expects to be fully exonerated."

System Senex Prime Minister Rodney Nessa publicly expressed a somewhat guarded confidence in Minister Pree. "A man is innocent until proven guilty," PM Nessa stated. "I am sure this is some kind of terrible misunderstanding, and that it will be cleared up."

# FORTY

Makko looked at his new head of security. "This the best image you got?"

The woman shrugged. "We're dealing with a pro here. She knew where the restaurant cams were, and she never gave them a clean view of her face."

Makko looked at the hologram floating above his desk. The woman captured in the image wore nice clothes, and looked to be trim under them, but the back of her head wasn't going to help them ID her.

"And Pree's townhouse cams were clean?"

"Like a puppy after a bath. They knew what they were doing. We got the guards' description of the couple fighting on the street, but no images of them, either—the traffic cam that should have picked up their vehicle was shot out. Pretty good marksman to hit it from the street with what was presumably a small-caliber blaster."

"This is not helping things. When the hand-picked candidate the Board plans to install as the new System PM gets busted in a sex-and-dope raid, it makes them look bad."

"Guy is not guilty," she said. "We got the guards' testimony. They'll all pass truthscans, and so will Pree."

"That doesn't matter. They can't use him now. If he let himself get conned into this, that's almost as bad. If he's not guilty, he's stupid; same difference, far as the Board is concerned. As far as the public is concerned, a minister got caught boinking a male alien, both of them stoked to the gills on mindbender drugs. Man on the street sees the charges get dropped, he's gonna think, 'Cover-up.' Why would the police bust him in the first place if they didn't have a reason? Pree is history. He's gonna resign from the Senex tomorrow and stay out of sight for the next couple years." He shook his head.

"I don't suppose any of the story the woman told Pree checks out?"

"Not really. There's a rich guy with the right name on Terzo, but his tastes don't run to the female end of the gene pool. He's not married, never has been, doesn't ever expect to be.

"They're good, whoever they are. They knew exactly what they wanted and how to get it. They played Pree like an electronic piano."

Makko nodded. Yeah, they did. Somebody was taking a serious run at the Board or one of the members. "Why" could be any number of reasons, from money to power to revenge. "Why" didn't matter, what was important to find out here was *who* . . .

"Get me something, Doobwa. These people are becoming a serious problem and, if I catch them, there will be a lot of gratitude shined in my direction—some of which will reflect on you."

"I'm on it, boss."

She left, but Makko didn't feel a lot of confidence. Whoever was playing them *was* good, maybe better than any of them, and that was bad. They had to be the same people who had blown up his liquor van, his clubs, and who had bollixed his bank accounts. It wasn't just about Susa and the Board, it was personal. He wanted to stomp their heads in, personally.

But first he had to figure out who they were, and then he had to catch them.

All right. Go back to what he knew. There were at least four of them. The woman who had conned Pree, that was one. The bird-watcher who had killed Neves. The man and woman who had suckered the guards away from the townhouse.

Could be some of those were hires, but he didn't think so. They worked too well together.

There was something else, though. Something just outside the reach of his memory . . . he couldn't quite put his finger on it. What was it . . .

Damn!

It was just there, down a narrow corridor of his mind, he was sure of it. Something to do with . . . the strike . . . ? Yes, that was it, the strike! On one of the stations . . .

He had it! On the station orbiting Vierde, the one protected by those dog-augs, one of the survivors had said something . . .

Makko waved his computer console to life and pulled up the file.

There, there it was:

"—dunno what the fook it was, never seen nuthin' like it. Big, hairy, nasty fooking teeth and claws, faster'n hell, it chopped the pack apart like they wasn't nuthin'."

Some kind of big, furry alien predator had been involved in the attack on that station, and big alien predators ought to be a lot easier to find than people. Maybe it was just muscle, but at least, if they could find it, they could ask it some questions that might help point them in the right direction.

Makko voxaxed his comm.

"Yeah, boss?" Doobwa answered.

"I'm sending you a file. Go find the Doom Dog survivors of the attack on the Vierde Station and get a detailed description of the alien that attacked them. Find an artist and come up with a picture that looks like it."

"Something?"

"A link to the guys giving us grief, maybe."

"I'm gone," she said.

He discommed. Finally. Something they might be able to use.

A big, furry clue . . .

# FORTY-ONE

The envelope the messenger brought was small, a standard letter-sized plastic mailer. There was no return address, only Jasmine's name and the name of the casino on the outside.

She gave the messenger a ten-cee note, and closed the door to her office.

Inside the envelope was a short letter, handwritten on thin scribbleplast.

> *Jasmine—*
>
> *If you are reading this, then I am dead. My attorneys should have already contacted you.*
>
> *Not much to say, except that I really liked you and had fun when we were together. I hope you have a long life—though given your profession, that doesn't seem likely, which is pretty much why I left the casino to you. Enjoy it in good health— you don't have to work anymore, if you don't want.*
>
> *One other thing. While poking around in my father's stuff, I came across something that might*

*be useful. I don't know what it means, but it was
tucked away in his personal Bible, and I've enclosed it here. Maybe it'll help you find who killed
him. And probably killed me, too.*

*Good luck. Take care of yourself.*

The note was signed "Joe."

Clipped to the note was an old-style 2-D graphic. It
was of a woman who looked to be about thirty. She
was handsome. She was smiling, standing in a room
in front of a big window, facing the camera—and
naked. The light was artificial, and it appeared to be
night, or at least dark outside. She had a pretty good
body, not voluptuous, but not skinny, either.

She looked familiar. As if she were somebody that
Jasmine had met.

The print was old; at least it felt old, the colors
faded a bit. Odd thing to keep in a holy book. In
the lower right-hand corner were written two words:
"Love, Lispeth."

A girlfriend? She didn't see much help coming from
that. The image could be forty or fifty years old—
impossible to tell by looking at the woman; there were
no clothes or other images to time-stamp and date it.
There was something visible outside the window in
the distance, a smear of red and blue color that looked
like some kind of advertising sign, but it was too small
for her to read what it said.

She didn't see that it was any help.

Still, she would check it out. You never knew but
that there might be something useful to be found.

She stared at the letter again, and blinked away
tears that welled suddenly. She had liked Joe, too.

* * *

Grok, on his way back from a run in the forest hunting the local version of deer, was a little tired. He had chased half a herd of the things for twenty or thirty kilometers all told, and gotten a pretty good workout. He hadn't killed any of them—there was no sport in that—but he had given them some pretty good stories to tell, if they could but communicate them.

"Oh, you should have seen it, son! It was huge, fierce, had teeth as big as your ears, claws as long as your forelegs! No matter which way I ran, it was there! And, when exhausted, I stopped and waited for it to kill and eat me, it just . . . patted me on the flank and then walked away. A miracle, I'm telling you, it was a miracle . . ."

Grok smiled at the image of a deer-thing telling that tale to its offspring. Never happen, of course, they were only marginally sentient, but it was a funny picture . . .

Because he was tired, and because he was daydreaming, he didn't see the box until it was closing.

In a moment, his senses went on alert, and he became aware that there were suddenly four vehicles on the previously empty country road traveling in the same direction as his car, and the ones in front were slowing down as the ones in back speeded up.

A box, no question, which meant several things, none of them good.

Somebody was trying to capture him. Which meant somebody had reason to do so—and was willing to spend a fair amount of money to set it up. Which had to mean Star Risk was in trouble.

He waved the car's comm on to call and let his friends know, but the unit chirped and said, "Unable to connect to the network."

They were jamming him! More bad news.

Well, he'd just have to show these thugs some fancy driving, was all. A jink here, a zag there, he'd take it off the road, and then let them try to—

But before he could do more than think that, there was an explosion in the rear of his vehicle.

The gauges on the heads-up blinked, and when they stabilized, Grok saw that the harmonics were Dopplering down, the lube pressure was falling, the superconductors were off-line, and the temperature in the engine was shooting into the red zone.

Crap! They had cooked his engine!

The vehicle started slowing as the power failed. The emergency landing wheels deployed just as the car dropped the last few centimeters to the road's surface. The impact bounced Grok's head off the interior of the car's roof. There came a rubber screech as the wheels touched down, and the smell of burning metal filled the cab.

Well, fine. He'd bail out before the car came to a stop and head across country on foot. There were some trees only a few hundred meters away, to the right. If he could get that far, he could lose them. A pity he had burned all that energy chasing the deer, but it was not to be helped. He'd just have to dig a little deeper, was all.

He pulled his blaster, flicked the safety off, and slapped at the console controls, lowering the side windows.

The vehicle pacing him on his left was pretty much

dead even with him. He shoved the blaster through the open window and fired.

The bolt shattered the passenger window on the pace car just as the driver swung it into a hard turn away from Grok's fire.

Guy might be fast, but not faster than a blaster bolt. The pace car yawed across the road and onto the shoulder, bouncing a little as the cushion lost the flat road's support and dispersed somewhat over the softer ground. The car slowed, doubtless because the driver's foot had slipped off the accelerator after the blaster shot that probably took half his head off.

One down, three to go.

His engine was dead and the vehicle was coasting to a stop, probably rolling along at fifteen or twenty klicks an hour, so it was time to leave. Grok steered the slowing car off the road, shoved the door's emergency pop-up lever, and dived out.

He hit the ground on his shoulder, rolled, dived again, rolled a second time, and came up running. Nothing felt broken, and he found a sudden reserve of strength and speed despite all the deer-chasing earlier.

As he ran toward the cover of the trees, he snapped off three rounds from his blaster in the general direction of the cars chasing him. They were slowing to a halt, their doors opening, and while he didn't have time to examine them carefully, at least half a dozen passengers boiled out. They made a lot of noise, yelling and such, and he fired a couple more bolts over his shoulder, speeding up as he did so. That ought to keep their heads down—

Eighty meters left to the trees, fifty; this was going to work out fine.

He risked a backward look, and saw that the pursuers were a good fifty meters back and just starting to move after him.

It would take a lucky round to hit him, and so far, nobody had been doing any shooting—they wanted him alive, else they'd never have tried that box.

He grinned. You had to get started early in the feeding cycle to outeat Grok, thank you very much. He was faster, stronger, smarter, *and* a better shot.

He was almost to the safety of the trees when he realized his mistake. He'd been so busy congratulating himself on escaping that he hadn't asked himself a necessary question: *Why had they tried the box here?*

Doubtless it was because of the three men hidden in the trees right square in front of Grok. He raised the blaster, and even though he was fast and accurate enough to nail two of them, the third man's dart gun thrummed half a dozen times on full auto. He felt at least three of the needles hit him, and there was no doubt they were full of chem. The only question was, was it a fatal poison or just knockout juice?

He felt the chem claim him, slowing his run, making him dizzy.

Okay, faster and stronger, but maybe in just this one instance, not smarter . . .

He managed to shoot the last of the treewhackers as he fell, which was mildly satisfying. If he was going to the Other Side, these three would be there holding the Gate open for him when he arrived.

Not much consolation, but better than none.

Lying on the ground, he managed to turn and line his blaster's sights up on one of the men running toward him. Maybe he could take a few more with him . . .

That was his last thought as things went dark.

# FORTY-TWO

Jasmine scanned the 2-D graph Joe had sent into her computer and opened the HoloSuite software. With the image sharpened, she examine the figure of the nude for identifying marks—tattoos, moles, birthmarks, but didn't see any of which to speak. Her hair was dark, and worn long, a natural and timeless style that didn't offer any clues.

The room had curtains next to the window, but they were simple, white cloth; no designs in them.

The window itself appeared to be a standard residential rectangle, probably aluminum- or vinyl-framed, with two panes of glass, one above a locking bar, one below.

In the night, there was only that distant splash of primary colors.

She highlighted the scene outside the window behind the woman, who was presumably "Lispeth," and enlarged it. The resolution wasn't very good, but the software had in it an extrapolation program that filled in gaps using a faux hologrammatical process. She programmed the extrap software with the parameters of "outdoor advertising, lighted," and used the planet Una as a reference. The picture could have been recorded on any of a hundred planets, but she couldn't begin to cover them all, and she might as well start with the one she was on.

According to the software, what the sign said was "9-Up Bottling Plant."

She opened the planetary database and plugged in the term.

A moment later, the holoproj lit with a datascan.

9-Up, it seemed, was a sugary, carbonated fruit drink. Or it had been. According to the scan, the company that had produced the drink, along with Kava Cola, Professor Prune, and ShockAde, had sold out to a larger soft drink company thirty-one years ago, and had ceased producing its line at that time.

9-Up had apparently been quite popular in its heyday; there were nine bottling plants in the capital city seventy years ago. When the company had been sold, however, there was but one of them still in operation.

Jasmine ordered up a map of the city, circa thirty-one years ago, and located the soft drink plant. She pulled up a second map, of Sarcid currently, and compared the two.

The plant's main building was apparently still there, but converted into a mini-mall full of high-end shops.

Jasmine plotted a straight line from what would have been the front of the building three decades ago and into the city. About two kilometers away was a residential development that had been in place for more than sixty years.

Things were slow. What the hell.

*     *     *

Jasmine drove to the development, which had a fair amount of new construction—plexes, multicube condos, single-family boxes—but also some rather lovely houses that were sixty years old. Most of these were everlastplast, stained or painted to look like wood or stone, set in small grassy yards with short fences, trees, and bushes.

She had the original picture and a holographic enlargement of it, and she walked up and down a few streets until she found a spot where three houses appeared to have a matching view of the former 9-Up plant.

Jasmine walked up to the first one and activated the door chime. A young woman holding a baby on one hip answered the chime. "Yeh?"

It was a million-to-one shot, but she said, "I'm looking for Lispeth."

"Next door, to the right," the young woman said.

Jasmine thanked her. Son of a bitch! What were the odds that the woman would still live in the same house more than thirty years later?

Jasmine moved to the next house and activated the chime. The yard was full of flowers, herbs, a riot of plant growth, all carefully tended, and shaded by the crown of a huge oak tree.

The woman who answered was maybe seventy, her hair snow-white, her face tanned under a lot of smile lines and sun wrinkles. "Hello? How can I help you?" She smiled.

Jasmine said, "I have a picture I think belongs to you."

"Really?"

Jasmine held out the 2-D graph.

The old woman's smile faltered. "Oh, my. I was so young. And not unattractive. I can't believe he kept this all this time. Almost forty years." She looked up at Jasmine, her eyes brimming with tears. "Do come in, dear. I'm sure we have things to talk about."

Doobwa said, "You want me to wake him?"

Makko shook his head. "Oh, no. We aren't going to risk screwing this up. Keep him in the van. I'm calling Susa, and we're going to see him with our fuzzy friend. If he drops dead while we are asking him questions, it isn't going to be on our heads."

She nodded. "Good thought."

Makko reached for his comm. Susa would want to be kept in the loop on this in any event, and while it wasn't a guarantee that it would give them what they wanted, it was the best lead they'd gotten so far. At least it was still a live lead . . .

"Yes?"

"I have one of the players in the game against us," Makko said. "I thought I might bring him round and we could speak with him."

"My estate," Susa said. "How long before you can get there?"

"Forty minutes."

"Good. I'll see you there."

Awake, but pretending to still be out, Grok considered his situation. He was bound—some kind of high-strength tape over his mouth and around his wrists and ankles—and unable to reach the bonds with claws or teeth. A quick flex, and the stuff creaked but held, which told him he wasn't going to break free on his own.

He was in the back of an enclosed van, with a tiny bit of light seeping in from a covered window in the rear door, enough to show him where he was.

It didn't take a very bright thinker to realize that his captors had a good idea of who he was in general, if not the specifics, and that they wished to discuss those specifics with him.

Fortunately, the truth drugs and face-readers that worked on humans didn't work on Grok's people, so they'd have to do it the old-fashioned way, with torture. He could stand a certain amount of that, he supposed, but he would prefer other options. They had stripped him of his carry pouch and belt, and since he wore no other clothes, they had probably reasonably assumed that he was disarmed.

Grok grinned against the tape binding his mouth. That would have been their second mistake.

The first mistake was in coming after him in the first place.

He inhaled sharply and sucked the tape past his lips. Then he began to chew on it. With teeth like razors, it wouldn't take that long to free his mouth.

He heard somebody approaching and went still. There was a flash of light as somebody lifted a covering over a window.

"Still out," a voice said. "He took three needles; he ought not be coming around for a couple more hours, at least."

"Good. Let's roll."

After a moment, the van's fans cranked and Grok felt the vehicle lift and start to move.

He went back to his lunch of binding tape . . .

# FORTY-THREE

"My name is Lispeth Vauly," the white-haired woman said. "How did you come by this?" She held up the flat image.

Jasmine said, "A friend sent it to me."

"A friend?"

"The son of the man who had it tucked away in his Bible."

Lispeth sighed. "Joe, Junior." The tears that that been gathering spilled.

"You knew him?"

There was a long pause, and Jasmine realized what the relationship was. Why the picture, and now the old woman, looked familiar. There was a strong family resemblance; she could have been Joe's sister. That was what Jasmine had seen in that picture, that they were related.

But she wasn't Joe's *sister* . . .

"You are his mother."

Lispeth nodded. "Josiah and I were from different backgrounds. My family was rich, my father influential. Josiah and I would have left it all and married, but my father saw to it that he was arrested and charged with some trumped-up crime. He was given a choice—join the military and ship out, or spend five years in prison."

"And the baby?"

"My parents never knew I was pregnant. I ran off, had the child, and arranged to have him sent to Josiah. He married, a good woman, and they adopted the boy. Never told him about me."

Jasmine shook her head. "How awful for you."

She shrugged. "It was what it was. I didn't want to see Josiah hounded into jail. Better a clean break for all of us. Joe had a father who *was* his father, and a mother who loved him."

"I'm sorry."

She said, "Don't be. I had a good life. Found another man who hung around until he dropped dead— we had thirty-eight years together. I would have missed a lot of joy if I hadn't met him.

"How did you come to know Joe?"

Jasmine told her.

"I see. And you are hunting for whoever it was who killed him?"

"Yes."

"And you will turn them over to the law when you find them?"

Jasmine looked into the old woman's tearful eyes. "No."

Lispeth nodded. "Good. Wait here a moment. I have something for you."

Jasmine looked at her quizzically.

"I'll be right back." She left the room, and returned shortly. She had a small, black plastic box. She handed it to Jasmine.

Jasmine looked at her.

"Take a look."

She opened the little box, sliding the lid off. Inside, nested in a hard plastic formsheath, were two computer chips, each a square no bigger than a tenth-credit coin.

Jasmine blinked.

"Josiah sent them to me months ago," Lispeth said. "He called now and then. Wouldn't come round—he was worried about putting me in danger, he said. But every so often, he would call."

"Do you know what this is?" Jasmine looked at the box.

Lispeth shrugged. "No. Something important. Somebody would eventually show up to retrieve them, he said. Since he and Joe are dead, neither of them are coming back. You should take them. If they are any help in finding and punishing the person who caused Josiah and Joe's deaths, then you are welcome to them."

"If these are what I think they are, they are quite valuable."

"I own this house. I have my garden, and more than enough to live on comfortably. No amount of money can bring them back, can it?"

"No."

"Go, dear. Find out who did it. Make them suffer."

"Yes, ma'am. I intend to."

\*    \*    \*

Jasmine was on her way to her vehicle when her secure comm blipped. Freddie.

"What's up?"

"Grok missed his check-in."

"No way." Grok never missed a check-in.

"Not answering his comm. GPS sig is dead. Nobody we know has seen him today."

"Crap!"

"Exactly. I think maybe you better get back to the casino. M'chel and Chas are both on the way. I can't help but think we've got troubles."

"Crap," she said again.

# FORTY-FOUR

Once Grok chewed through the mouth covering, the next part was a little more painful. His hands were tied behind him. He didn't have the anatomy to dislocate his shoulders and bring them over his head, so he squeezed himself into a ball and worked his bound wrists under his butt and then along the backside of his legs. Grok wasn't as flexible as he had been when he was younger—his hamstrings were very tight, and the muscles started to cramp as he worked his wrists toward his knees, causing more than a little discomfort, if not to say a fair amount of outright pain.

On a scale of one to ten, call it about a four. Bad, but bearable.

He lay on his side and waggled his arms and legs, eventually working himself into a position much like some kind of yoga adept reaching over to touch his head to his knee. Unfortunately, he *wasn't* a yoga adept . . .

The cramp in the left leg abated a bit; alas, the one in his right leg got worse, and it was all he could do to keep from screaming curses aloud. Up to a five on the scale now. Maybe a six, even . . .

The van flew along, an occasional gust of wind from a truck passing them in the opposite direction rocking the vehicle a little.

Finally, he got his hands over his feet.

It took all of forty-five seconds to chew through the binding, and once his hands were free, he quickly ripped the rest of the tape off his mouth—ow! that took a goodly patch of hair with it!—and then used his claws to free his ankles.

Now he had to come up with a strategy. They had been on the road flying for more than half an hour. Presumably they were going somewhere quiet and private, whereupon they could force their captive to speak without fear of his screams being overheard.

Once they got there, men would come to fetch him, and there really wasn't any place to hide in the back of the van. His best chance, he figured, would be to wrap the torn tape around his wrists and ankles and mouth again, arranging it so that it looked as if it were still binding him.

There was a chance that they would dart him as soon as they opened the door—that's what he'd do in their place, shoot first and don't worry about it later. But if they thought he was going to be unconscious for another hour or two and they stopped anytime soon, maybe they wouldn't want to risk overdosing him.

If they thought that way, they'd come in and maybe bring something to carry him out with; a dolly, or three or four weightlifters. Once the door was open and there were people who could be used to block blaster bolts, he was in good shape. Yes, he was tired, and the dart drugs had given him a terrible headache, plus that cramp had made his leg real sore; still, Grok free, and armed with naught but his teeth and claws, was not an inconsiderable foe . . .

It was what he had. It would have to do.

Once he was free it would be easy enough to escape, perhaps pick up a weapon, and do some serious damage until he could rest up a bit, maybe get some help from the other Star Risk members. He had missed check-in; they would be concerned and gearing up to go find him.

Grok felt the vehicle slow. He lay down and arranged the tape loosely over his ankles, put his hands behind himself and turned so he was on his side, his chest facing the door.

The van paused but a moment, however, and then started up again, moving slower. He considered going to the window to try and see out, but didn't want to risk it. The driver might feel him moving around, and he didn't want that.

No matter. They would get wherever they were going soon enough. And whoever came to collect him was going to get a big surprise when that happened . . .

In von Baldur's office, Jasmine was the last to arrive. She came in, looked around, and nodded. "Anything new?"

Goodnight said, "We backtracked his GPS sig this morning. He went out into the Emerald Forest at dawn."

"Chasing deer, probably," Riss said.

"The sig shut off on the way back. I took a run out there. Spotted some crush marks where it looked like a hopper set down hard, off the side of the road. You could smell burned lube. There were splotches of almost-dried blood not far away. I put a DNA scanner on it, and it was human. Not . . . whatever Grok is . . ."

"What do you think?" Jasmine asked.

"No way to tell."

"Speculate."

Goodnight shrugged. "Our friendly neighborhood hairy boy went out to play tag with the local ruminants. He got done, headed back to town. Somebody ran him off the road and collected him. Must have been more than one of them, and I'd guess that Grok took a few of 'em out before they grabbed him."

"You don't think he's dead?" Riss said.

Goodnight shrugged again, as if that question was no big deal. "I don't think he died there, otherwise, why'd they keep the corpse? Bother to clean the place up? I think they have him somewhere, and the only reason I can think of that somebody'd snatch him is because they connected him to what we've been doing. I dunno how, but Grok is hard to miss. Maybe he stepped in front of a camera at the wrong time. Maybe somebody we thought was fertilizing daisies somewhere survived and fingered him. Doesn't really matter how they got him, only that they did."

Jasmine blew out a sigh. "Freddie?"

"Time will be critical," he said. "At most we'll have a few hours before they try to open Grok up. He's immune to truth chems, and he has a high enough pain threshold that he can hold out for a while. He might even kick off before he'd give us up, but I confess I have grown fond of the big fellow."

"How do we find him in time?" Jasmine said.

"Chas's earlier suggestion merits reconsideration.

We go see Mr. Makko and see if we can't persuade him that, if Grok dies, he does, too."

"Even if he doesn't die," Goodnight said, "I am inclined to kill the bastard anyway."

"We'll see."

"We have enough guns?"

"For a surprise attack, I believe we can muster enough force ourselves."

"Okay," Jasmine said.

"Grab your hardware, back here in five minutes?"

"No sweat," Goodnight said.

Both Riss and Jasmine nodded.

Jasmine thought, *Hang in there, Grok. We're coming for you.*

# FORTY-FIVE

Susa's mansion was huge, a veritable castle in the middle of a thousand-acre estate. They parked the van. Doobwa alighted and went to meet a group of Susa's troops headed their way.

Makko climbed out of the van and was heading to the back when the first of Susa's men opened the cargo door. He heard one of them say, "Man, that's a pug-ugly hairball, ain't it?"

Another man laughed—and then the van shook and rumbled and the men screamed—

Makko heard a blaster go off, and he dug for his own weapon, crouching, looking for the danger—

He sensed motion and caught the hint of a dark blur. He thrust his blaster in that direction, but it was gone in a heartbeat and he held his fire.

Somebody cursed like a pub full of drunk asteroid miners.

Makko, gun leading, moved toward the back of the van again—but slowly and carefully. He saw Doobwa, her own sidearm out, but pointed up.

"What?"

"Thing was awake. Had gotten loose somehow." She waved at four bodies on the ground and two inside the truck. "It went through Susa's men like a *vibroknife* through a steak."

Makko could see that. Nasty beast. A *dangerous,* nasty beast. "I heard shots. Somebody hit it?"

"Not enough to slow it down, apparently."

"Crap."

More men came running, waving carbines and plasma rifles.

"There's an eight-meter-tall electrified chain-link fence around the estate," Makko said, "topped with high-voltage razor wire and auto-laser cutters. It can't get away."

"Maybe," she said. She sounded doubtful.

Makko nodded. He could understand that. It looked like somebody had gone to work on these men with knives—blood was everywhere.

Susa arrived. He wore an antique handgun in a leather holster strapped around his waist. The gun was shiny, nickel or stainless steel, Makko guessed, with what looked like a pearl handle, shaped something like a bird's head, without a beak. Lord knew what it fired. Susa collected such things; he had dozens of them hanging on the walls of his mansion.

"My men were told the creature was unconscious and bound," he said.

"It was when we left it in the back of the van," Makko said.

Susa nodded. "Resourceful, isn't it? Well. They should have been more careful, shouldn't they?"

Makko didn't speak to that.

Susa turned to one of the men standing there.

"Issue everybody dart rifles and pistols—no blasters, copy? We still need it alive, and any man who kills the thing will be joining it in short order—is that clear?"

"Yes, sir."

Susa raised his voice so all around him could hear. "Five thousand credits and a month's vacation first-class in the SolarDome to the man who darts it first!" he said.

He turned back to Makko. "We'll just have ourselves a little hunt and bag us an alien."

Susa headed off to collect a weapon, leaving Makko and Doobwa alone. "Five thousand credits and a month in a pleasure dome," Makko said. "Not bad. You're a pretty good shot, right?"

"Yeah. And it would be my guess that the first person who gets close enough to hit this alien might quickly get to be a mound of fresh ground meat piled up around the base of a rosebush somewhere." She nodded at the dead men. "Tell you what. I'm not going to be trying real hard to be the only thing between this monster and wherever it wants to go. I don't need a vacation that bad."

Makko nodded. Yeah. He heard that. He had captured it and it had killed several of his boys. He had brought it here. Now it was Susa's problem . . .

Grok had run like his tail was on fire for the nearest patch of trees, stutter-stepping, dodging, jinking left and right in an evasive manner. A couple of blaster bolts had zipped past him, but not close. He had taken a slight hit while leaving the van, a glancing shot that singed the hair over his left hip and dug a thin line in the skin, but nothing major. He wasn't even bleeding.

As soon as he reached the woods, he cut to the left and did some more broken-field dancing at speed, zipping around the tree trunks and leaping over short bushes, circling out of the trees three hundred meters to the left of where he'd gone into them. He checked, didn't see anybody, and scooted out and behind a gardener's shed.

The one thing about looking like a big, dumb animal was that sometimes people thought of you that way. They'd expect him to run straight away from danger in full panic, heading for the deepest part of the forest. True, he had been in better circumstances, but then again, he had also been in worse ones. Using what cover he could find—bushes, buildings, a lawn mower, he worked his way back toward the van in which he had arrived. They wouldn't expect that.

A herd of humans appeared, emerging from the huge structure, and all of these men—and a few females—were armed, but with what appeared to be pneumatic dart weapons, rifles, and pistols.

Ah. They still wanted him alive.

And leading the human pack, Grok recognized Susa.

Well, that told him something. At the very least, Makko, who had been responsible for kidnapping Grok, was telling Susa that much, and bringing him here was a telling point as well. So whether or not he'd had anything to do with the deaths of Josiah Williams and his son Joe, Susa was now in the mix. Once you started shooting at one of Star Risk's team, you were shooting at them all, and what happened to you was on your own head . . .

Thinking of Star Risk, best he find a comm and give

them a call. They would be worried, and they might also waste a certain amount of time looking for him in the wrong places.

And a gun of some kind, that would be nice. True, his teeth and claws were most effective, as witnessed by those fools who opened up the van; still, a longer-range reach was better when facing multiple guns, as he was here.

That there were many to his one? Well, that wasn't a problem. The more there were, the easier it was to find a target . . .

It would be too much to hope for that the house would be unguarded, but there were all those dead men there by the van who weren't using their weapons and comms. And who would expect to see him there?

The door to Makko's club blew down in a blast of smoke and sparks, and Goodnight, in bester, was first through it.

Save for one guard who couldn't hit the side of a tanker ship from ten meters, the place was empty.

After the guard emptied his weapon and did nothing more than ruin some of the interior decor, Goodnight grabbed him, whacked him a couple of times hard to get his attention, and shifted out of bester.

"Where is Makko?"

"He's not here!"

Goodnight shook his head in disgust, then slapped the man again. "I can bloody well see that! Where *is* he?"

"He—he left."

Goodnight raised one hand. "I can do this all day."

"Wait, wait! He and the new security chief, they went to Susa's estate. I heard them talking!"

"Why?"

"I don't know! They took one of the big vans, the two of them. They had something in the back—I didn't see what!"

This time Goodnight hit the man hard enough to knock him unconscious as Riss, Jasmine, and von Baldur entered the club.

"They took him to Susa's estate. Do we know where that is?"

Von Baldur nodded. "I'll drive."

"Let's hit it," Goodnight said. "Poor old Grok is probably getting his nads wired for electricity even as we stand here."

"Hold up a second," Jasmine said.

"Why would I do that?"

"Because we don't have enough muscle to mount a straight-up assault on Susa's estate. He's got more than a hundred men out there, the place is fenced, and he could hold off a small army. We'd never be able to get to Grok in time to save him."

"So what is our option?"

Jasmine held out her hand. In it was a small plastic box.

"And this is . . . what? A make-nice gift for Susa?"

"Sort of. It's the missing plates. The chips for the mint."

That got their attention.

"Whoa," Goodnight said. "Where did you get those?"

"It's a long story, but the point is, I have them."

"And that's good for our bank accounts," Riss said. "But how does it help Grok?"

"The Alliance wants them back, bad. What if they knew that Susa had them?"

Von Baldur smiled. "Ah, clever."

"And how are you gonna convince the Alliance that Susa has them? He's thick with influence. You can't just com up the local Alliance garrison and allow as how they ought to go out there and look, now can you?"

"That's exactly what I can do," Jasmine said. "I have the chips. Which means I have all the codes and programming in them. Only somebody who has her hands on them can possibly know the program codes. I call up the Alliance, tell them I'm Susa's girlfriend, that he's got the chips at his estate, and give them proof!"

"Gods save me from devious women," Goodnight said.

"It still could take too long," Riss said. "The local Alliance commander will want to check with HQ before that kind of mission."

At that moment, Goodnight's comm chirped.

"You left your comm on?" Riss said.

"Grok might have called." He looked at the unit. "I don't recognize the name or number." He started to thumb it off.

"Wait," von Baldur said. "Answer it! How would anybody know your private number?"

"Goodnight here," he said. His face lit in a smile. "Grok, you motherlickin' furball, where the hell are you? Uh-huh. Uh-huh. Really? Uh-uh. Hold on a second." He looked at the others. "Grok is at Susa's estate. They grabbed him, like we thought, but he got loose. He's running around and they are trying to find him. He's got a comm and gun."

The others all smiled.

"Listen up, Shaggy. Can you stay loose for a little while? We'll send in the marines, get their attention. Right, right.

"Try not to kill *every*body, okay? And don't shoot at the Alliance boys when they get there. I wasn't kidding about that—they are legit."

Goodnight's grin was bigger than anybody's when he discommed.

"Son of a bitch, he's out there chopping down bad guys, doesn't have a care in the motherlickin' galaxy. Looks like we might have time to do Jasmine's plan."

"Let's find a reader and have a look at those chips," Jasmine said. She looked at the others. "We can't keep the plates, you know."

Von Baldur nodded.

Goodnight said, "Why the hell not? You give 'em the info, the Alliance goes out there and stomps the crap out of Susa, but they don't find 'em . . ."

"No, she's right. If they don't find them, they start asking hard questions, like, where is Susa's girlfriend who called them? And where are the chips, because somebody has them if they knew the codes. And they muck around and maybe we get caught up in the back-wash. No, if they recover the missing chips, then the Alliance is happy. Jasmine can call them later and claim the reward, since she'll know all about the call, who she talked to, like that. That's clean, honest money, millions."

Goodnight nodded. "Yeah, okay. No point in being greedy."

They went to find a chip reader.

# FORTY-SIX

Grok hadn't had so much fun in years. Hiding in the brush, leaping out to cook a couple of guards, then hauling ass and finding a new hiding spot. The place was filthy with sensors and they'd have found him pretty quickly using those, but he snagged a beacon from one of the dead guards, and with it he gave off a signal that identified him as one of Susa's men—how great was that?

He had one particularly exciting match that he would sit and savor at some length when he had time to meditate upon it. The female who worked for Makko—what was she called? Doobwa? He had circled back to the yard near the mansion, and spotted her. She was leaning against a tree, her sidearm holstered, not out looking for him. Wise decision.

He sneaked up behind her, and raised his blaster. "Hello," he said. "New in town?"

She spun and snatched her weapon out—very fast for a human—and at the same time leaped to the opposite side.

Grok fired, but because she was moving, missed the

center-of-mass shot. In a fluke of an event, the bolt smashed into her pistol and blew it from her grip.

He expected her to turn and run, and he took a more deliberate aim. A shame to shoot her in the back, but— Then she surprised him. She pulled a short knife from her belt, the blade no more than one of her finger lengths long, and charged him.

He had to smile at that. What a brave human she was! Charging something as big and deadly as Grok, who had a blaster still aimed at her, with nothing but that itty-bitty knife?

No points for brains, but many for guts.

He held his fire, waited until she was almost on him, then sidestepped and tapped her temple with one knuckle as she swiped at him with the blade.

He had the reach by a long margin.

The impact knocked her sprawling and unconscious. Carefully, Grok squatted, picked her up, and carried her to a shady patch of grass. He laid her down there and arranged her limbs so that she appeared comfortable. Her heartbeat seemed strong. "Such bravery deserves recognition, human. So you live to fight another day." He patted her shoulder, and then turned and loped off.

He hoped that whatever plan his Star Risk friends had didn't happen too soon. He had gotten a second wind; he wasn't tired at all. There were still so many targets.

"Okay, it's done," Jasmine said, cradling the comm. "A company of the Alliance's finest is mounting up even as we speak. They will take care not to shoot the, um, undercover agent who looks like a furry creature from a monster entcom."

Riss said, "Susa is bound to have some kind of spy in place at the Alliance base. He'll know the marines are coming."

"Almost certainly," von Baldur said. "He might not know the particulars, but I would also bet he won't want to be there when the Alliance shows up. He knows he can't punch it out with them—he can't buy enough guns—so he'll take off."

"To where?"

"Where any rich man goes when he feels official heat."

Goodnight shook his head, puzzled.

"Who's the first person you'd call if you got caught by the police breaking into a jewel mart?" Jasmine said.

"Ah," Goodnight said, getting it. "Right."

"You and Riss go collect Grok," von Baldur said. "I think Jasmine and I can handle Susa and Makko."

"You sure?"

"One or both of them are mine," Jasmine said. "That was the deal."

Goodnight nodded. "Yep, it was. See you later."

# FORTY-SEVEN

Makko was more than a little nervous, and that hadn't improved on the frantic thopter flight from Susa's estate back to town. First, that hairy monster was still free, killing people left, right, and center. Second, that the Alliance was sending marines to have a little talk with Susa? That had come like a punch to the gut.

"I don't *know*!" Susa said as the thopter whirred away from the estate. "My spy doesn't have anything other than that they are coming and they are coming hot—if anybody tries to stop them, they will engage. Since I don't want my house turned into a smoking crater, nobody is going to try and stop them—if that hellish alien hasn't killed them and made the point moot."

Makko shook his head in disbelief. The Alliance? Why? They were very careful not to step on those toes—what did they think Susa had done?

And, by proximity, what Makko might have done?

"Windom will get it all sorted out," Susa said. "That's why he gets a million-credit-a-year retainer. He's got clout as high as you can get. We'll be fine."

Windom Windom the Fourth was as hot a criminal lawyer as there was on this world, or on any world, from his reputation. He had never lost a case, had argued before the Galactic Supreme Court six times, and if he couldn't walk on water, he could probably stand on it without sinking.

Of course, Win IV, as they called him, wasn't Makko's attorney, but then again, the Alliance hadn't been about to knock on his door. It was Susa who had that problem.

He hadn't seen Doobwa when he piled into the thopter and left in a hurry. He hoped the monster hadn't gotten her. He would have to come up with another security chief if that happened, and that would be a pain in the butt . . .

"Sir," the pilot said, "we are approaching city airspace. Do we want to land on the Legal Tower?"

"Hold on a second." Susa used his comm.

"Win? Susa. I need to see you right now. Uh-huh. Right. Good. Ten minutes."

To the pilot, Susa said, "He's knocked off for the day. Get clearance and take us to his house."

"Yes, sir."

While Windom's house was not nearly as opulent as Susa's, it was large enough to have its own thopter port, Makko knew, even though he had been there but once, for a party.

Windom Windom IV was not a happy man, but because he was a very powerful one, used to getting his way, he didn't seem overly worried. He looked at Jasmine and von Baldur and said, "All right. He's on his way. You want to tell me what this is all about?"

"Not really," Freddie said, "but suffice it to say, if you intended to keep Mr. Susa as a client, you will soon be suffering your first defeat in a criminal courtroom."

The lawyer laughed. "Are you serious?"

"As ventricular fibrillation. Susa is on his way to see you because a company of Alliance Marines is about to storm his estate and take it apart, looking for something the Alliance *really* wants. Defending a local crook against problems that arise on a planet as bent as this one is one thing; standing up against the heaviest guns the Alliance can bring to bear on galactic charges? That's something else."

Jasmine watched the lawyer, who was probably arrogant enough to believe he could beat the Alliance or anybody, given how many times he had before. Sure enough, Windom grinned. "Mr. Susa has a lot of money. We could keep the fight going for a long time."

"At the end of which I guarantee you would lose," Freddie said.

"We'll see."

Jasmine said, "That's assuming your client is still alive to defend after this meeting."

Windom frowned at her. "What?"

"That will be his choice," Freddie said.

Windom shook his head. "You don't think you can get away with this."

"I don't see any reason why not," Freddie said, smiling. "The Alliance wants your client in the worst way, dead or alive, doesn't matter. And my blaster has more than one bolt in it."

"Are you threatening *me*?" He seemed astounded by the idea. "Do you have any idea who I am?"

Jasmine said, "Yes. You're a pretty good lawyer who represents the biggest crook on this planet. He's as dirty as a backworld sewer and you know it. If the Alliance finds Susa dead and his shyster lawyer dead along with him, they aren't going to burn two calories trying to find out who did it. And—trust me here—if they do bother to look, they'll find all kinds of evidence linking you to the crime they want to nail Susa for."

"Like hell they will!"

"Oh, it'll be there," Jasmine said. "The choice is yours, too. We spray you with a little narcogas and you take a nice nap, and when everything is done, you wake up, take a pill for your headache, and forget you ever saw us.

"Or you eat a blaster bolt and, when the Alliance investigators start poking around, they find that you were as dirty as Susa."

Jasmine saw him roll it around in his mind. He hadn't gotten to be a top dog in the legal profession by making stupid decisions.

"I could be having every word of this recorded," he said.

"But you aren't, and even if you were, we'll sweep the house before we leave. None of your security cams will have anything on them, and if we wanted to be real nasty, there might be some kind of terrible accident—a gas line or battery nova that blows the place into little pieces. They'll have to identify you and Susa from your DNA.

"We are serious people, Windom, and direct in our methods. All your dancing in a court won't help you here. Take a short nap, or take a permanent one—same to me either way. Choose."

He swallowed. "All right," he said.

When Grok saw the Alliance Marine transport do a fast overflight, he decided it was time to leave the party. The marines sometimes were trigger-happy; they'd shoot first and offer mea culpas later, being big on the philosophy that it was easier to ask forgiveness than permission.

Grok had pretty much fished out this pond anyhow.

He took off at a fast lope for the fence. Yes, it was tall and full of enough voltage that even he wouldn't enjoy trying to climb it and avoid the razor wire at the top, but the problem with a fence like this was that it had been designed to keep out people who didn't want anybody to know they were trying to sneak past it. At this point in the evening, it wasn't likely that anybody was worried about that.

Grok reached the fence. The metal posts were spaced about five meters apart. He walked along the wire and started blasting. By the time he had taken out six posts, the fence had begun to sag considerably. By the tenth post, the top of the razor wire was only a meter or so above the ground. Even a human could clear that. Grok leaped over the sagging barrier. He ran directly away from the estate, and as he did so, he pulled the borrowed comm.

"What's up, pal?" Goodnight said from the comm.

"Grok has left the estate," he said. "Heading north. I see a road in the distance that curves around. I would appreciate a ride. It has been a long day."

"Copy that. Riss and I happen to be in the area. We'll see you soon."

Grok smiled. A long day, but very fulfilling, to be sure . . .

# FORTY-EIGHT

The pilot set the thopter down on the landing pad. Susa stepped out, followed by Makko, while the down-draft still blew hard, ruffling their hair and clothes. They started toward Windom's house.

"Where are his guards?" Makko asked.

"He doesn't believe in them. Got all kinds of high-tech electronic security. He's a very private man."

At the door, Susa said, "It's me."

The lock snicked and the door, a heavy, durasteel slab, slid open quietly on runners.

"Windom?"

"In here!" a voice called.

Susa and Makko headed toward the sound.

In a large living room, they found themselves alone. "Win?" Susa called out again.

"I am afraid he is . . . indisposed at the moment," a man said.

Makko turned, and saw a man holding a blaster, pointed at them.

Almost unconsciously, he let his hand drift toward his own hidden weapon.

"I wouldn't," a woman's voice said.

He turned his head slightly and saw her, a blonde in thinskins, also with a blaster. Hers was pointed right at his face.

"Lose the hardware," she said, waggling the blaster half a centimeter. "Both of you. Twitch while you do it, and I'll fry you."

Makko believed her. She had that look.

He'd seen her before . . . Where . . . ?

Of course! At the casino opening—he had hit on her, trying to chat her up. She'd chilled him.

Carefully, using two fingers, he pulled his blaster from his waistband and dropped it onto the thick carpet.

Susa did the same with his own sidearm.

"Keep your hands clear of your body," she said. "No sudden moves."

Makko still had his gravity knife, tucked into a back pocket. If she got close . . .

"Who are—? Wait, I know you," Susa said.

At the same moment, Makko realized that he also knew the man with the gun. The new casino guy . . . Smith . . . ?

"Windom the Fourth sends his regrets," the man said. "He was feeling extremely fatigued, and had to lie down for a while."

"What do you want?" Susa asked.

"Peace, harmony, and brotherly love," the man said, smiling. "But that would put all of us out of work, wouldn't it?"

"You're the guys been screwing with our biz," Susa said. "Why?"

"Somebody killed Josiah Williams," the woman

said. "And his son, Joe. We know who dropped the hammer, and he is no longer among the living. What we want to know is who ordered it."

Susa frowned and glanced at Makko, then said, "Listen, friends, whatever the deal you have going with whoever, I can double it. You're good, you caused us a crapload of problems, but we're all reasonable people here. We can do business. Name a price."

Makko allowed his widespread arms to sag a little.

The woman said, "Another centimeter and you'll be smoking meat on the carpet."

Makko froze. What the hell was this about?

"Surely this can't all be because some old activist preacher got himself killed?" Susa said.

"He was our client," the man said. "And then his son was our client. It's bad business to let people kill off our customers. Scares away potential users of our services if word gets around."

"How much?" Susa asked. "To make it all go away? Ten million? Twenty? Call it."

The woman said, "You don't have enough to make it go away."


Jasmine had caught the look Susa gave Makko, and she wasn't sure what it meant. It was time to finish this. "Ten seconds," she said. "One of you tells us who ordered them killed, or we cook you both where you stand. We know one of you is responsible, so either way, we get him."

Susa said, "He did it. I warned him against it."

Makko stared at his boss, sudden rage painting his face. "Bastard!"

He looked at Jasmine. "It was an accident! I didn't

want the preacher dead! He had something that belonged to us! We were trying to get it back! The kid got hit in a shootout. I tried to keep my guy from doing it, but he wouldn't listen!"

"Kick that blaster over this way," Jasmine said to Makko.

"You don't want to do this!"

"Kick it or join it on the floor."

He shoved the fallen blaster in her direction. She didn't look at it as it slid past her.

Freddie said, "That item you were looking for? I have it." With his free hand he produced the plastic box with the chip plates in it.

Despite his personal danger, Susa stared at the box with an intense hunger.

"Tell you what," Freddie continued. "I'm a gambling man. You and I will play a hand of cards. You win, you get these and a head start—the Alliance will be sending investigators here shortly."

"And if I lose?"

"The Alliance won't have to go far to find you—you'll be trussed up like a gift package waiting for them. They believe you stole these, you know." He waved the box.

"Ah. That explains it. You aren't going to kill me?"

"Why would I do that? You didn't take out our clients. We are all professionals here."

"What about Keven?"

"Mr. Makko and my associate are going to discuss his options."

"Windom keeps cards in that drawer over there," Susa said. He smiled.

"Have a seat there," Freddie said. "I'll fetch them."

# FORTY-NINE

Jasmine said, "You have a knife?"

Makko nodded. "Yeah."

"You know how to use it?"

"Yeah."

"Show it to me."

Makko reached his right hand behind him, into his hip pocket, and came out with a gravity knife. He touched a stud on the handle, flicked his wrist, and the blade slid out and locked into place with a *click*. It was a dagger-style blade, eighteen or twenty centimeters long. He gave her a wolfish grin.

Jasmine tossed her blaster behind her and, with the same move, pulled her own knife, the Tiger's Claw, from its belt sheath. She held it point down, edge forward, and she turned slightly to put her right side forward, but behind the knife.

"You win, you walk," she said.

"What about your friend?"

"You heard the deal. He won't stop you."

He was four meters away. He charged—

Jasmine waited until he was almost upon her, then

she jumped to her left as he slashed for her face. She spun the knife in her hand and, with a fencer's grip, jabbed the point into his ribs and raked it down, hard. At the same time, she slammed her free hand into his shoulder, deflecting his slash and knocking him a hair off balance. He stumbled past her—

He recovered, spun, and did a wild backhanded slash, but she had already leaped back out of range.

When most people saw a knife, they didn't expect you to use other tools. The knife was the weapon, and attackers tended to forget they had fists and elbows and knees with which they could back up the blade . . .

The wound on his side was not deep, but it was bloody, running from just under his armpit to his hip and splayed wide.

Makko stopped and regarded her. His charge had cost him—and she could have killed him with a well-placed stab. Maybe he knew that, maybe not, but he wasn't going to make that mistake again. He edged slowly forward, waving the knife.

Jasmine reversed her grip on the knife again. She stood her ground, waiting . . .

Von Baldur, keeping his blaster pointed at Susa, opened the drawer in the hand-carved antique armoire against the wall and removed a deck of cards. The package was enclosed in plastic, the seal on the box unbroken. He tossed it to Susa, who caught it.

Behind Susa, Makko yelled, "Bitch! You cut me! I'm going to slice your eyes out!"

Seated at a small table, Susa glanced that way, then

back at von Baldur. What happened to Makko and the woman wasn't at the top of his list, obviously.

"Open them, shuffle them," von Baldur said. He moved to sit opposite Susa.

Susa riffled the deck. Split it, shuffled the edges together, squared the cards. Did it twice more. Put them on the table.

Von Baldur reached over and picked up the cards. He cut them one-handed and restacked them. Gave them back to Susa.

"You deal," he said. "I don't want you to think I'm not playing fair. Besides, I need one of my hands." He waved the blaster a hair. "Five-card Showdown, all right?"

Susa shrugged.

For all his threats, Makko moved more carefully on his next pass. He feinted high to draw the block and then shot in low, stabbing at her groin—

Jasmine stepped in and turned, blocked the stab, and sliced upward with her blade, aiming at his throat—

Makko turned the stab into a rake, dropping his blade lower, and she was a hair slow. The tip of the blade dug a line a hand span long across her thigh, right over the quad—not deep, but she felt it.

Makko got an arm up to block her cut at his throat and that saved his life, but it cost him—she flayed his triceps to the bone—

Von Baldur's first card, laid faceup, was the nine of hearts.

Susa's was the ace of clubs.

Von Baldur's second card was the six of hearts.

Susa's second card was the ace of diamonds. He grinned.

Von Baldur's third card was the eight of hearts.

Susa laid down in front of himself the ace of hearts.

"Three aces to your . . . nothing," Susa said. "Looks like it's going to be my lucky day."

"Game isn't over yet. Deal."

Makko was worried. His ribs hurt like hell, his left arm was laid open to the bone, and he was losing a lot of blood. He had to finish this bitch soon or he was going to pass out; already he was feeling light-headed. If he could maneuver her into a corner, with a chair or something blocking her so she couldn't jump out of the way, he could overpower her. He was bigger, stronger, and his knife was longer. Plus, he had scored; *she* was bleeding, too.

He edged to his left, keeping his knife up. There was an overstuffed chair behind her, close to the wall and to her right. He could back her up a little, feint from his right. She would be blocked and he could roll over her. Might take a cut himself, but he could finish her.

He edged toward her.

She backed away. *That's right, bitch, that's exactly where I want you to go . . .*

She was almost there, almost . . .

He had her. He took a deep breath, gathered himself—

Von Baldur's forth card was the ten of hearts.

Susa turned the ace of spade over for his fourth card. "My, my," he said. "Four bullets."

"One more card."

Susa shook his head. "Get another heart, you have a flush, not good enough."

"Deal."

Susa flipped over von Baldur's fifth card.

Seven of hearts.

"My, my," von Baldur said. "Look at that. Six, seven, eight, nine, ten, all of hearts. Straight flush. Beats your four aces, doesn't it?"

Susa upended the table. He was big and strong and it would have knocked von Baldur on his ass—if he hadn't been expecting it.

Von Baldur was already moving, stepping out of the way of the flying cards and table—

Makko charged, intending to take the woman's head off. He took the angle and thrust the knife in front of him. She had nowhere to go—she couldn't back up, couldn't move to the side—he had her, he had her—!

She dropped like a stone. He had time to realize his mistake as she stabbed at his groin, first the left leg, then the right, ripping open both femoral arteries before he could bring his knife down, and when he did, she already had her blade point up, toward the ceiling, and he spiked his own forearm on the steel. She twisted her hand, and his knife fell from his suddenly dead fingers. Oh, *crap*—

Susa was big and fast and very strong, but not blasterproof.

Von Baldur shot him three times, the classic Mozambique drill: two in the chest and one in the head.

Susa collapsed.

\*     \*     \*

Jasmine pulled her knife free of Makko's arm, swept his bleeding limb out of the way, came up from her crouch, and, as he grabbed her in a final, desperate attempt to hold himself up, she drove the point of her knife into his right eye.

He convulsed like a caught fish flopping on a dock and fell backward. He hit the floor hard, but bonelessly. He wouldn't be getting up again.

Jasmine bent and wiped the blood from her knife on the man's shirt. She didn't want Mushtaq's knife to rust. . . .

"Say hello to Joe and his father if you pass them on your way to Hell," she said.

She looked up. Freddie was looking down at Susa's body on the rug, smoke curling from the muzzle of his blaster. "He was a poor loser," Freddie said.

"You cheated, didn't you?"

"Of course." He looked at her. "You okay?"

"Yeah. A little orthostat glue—I'll be good as new."

"And Keven has gone to his reward?"

"Oh, yeah."

Freddie shook his head. Mumbled something.

"What was that? I didn't catch it."

"I said, 'If you are captured by the savages, don't let them give you to the women . . . '"

She smiled at him. "Absolutely true."

"Well, we have things to arrange. Let us be about our business. Not a bad day's work, hey?"

She nodded. Life was seldom fair, but they had dispensed some justice here. Not a bad day's work at all . . .

# FIFTY

The Star Risk team had lunch in the private dining room at the casino. They had broken out the good champagne, and the smiles to go with it.

"So," Goodnight said, "exactly how rich are we?"

"Well, moderately so," Freddie allowed. "The reward for the missing plates was ten million, and that is on its way into Jasmine's account."

"Which plates were found on the body of the late and unlamented Mr. Susa?" Riss said.

"Yes. A shame to have to give those up, but that satisfied the Alliance, and we won't have them buzzing around like angry hornets."

"Two million each," Goodnight said. He raised his champagne flute. "I'll drink to that."

"Well, actually, only one point eight million each," Jasmine said. "I thought it only fair that Lispeth get a share, so a million went to her."

Goodnight shrugged. "What the hell. I won't begrudge the old lady a few credits."

"The casino's value, given the improvements and current upcoming operations, is about eight million,"

Freddie said. "And we are clearing somewhere in the neighborhood of three-quarters of a million a month, after all the bills are paid."

Riss shook her head. "Who would have ever thought it? We're millionaires. Rich, and getting richer."

"Hear, hear, I'll drink to that, too," Goodnight said.

They all sipped their champagne.

"So, what now?" Jasmine asked.

"I'm happy running the casino," Freddie said. "For a while, anyhow. Be nice to have a place to call home, where I can gamble and make money even if I lose."

Grok said, "As a being of means, I can return to my homeworld and finally accumulate a first-quality harem. At my age, spawning sounds like an excellent way to spend a few years. Six, eight, maybe ten wives, maybe a couple dozen offspring—I don't want to spread myself too thin."

The others all laughed.

"What about you, Riss?" Goodnight asked.

"I've always wanted to see the autumn foliage on Badji's World. I understand the binary stars make for the most beautiful sunsets in the galaxy. Costs ten thousand credits a day to stay there, but—a week or two—hey, who's counting?"

"I hear the Clarke Diamond is being sent out on a museum tour in the Inner System," Goodnight said.

"C'mon, Chas," Riss said. "You're a rich man now."

"Yeah, but even a rich man needs a challenge. I can get my augments tuned, add some top-grade military bioware upgrades, hell, I'd be that ghost I played. The

Clarke is as big as a man's fist. Make a great night-light."

They smiled at that.

"What about you, Jasmine?" Riss asked. "You have any plans?"

"Not really. I think maybe I'll find a nice house in the neighborhood where Lispeth lives, settle down for a while and . . . raise my son."

They all stared at her.

"Say that again?" Goodnight finally said.

"Yes. I'm pregnant, didn't I tell you? I think I'll name him Josiah—after his father . . ."

She grinned.

"Maybe we'll come to visit you in jail, Uncle Chas . . ."

Goodnight shook his head. "Don't you dare let the kid call me 'Uncle'!"

They all laughed. Even Chas . . .

# ABOUT THE AUTHORS

**Chris Bunch** was a full-time novelist following his career as a television writer. A military veteran, he was the author of such popular works as the Sten series, *The Seer King,* and *The Demon King,* and lived in Washington state on the Columbia River. He passed away over July Fourth weekend, 2005.

**Steve Perry** has sold dozens of stories to magazines and anthologies, as well as a considerable number of novels, animated teleplays, nonfiction articles, reviews, and essays, along with a couple of unproduced movie scripts. He wrote for *Batman: The Animated Series* during its first Emmy Award–winning season, and during the second season, one of his scripts was nominated for an Emmy for Outstanding Writing. His novelization of *Star Wars: Shadows of the Empire* spent ten weeks on the *New York Times* bestseller list. He also did the bestselling novelization of the summer blockbuster movie *Men in Black,* and all of his several collaborative novels for Tom Clancy's Net

Force series have appeared on the *New York Times* list.

Despite being an avid reader and growing up in a family of writers, **Dal Perry** hated writing until he was well into high school, where his feelings moved from active dislike to tolerance. That gave way to enjoyment when he finally figured out that the process could be fun, too. Dal has enjoyed four other careers in addition to writing, including computer programming, technical theater, apartment management, and project management, taking place in locations ranging from Los Angeles to London to Portland, Oregon. He lives in the Pacific Northwest with his wife, Rachel, and his sons, Zachary, Bretton, and Nathan. It's a busy life.